Y0-ABJ-273

THE LAMENT
OF
CHARLIE
LONGSONG

Roch Carrier

*translated from the French
by Sheila Fischman*

VIKING

VIKING

Published by the Penguin Group

Penguin Books Canada Ltd, 10 Alcorn Avenue, Toronto, Ontario, Canada M4V 3B2

Penguin Books Ltd, 27 Wrights Lane, London W8 5TZ, England

Penguin Putnam Inc., 375 Hudson Street, New York, New York 10014, U.S.A.

Penguin Books Australia Ltd, Ringwood, Victoria, Australia

Penguin Books (NZ) Ltd, cnr Rosedale and Airborne Roads, Albany, Auckland 1310, New Zealand

Penguin Books Ltd, Registered Offices: Harmondsworth, Middlesex, England

First published 1998

10 9 8 7 6 5 4 3 2 1

CANADIAN CATALOGUING IN PUBLICATION DATA

Carrier, Roch, 1937–
[Petit Homme Tornade. English]
The lament of Charlie Longsong

Translation of: Petit Homme Tornade.
ISBN 0-670-87350-0

I. Fischman, Sheila. II. Title. III. Title: Petit Homme Tornade. English

PS8505.A77P4713 1998   C843'.54   C98-930780-8
PQ3919.2.C3294713 1998

Visit Penguin Canada's web site at **www.penguin.ca**

Other works by Roch Carrier
available from Penguin Books Canada

THE LAMENT
OF
CHARLIE
LONGSONG

1 Unless you were born here, you have to be lost to end up in this Arizona hamlet. Along the single street, sequoias lift their thorny arms towards a sky that reflects the grey earth. The dilapidated wooden fences do their best not to collapse. There are six or seven shacks covered over with rusted old billboards. All around sit the skeletons of abandoned cars, while behind, all the way to the horizon, is the desert. And yet the traveller discovers the place with astonished pleasure. There's nothing on the map to indicate he'll be able to enjoy a cold beer under the sun that will melt the roof of his car. And he's relieved that he can finally fill his gas tank. There's a long road ahead of him in this uninhabited region.

To the north, evaporated rivers, relentless winds and the insistent passage of millions of years have carved out mad castles, extravagant cathedrals that have inspired religious fervour in some travellers. Here the earth is worn-out, tired, poor. Even the cactuses look woebegone.

The trading post serves as post office, restaurant, gas station, grocery store and antique shop; magazines, books, erotic videos, alcohol, boots and tools are all available too. Who buys these things? The traveller hasn't noticed a single dwelling anywhere. Winding trails cut through the bushes only to be lost in the desert where nothing seems to have been built. Only cactuses inhabit this territory. Yet several customers are gathered here and they seem to be in a cheerful mood. They're teasing one another the way people do in villages where everyone is as close as brothers and sisters, where they tell each other the same jokes day after day and laugh at them year after year. Their faces are baked and deeply lined. Sun, wind and time work on them as they work upon the earth.

The traveller wipes his blazing forehead, where he's amazed not to find any sweat. The air is so dry. He drinks with delight. The cold drink in his hand and in his throat makes him yearn to linger here rather than continue along the softened asphalt road that sticks to his tires, under the scalding sky.

"Take whatever you want, young fellow! I'm giving it to you. Everything you see here belongs to me."

Who is this very tall individual with the long white hair? He resembles an old, fallen prince, miserably dressed, who moves and talks like a drunk. The idlers are keeping an eye on him; on their lips is a smile that's about to burst into coarse laughter.

The old man who seems to have had too much to drink sets down on the counter an armful of products he'd been clutching in his one arm.

"All this belongs to me," he mutters. "I can give it all to you."

Though his back is hunched, his shoulders are those of a man who will be able to bear the burden of life for a long time yet. His hair bestows a majesty on him that's contradicted by his behaviour. The old Indian steps up to the traveller.

"Take what I'm giving you, stranger."

The traveller feels ill at ease. The locals are following the show attentively. Distractions are no doubt rare here in the desert. Perhaps this is their theatre? They all carry revolvers. Who are they protecting themselves against in this empty territory? Who do they want to kill?

"This is my bread, stranger, and I'm giving it to you. The store's mine. This village is mine. This whole territory belongs to me."

The traveller drinks more quickly than he wants because he senses it would be best if he left. In the shadow cast onto these faces by the broad brims of their hats shines a mocking smile that shows teeth yellowed by tobacco.

"Of course, you're right," says the cashier. "And now, Charlie Longsong, you're going to put it all back. That's right, there, on the shelves."

The old Indian obeys her. The traveller thinks: that man's body is filled with the power of a sleeping animal. Taking small, hesitant steps, like a child who is at once rebellious and obedient, he puts all the articles back where they came from. The idlers don't like to see a man obey a woman. At the same time, they enjoy the sight of this old Indian submitting like a well-trained dog.

"Tell me, Charlie Longsong, do you remember the last time you saw soap?"

"Charlie Longsong, you'll smell better as a corpse than you do alive!"

The traveller is irritated by what he's witnessing. He hates this kind of torture through teasing that people resort to in villages that are too peaceful. He becomes impatient as he gathers up his change.

"Charlie Longsong's slightly crazy," explains the cashier. "He lost his mind a little when they killed his father. That's the story that's always been told. Probably I'd have gone crazy too if I'd seen my father killed before my eyes. The guilty parties have never been caught. . . . It was a long time ago."

The traveller tells himself he'll never come back to this spot on the planet. He will forget its name. In fact he doesn't even know it. He's anxious to leave. He has to fill his tank. He backs the car up to the gas-pump. It's covered in rust. A relic. The cashier comes along.

"Is it far to the next village?" asks the traveller.

"Depends what you call far. . . . You have to find it. The Government builds the roads. It builds them the same way it makes up its tax forms. Nothing's simple."

"Is there a decent place to spend the night around here?"

"Depends what you call decent."

The white-haired old Indian looms up from between the pumps.

"Take all the gas you need; I'm giving it to you."

"Charlie Longsong, don't you think it's time to crawl back in your hole?" asks the impatient cashier.

"Aren't you being a little hard on the old man?" asks the traveller.

"He's an old fool. We've been putting up with him for a hundred years now. There's a limit to a person's patience. Every time he lays eyes on a stranger he goes into his act. Is it my fault his father got killed? Do I know if somebody stole his father's land? My own father wasn't even born yet. Life's complicated enough as it is. Do I have to worry about the past as well? Charlie Longsong isn't living in the present. His brain's in the past like a fish in a jar. That's his craziness. He spends his nights hiding behind his cactuses, on the lookout for his father's murderers. He's convinced they'll come back. Is that any way to live? . . . The nearest motel's the Universal. The name's written in red neon. Anyone who gets lost around here ends up at the Universal Motel."

The old Indian has crossed the road and now he is walking into the desert that stretches out to a distant blue wall like a high wave in the ocean.

2 At the Universal Motel, the traveller signs his registration form.

"God in Heaven, what terrible handwriting. You must be an educated man. I can let you have room 13, on your left at the end. Only educated people will take room 13. Education cures superstition. I don't know as I'd spend a night in there myself."

Robert Martin shuts his door. He switches on the light. The choking smell of tobacco joins those of mustiness and the acrid fumes of cleaning products. The walls are yellow. The red wall-to-wall carpet is strewn with the scars of cigarette burns. Here in the desert this is at least a roof over his head and a door that locks. He sets down his bags. Small, slightly greasy insects make way.

He was glad to set out on this journey, but now his searing pain has caught up with him. In the past, he liked to travel with his wife and then, in the evening, to go over the high points of the day. Today, he's alone in this loathsome hotel. She's not there to recount the day's itinerary as they sip a nicely chilled drink. She is demanding the house, the car. He shouldn't have called his lawyer. . . . He hates her now more than he's ever hated anyone, though he once dreamed of loving no one but her for the rest of his life. She wants to rob him like a pirate, send him to the gallows. He is too lonely. He was an idiot not to buy something to drink at the trading post. . . . If she'd been with him she'd have tried to talk to the old Indian, a man who has already travelled some distance on the road to paradise. She is curious about everything. She can approach people with an ease that he doesn't possess. She has usurped the children, the chalet by the lake, the boat. . . . What will be left for him? Where will he sleep? Where will he work?

"The witch wants to skin me alive."

For how much longer will he be able to run away? Will she take advantage of his absence to finish ruining him? Will she accuse him of abandoning his children? It was to discuss that possibility that he spoke to his lawyer—an upsetting conversation. He feels like heading north again, returning to Canada. Arizona doesn't protect him. He has run away, but his journey brings him no pleasure. She has kidnapped his children. What will she tell them about him? His children love him. They certainly ask for him. He is sneaking away. Yet even if he'd stayed near that conjugal hell, in Montreal, he wouldn't be able to see them. He wanted to live with her, perhaps have another child, then wait for the grandchildren whom one apparently loves more than one's own. He saw himself with a long white beard, old as an ancestor, surrounded by them all. What happened? In just one day the woman had become an earthquake, a typhoon, a boa constrictor, an executioner, a bandit.

Robert Martin has lost everything. Friends urged him to put some distance between himself and what happened. And so he went away. When he comes back, he'll see things more clearly. For the time being, here in room 13 of the Universal Motel, he is crying because he wanted to be with his wife and his children. His entire body is in pain, as if his soul were covered with sores. He has to get out of this room.

No dining room. All he finds is a counter where fat, sleepy men on stools are busy stuffing their faces. The plate that's shoved under his nose is enormous. In this part of the world nothing is small. Everyone is as silent as a monk. No women except the waitress. Each man is busy straddling his vast thoughts. No one's drinking but they seem drunk. Robert Martin is drunk too. On sorrow. But if he had stayed in Montreal he'd be even more unhappy. Crying when you go away hurts less than crying when you stay behind. He will go back. For the time being, he's in pain as if he'd been beaten up by thugs. He has been assaulted in full daylight by the person he loved the most. No stranger could have been so ferocious.

It would be better to go to sleep than to twist again and again this mill that is grinding the same thoughts. In the light of the Universal Motel's neon sign, the cactuses seem phosphorescent. The night is a beautiful, smooth blue desert sparkling with hundreds of pebbles.

After scribbling a few words in a notebook and marking some reference points on his map, Robert Martin cautiously gets into bed. Many have slept here before him. The covers are steeped in the smells of their fatigue and their nightmares. The mattress is lumpy from their restless tossing and turning. Many others have, like him, gone to bed early to escape the interminable day.

Since she's decided to make him a free man, he must assume that freedom. His wife is taking everything but his freedom. She wants him to be free, but ruined. No, he mustn't replay that record again. Whenever he thinks about the divorce, his brain is nothing but a lump of dough kneaded with suffering.

Taking off aimlessly like that was something Robert Martin had never done before. With her, there always had to be a plan. A plan for the day, a plan for the hour, a plan for the year, a plan for life. Ah! how good it is not to be hobbled by a plan! First, he has to tire out his pain. After that everything will be possible. He'll also have to overcome the giddiness of being alone, without her; it's like being an adolescent. . . . His children will come back to him. She wanted to keep them as hostages. They will escape to their father. . . . No plans ever again! Were the canyons, the fabulous rocks that were as beautiful as sublime cathedrals, were Arizona's fantastic palaces built according to a plan? No, everything was done in the way that the ocean waves are done and then undone, in the way that a life is done and then undone. The sea has no plan, nor does life. Ah! how hard it is to sleep when one is free.

This journey will restore his strength. The force that has fashioned the rock, the space where the light is reflected, the wind that has erased history, all will come back to him. They will permeate him, nourish him.

During his journey the historian has often thought about the hundreds of thousands of his French-Canadian compatriots who fled the misery of their ungrateful northern land. Fascinated by the United States, where dreams were transformed into fortunes, hypnotized by hope, they followed old paths and created new ones. In the mountains of Colorado, at the end of a zigzag road his car was much too wide for, Robert Martin visited a ghost town's humble museum. On the first page of an old school scribbler where the minutes of the hamlet's council meetings were piously inscribed, he read with emotion an account of the first transaction recorded in this place. A farmer had bought from a trader fifty-nine head of cattle and a plough. The farmer signed his name: Joseph Dubois. A French-Canadian name.

How fascinating it would be to follow this farmer from Canada to Colorado, this man who roamed from farm to farm and from state to state and then decided to build his nest here, in this godforsaken valley nestled in the mountains. The rocky paths exhausted horses and broke wagon wheels. The most intrepid dreamers exhausted themselves digging the land, hoping they'd find shovelfuls of gold. The first house these adventurers constructed was built to accommodate the girls from the brothel. People came to these places from all over the world. The miners were Russian, Polish, Italian, Australian. What brought them to this unknown region? How did Joseph Dubois end up in this hamlet?

The historian Robert Martin hasn't published anything for several years. Wouldn't it be fascinating to walk in the footsteps of this Dubois? Wouldn't it be exciting for a man from our weary age to walk in the footsteps of a man who lived dangerously more than a hundred and twenty-five years ago? What was he running away from? Who was he trying to escape? What was he leaving behind? What was tormenting him?

Farmer Dubois represents an entire historical period. Expeditions, great displacements, epic rushes, immigration, caravans. . . . All those lavish movements, like shuttles on looms, wove the great tapestry of America. Robert Martin should relate this story. By bringing together the fragments of this unknown life, perhaps he'd be able, for a while, to forget his own life, his own sorrow.

He nearly has a plan in mind already. He falls asleep.

3 At the time of his father's death, Little Tornado Man was not yet known as Charlie Longsong. He didn't want to go back to the mesa with the others. He waited under the bright sky, crouching behind a clump of sagebrush. The heat of the day that had seeped into the dry gravel was baking his legs, pricked by the thorns on the low-growing calamints that shone in the brightness of night. Gradually, the child's eyes closed against his will. Then his legs were drawn up to his chest. Alone, he was afraid in this night with its looming terrors. With his hand on his rifle, Little Tornado Man had finally fallen asleep.

Sometimes his father would come to visit his dreams, riding the black mare that had disappeared with him. Holding out his big hand, he would beckon to him to come closer. Little Tornado Man grasped the hand and his father lifted him up as if he were a mere twig and he'd land on the mare's back. Then she would hurl herself forward and the two would enjoy a fine horseback ride. The mare's hooves were silent now. The pebbles didn't ring out.

"All this is yours, Little Tornado Man; I'm giving it to you because it used to be mine."

His father's lips did not move as they spoke the words. He spoke the way he'd spoken when they were still together. To the child on the black mare with his father, it was as if they were soaring above the desert on the back of a great black bird. Never in his life had Little Tornado Man travelled so far. At times it seemed that he'd gone beyond the borders of his Arizona.

What Little Tornado Man didn't like was to come back from these rides. His father would push him till he slid off the horse, then disappear so fast that Little Tornado Man was afraid he would never return. After that he'd get up and look for his rifle. The brambles rustled as some hares came out into the starlight. Here, a mouse was scratching at a stone. In the distance, a coyote was proclaiming his hunger. Sometimes it was so dark that the child could see no better than if his eyes had been closed.

When the sun returned, Little Tornado Man walked so he could read the signs in the grey earth. He spotted the narrow path of lizards, the quick winding path of the snakes, the fearful steps of mice, the cautious prints of a coyote that had stopped to sniff his victim's scent in the air. But he never spied what he hoped to see: the marks left by the hooves of a mare. He wished he could sit down beside her, think about his father and wait for his return. He tried not to be sad. He kept telling himself his father would come back to visit him.

As autumn approached, the wind irritated the crows and the bats and stirred up clouds of cold dust that wrapped themselves around him. Little Tornado Man decided to build himself a shelter, for he didn't want to go back to the mesa with the others. He remembered what his father had taught him. He gathered a pile of big stones and set them one on top of the other to make a low wall. Depending on which side the wind attacked from, he would stretch out against the stone, rolled up in his woollen blanket. Even as he continued to hope for his father's visit, he feared the return of the men who'd attacked him. He kept his rifle close to him under the blanket. Little Tornado Man still had his father's weapon. Those men who had come—strangers, *bohanas*—had tried to take it from him. That was what his father called Whites, because he didn't like them. Little Tornado Man had hidden the rifle in a nest of thorns near the hole where the snake lived. He had prayed to the snake to guard it.

Just before winter, Little Tornado Man had to go back to the mesa with the others. An uncle had come to live with his mother and his brothers and sisters. No one liked the uncle. He used to be entertaining, with his funny stories, when their father was alive. But now the uncle no longer told stories, and he beat the children. If their mother tried to protect them, even with just one word, he'd beat her as if she were a child. The house was small; when the uncle lost his temper no one was safe from his hand, which was as hard as a stick. None of this would have happened when his father was alive. He wouldn't have let the uncle do that.

When the storm had passed, Little Tornado Man went to the highest point of the mesa's plateau and gazed down at the earth at the base of the rocky column. It was flat, and it stretched all the way to the circle of the mountains on the horizon. He lingered in particular to look at the piece of earth he knew best, his own piece of earth, where his father had fallen and never got up again.

One day he decided to run away from the mesa. He found his rifle safe under the pebbles, near the snake's nest. He had to wait for the snake to emerge before he could pick it up. The men who'd come to attack his father had set fire to his cabin. Everything had burned, except some blackened tree trunks. Little Tornado Man hadn't dared touch the debris. He didn't want to complete the destruction of his house. Even in ruins it was his house. Maybe one day his father would come back and repair the damage. Maybe everything would be as it had been before. Maybe the uncle would stop beating his brothers, his sisters and his mother and start telling funny stories again.

Some distance away—you could get there on foot—was the hamlet where everyone looked like the *bohanas* who had come to wage war on his father. He decided to venture on his own into this foreign territory where he'd gone a few times with his father. Wary, on tiptoe, he entered the trading post. All kinds of coloured boxes were stacked on the shelves. He didn't remember seeing all these things when he'd come with his father. He didn't remember smelling all these perfumes. He also saw all sorts of bottles and he recognized the one his father used to drink. He noticed clothes in amazing colours. And over there was the ice cream. His father had bought him some once. It was cool and delicious in your mouth. The child wished he knew the words his father had said when he needed to buy something but had no money.

One of the loafers saw him longing for ice cream and understood that he hadn't a cent to pay for it.

"Sing us a song and I'll buy you whatever colour ice cream you want."

Little Tornado Man shot a look at the *bohana* and knew he wasn't a good man, but he wanted that red ice cream he'd eaten when his father was with him. So he planted himself in the middle of the trading post and he sang as they'd sung in his house on the mesa when his father was still there with the brothers, the sisters, his mother, the cousins, the aunts and even the uncle who would never have dared to beat Little Tornado Man or his brothers or his sisters or his mother. He sang. And along with the music came memories that mingled with his song until all at once there were tears on his cheeks as he murmured it. Everyone tossed him some coins. He paid. His ice cream tasted as good as it had that time when, mounted on the black mare, snuggled in his father's arms, he'd experienced happiness so great it seemed that it would last forever, like the eternity of the gods.

When he came out of the trading post he heard someone call out:

"Sing us another song, Charlie Longsong!"

The child had never heard that name before.

"That was a real pretty song, Charlie Longsong."

"Real pretty but kinda long, Charlie Longsong."

"Come again tomorrow, Charlie Longsong!"

Now no one called him anything else. He went back to the trading post. He sang again. He helped out. He ran here and there to deliver messages. He filled tanks at the gas-pump. He cleaned windshields. He made himself useful. He got paid a little. Above all he was an amazing hunter. In places where no one else had noticed anything, Charlie shot hares, porcupines. He knew how to cook the tender flesh the way it was cooked in the house on the mesa. Sometimes he'd hit an antelope or a fawn. That was a long time ago. The antelopes hadn't all been shot yet. Often he was asked to sing. He realized now it was to make fun of him. When people made fun of him it pained his soul as much as when he thought about his father who was no longer with him or about the uncle who beat his brothers, his sisters and his mother. Little Tornado Man knew that the day would come when he'd be strong enough to defend himself. He hadn't gone back to the mesa. He hadn't seen his mother again or his brothers or his sisters. No one had come to fetch him. He would go back up to the mesa when he was strong.

Charlie Longsong became a long adolescent. His legs were swift. His biceps were hard as stone. As soon as he was no longer a child, his father didn't come on his black mare to visit him so often. Little Tornado Man moved into the fire-gutted shack. He gathered up the charred debris, he added rows of stones, he salvaged some construction supplies in the hamlet: wood, pieces of corrugated tin, cardboard. All these materials, clumsily amalgamated, made him a shelter from the overly violent sun, from the overly strong winds and from everything that might loom out of the night. It would be his *hogan*.

Little Tornado Man turned eighteen. At that age the nights are long if you don't sleep because you're trying to comprehend the mysteries of the world. Sitting outside his cabin with his rifle close at hand, he spent long days waiting. Nothing came but the dizzying columns of sand, rolled by the wind, that swirled like lost souls. He wondered if a man could spend his whole life waiting.

One day, the men who had assaulted his father would come back to attack him. Little Tornado Man was big now, and strong. He was a very skilful marksman. Let the bandits come! He would fire bullets into their hearts. He would watch them drag themselves through the desert, wounded, bleeding. He'd make them pay for his father's death, for his childhood sorrow and the suffering of his mother, his brothers and his sisters. Had the men who'd come to seize his father's land talked about oil? He wasn't sure he remembered correctly. Had his father talked to him about oil? He was so young. Those events had happened so long ago. How could he remember everything that had happened, everything that had been said when he was still just a Little Tornado Man who couldn't even blow his own nose?

4 "After coming down from Canada, what detours brought Joseph Dubois here to the middle of the inaccessible Colorado mountains?" asks Robert Martin. "Farmer Dubois probably set out from the countryside somewhere in the province of Quebec. What made him head for Colorado? He did what thousands of other adventurers from foreign continents were doing. Is there a voice that travels the world like the wind and whispers to the desperate to go where they will find a better life?" the historian wonders. What a research project! What a fantastic way to get inside the soul of America, to penetrate like a curious microbe into the deepest fibres of the American fabric! What an epic! Telling the story of Farmer Dubois would rekindle the fabulous legend of the millions of French Canadians who emigrated to the United States. If he published Farmer Dubois's story, Robert Martin would resume with dignity his place in the forum of the nation's historians. Robert Martin hasn't published a book or even a major article for years now. In fact, his dean at the university reproached him for his intellectual silence when he refused to promote him. Time flies. . . . Not all that long ago, wasn't Martin the "young white wolf of history"? His sharpened fangs flayed the old people who wrote history as if they were writing pious tracts. Why had the farmer left his province of Quebec? Had he run away because of a love affair?

For hours now Robert Martin hasn't thought about his unhappiness or about his children whom he is forbidden to visit or about the house he has lost or about his great love ravaged by hatred like a garden by thistles. "Thank you, Farmer Dubois!" This project has just been waiting for a historian. Many mysteries hide behind the events of a lifetime. Was it possible that, in the cycle of his own existence, some unknown force decreed that Robert Martin must lose everything in order to become a young historian again and embark on the most important project of his career?

At breakfast, mired in silence, the customers seem hypnotized already by the desert into which they'll soon charge, in a movement that will resemble immobility. Robert Martin gathers up his belongings. Farewell, Universal Motel! Fitted out with a shower that smells of urine and a TV station full of shrill commercials and performers who sing with a twang, this shack is still more comfortable than what Farmer Dubois must have known during his wanderings. He must have slept often under the stars, in the rain, in the snow, in the terrible Arizona hail, in sand storms and hurricanes. Pain returns to Robert Martin's soul: why did his wife suddenly become so furious?

Outside the godforsaken motel, sitting against a giant palm tree, the white-haired old Indian seems to be waiting for him. He waves his one arm.

"Yesterday at the gas-pump I noticed your foreign plate. Quebec . . . 33 Grande Allée, Quebec, Canada."

"What did you say?" asks Robert Martin, astonished.

"Will you take me to the mesa? When my father was alive it was a whole day's walk. I'll show you the village on the mesa."

Robert Martin hesitates. The old Indian has undoubtedly been sleeping in his clothes for several days. He doesn't smell like a rose. He's covered with sand and dried needles. And what problems is he bringing? Why has he followed Robert Martin to the Universal Motel? The old Indian is a hunter; Robert Martin doesn't want to become his prey.

"Thirty-three Grande Allée, Quebec, Canada."

The historian is stunned to hear this address in the mouth of an Arizona Indian, but he has other things on his mind. "Farmer Dubois," he reasons, "buys cattle. Which means he's settling down after a life of travel and adventure. If he's settling down, it must be because he wants to start a family. To start a family, you need a woman. To have a woman, you first must find her. Back in those days, in this town built in a day over the mine, there were no women. It was a town of men who roamed the continent with packs on their backs and rifles in their hands. They only stopped when their pack was filled with gold or when they fell, struck by a bullet or a knife. The only women were in the brothel. It was the most impressive house in town. The chapel was smaller. Had Farmer Dubois fallen for one of them? Tired from her long nights of labour, pregnant perhaps, had one of the girls accepted Dubois's invitation to turn herself into a farmer's wife and look after the turkeys, the hens and the calves?"

"Thirty-three Grande Allée, Quebec, Canada," says the old Indian again.

The historian turns the key in the ignition.

"Very well, get in."

"I'm going to show you my village on the mesa."

The old Indian's breath smells as strong as a barrel of whiskey.

"There used to be a missionary. He'd stop here now and then. He must've died long ago. When I was a lad he was as old as I am today. He'd tell me nobody's all alone in this world. He talked about an angel that was guarding me. My father protected me."

Robert Martin is annoyed with himself for letting this undesirable passenger get in his car.

"Is this the right direction?" he asks.

"You'd like it better if I wasn't with you."

The old Indian lets a broad grin settle onto his face, its skin furrowed like the desert.

"I'm sorry."

The road is straight. The ground is flat. The cactuses look like soldiers saluting an invisible general. At the end of the desert, rocks throw fantastic shadows, like cathedrals, onto the horizon. There isn't a cloud in the sky. Now and then a black crow soars past. Everything is still. "This region is fascinating because its stillness is never the same," Robert Martin muses. He has read that the desert is alive with an abundant and secret life.

"How do you manage to live in the desert?"

The old Indian thinks this over, then smiles as if he's chosen not to reply.

"Stop," he says, "I'll go and ask a cactus."

Robert Martin is amused. This old Indian is no fool. His trick worked; now the *bohana* won't tell him to get out of the car. And the trip continues along the rectilinear road, without words. It's as if the car is not advancing, as if the Earth isn't turning, as if time isn't passing, as if here on this vast planet the humans are too small, as if here on this old planet, the humans are too young. Robert Martin wishes he were somewhere else.

"You see that column?" asks the old Indian, pointing. "Up there. At the top is the mesa."

Under the sun that feels like the hot breath of the embers when you throw a log on the fire, the car turns onto a narrow, rocky road, all curves, that crawls along a cliff. It straddles crevices, clings to spurs, projects over the gulf, climbs the bumpy parts, climbs and climbs again till it reaches the plateau where an Indian village is built. Robert Martin understands why it's called a "mesa": it is as flat as a table. He knows that *mesa* is the Spanish word for table. Two or three winding paths are lined with small stone houses.

Robert Martin decides that they're huts. The car can go no farther. Now they have to walk.

"Blanche Larivière, 33 Grande Allée, Quebec, Canada," recites Charlie Longsong.

"What did you say?"

5 For years, Charlie Longsong hasn't bothered to remember all that. Since yesterday, though, he's been thinking of nothing but those days in the past. Many seasons have streamed by since then. Over time, all traces are erased from the sand. But ever since he spied that car with a Quebec licence plate at the trading post, he's been thinking about nothing but Blanche Larivière. "33 Grande Allée, Quebec, Canada." He feels as feverish as if he'd actually seen her get out of her car.

When he went back to his *hogan* yesterday, Charlie Longsong had the impression Blanche Larivière was walking with him. He could hear the rustling of her invisible dress. But only Charlie Longsong's feet were creaking across the gravel and crushing dried plants.

Behind a clump of sagebrush he spied a roadrunner. It's a bird that doesn't show itself often. Charlie Longsong slowed down. The bird was very busy. What Charlie Longsong saw Blanche Larivière had never seen. The roadrunner was attacking a snake. The bird doesn't use his wings. Instead of flying, he prefers to use his long legs and run. He only flutters his wings to frighten his prey. He shakes them, then dances, wriggles. Blanche Larivière used to dance too. Because of the beating wings and the stamping feet, the poor snake didn't know what he was dealing with. He dared not move. It was time to strike. The roadrunner began to stab the snake with his beak. Relentlessly he struck at the snake's head. The long body writhed. Slowly the snake coiled himself so his head was underneath his body, protected there. Blanche Larivière would have enjoyed seeing that. It was war. Blanche Larivière had known war . . .

The roadrunner seized the snake's head from beneath his coiled body and, squeezing it in his beak, began shaking the animal from left to right, to break it. The snake coiled and uncoiled till he grew numb and stopped moving. The roadrunner, frenzied now because of his victory, still squeezing the snake by the throat, thrashed the ground with the long, inert body. As if Blanche Larivière were there with him, Charlie Longsong explained:

"That bird is tenderizing his meat."

Charlie Longsong did not move, so the stones would stay silent. When he decided his meal was ready, the roadrunner calmed down, gazed triumphantly at his victim, then started gulping his meal. The old man mused:

"Animals die without complaining."

Ah! Blanche Larivière would have enjoyed seeing this conflict. She thought the desert was a place where nothing existed. "Where is rue Gît-le-coeur?" She had taught him to pronounce these words in her French language. It wasn't easy for him to make the foreign sounds. She teased him:

"You sound as if your lips were baked by the desert."

She warned him:

"One day you'll be lost in the city of Paris and if you don't know how to ask *'Où est la rue Gît-le-coeur?'* you won't be able to find me."

One evening, maybe because of the red wine, he no longer remembered which side of the river he was on. He'd forgotten on which side the rue Gît-le-coeur was located. And he searched. He tried to read the maps at the entrances to the Métro. Never had he been lost in the desert. He always knew where the sun was suspended. He could always spot the blue wall of the mountains and recognize the familiar touch of the wind. How was he going to locate the rue Gît-le-coeur, Blanche Larivière's street? In this city the streets all resembled one another, they crisscrossed, became entangled. Thousands of people were bustling about, but none of them could understand his language. Desperate, he dared to say in French: *"Où est la rue Gît-le-coeur?"* The sounds had emerged from his mouth perfectly formed because the person pointed him in the right direction. He told Blanche Larivière about his misadventure. She teased her Indian, who couldn't get lost in the desert but had lost his way just around the corner from rue Gît-le-coeur.

All these memories had come back to Charlie Longsong. He hadn't slept last night. Filled too full with his past, his feverish old body had no room for sleep. The springtime of his life was coming back to brighten the autumn of his old age. His memory was adorned with recollections the way bushes come to life and spill over with flowers in the spring. "We forget so many things!" he thought.

When he came home from the war Charlie Longsong had to dig down to enter the debris of his *hogan*, which was buried under the sand. Blanche Larivière never left his dreams. He told himself she would come back to see him. He would show her his land and how to hunt coyote. He would persuade her to stay with him. He had gone to put in an appearance before the people of the mesa, in his American Army uniform. Those who knew nothing but the rock of the mesa and the gravel of the desert couldn't understand what he had lived through. He told them how a shell had torn off an arm like a fire-wolf. The men laughed sadly: "Is a man with one arm still a man?" The women joked: "With just one arm can a man really prove to a woman he's a man?" Charlie Longsong, formerly Little Tornado Man, was patient. He demonstrated to the men that with just one hand he could still fire at a pebble flung into the air. As for the women, they'd have fallen silent if they'd seen him walking hand in hand with Blanche Larivière. For a long time, Charlie Longsong did not go up to the mesa. As he'd learned to do in England, he dug a trench around his hut. That way no one could attack him.

Blanche Larivière had told him about her city of Quebec in Canada. He had described his Arizona, with its sagebrush and *saguaros*—cactuses in which woodpeckers pecked holes where tiny birds nested with their families. He had described the brilliant flowers that adorn the cactuses in the springtime. She had told him how the snow is spread across the fields of Quebec for months at a time and how a river longer than the Colorado turns to ice during the winter. She had explained to him how on certain days, in her city of Quebec, the cold burns like fire. In that cold, a man, too, can freeze like water. She told him the story of a man who loved a woman. He went off to work far away in a forest where they felled giant fir trees. After being separated for several months, he decided to go and see the woman he loved. This was during a terrible winter. The lover fell asleep, surrounded by eddies of snow stirred up by the wind. He was lost. He couldn't tell where he was going or where he was. He froze to death. It was not a painful death. The man had fallen asleep, crying out the name of his beloved the way a child calls for his mother. Charlie Longsong had told Blanche Larivière he didn't want to freeze to death in the snow of Canada. She replied that she wasn't afraid of the desert.

Charlie Longsong had never said a word about that to anyone. In all Arizona he alone knew what had happened. He tried to convince himself he didn't need to write to Blanche Larivière. He refused the humiliation of asking for help from a woman on the mesa who knew how to write love letters. In the end, he reconciled himself to confiding to the woman at the trading post that he wanted to write to Blanche Larivière, whom he thought about day and night. He wanted to reassure her that he felt her close to him as if she were there with him on his walks. He wanted her to know that he no longer had to dream because the thought of her was more beautiful than a beautiful dream.

At that time he still had nightmares. His memory would explode all at once with things he remembered from the war. Like him, Blanche Larivière had come from America. Like him, she had crossed the ocean. Like him, she had encountered war. Like him, she'd gone back to her country to live. He thought about her constantly. Did he need to write? Thoughts don't need a stamp or envelope to travel. She was thinking about him, too. He knew it. He talked to her and she could sense it. She talked to him and he could hear it. For a long time he kept hoping to find a letter from her at the trading post. When a letter did arrive for him, it was a cheque from the Government—a compensation for the arm he'd lost in the war. If Blanche Larivière had written him, he wouldn't have been able to read all those pages on his own; he'd have had to ask the woman at the trading post for help. Thinking about that disadvantage, he preferred that Blanche Larivière not write him.

In his desert Charlie Longsong wasn't really alone, because Blanche Larivière was holding his hand, just as she'd held it on the rue Gît-le-coeur, in Paris.

6 Robert Martin is perched up high. Charlie Longsong had him climb onto the roof of the highest house. The others have just one storey. This one has two. Down below on the mesa, the grey desert plain stretches all the way to the horizon.

"That's my land over there," Charlie Longsong indicates. "They tried to take it away from my father. That would be like skinning a hare that's still alive. Men fight back. My father fought. While me, I still had my baby teeth. I fought back like my father. He fired. I fired too. I still had hands like a little girl. I fired. That day I lost my father. It was night. The men who wanted our land were *bohanas*, white men, white men like you. Those people only come out at night. I thought I should run to the mesa and ask for help. And then I thought it would take me a while to get there. If my father was all alone in the desert during that time, jackals would be attracted to his blood. So I turned back. My father wasn't where I'd left him. I cried. I looked for him. Even though the night was as black as the souls of the *bohanas* who wanted to take my father's land, I could see as clearly as if it were broad daylight. I could see the smallest twig that had been trampled by a foot. My throat was choked with all my childish sorrow as I cried out, I called to him. I was sure he'd answer me. I knew a father wouldn't abandon his son all alone in the desert. I'd tried to help him. I was just a child. I fired. It's not fair that a child should have to fire a rifle. All I knew was how to play with my little wooden horse. I knew my father would come back. And he did come back to visit me in my dreams. A man doesn't die. . . . That land is mine and I say so to all of Arizona, even though I know Arizona's not listening to me. . . . Here, have a drink."

Charlie Longsong takes a flask from inside his denim jacket.

"I don't want a drink," says Robert Martin, curtly.

Isn't it his duty as a well-intentioned white man to teach this poor Indian a lesson and stop him from destroying himself with alcohol?

Charlie Longsong takes a very long swig of whiskey.

"Everything I told you, I told Blanche Larivière, on rue Gît-le-coeur, in Paris. When the war was over she went back to her country: '33 Grande Allée, Quebec, Canada.' . . . After a while I forgot

Blanche Larivière.... A man forgets everything. A man forgets the day he was born, the most important day. A man also forgets the days of love. Yes sir, I loved a *bohana*, I loved Blanche Larivière, rue Gît-le-coeur, in Paris. Yes sir, I loved Blanche Larivière, 33 Grande Allée, Quebec, Canada. Yesterday at the trading post, when I saw the name 'Quebec' on your licence plate, my memory was resurrected like the missionaries' Jesus.... Here, take a swig."

During the short trip that brought him from the Universal Motel to the mesa with this Indian sitting beside him, Robert Martin felt an unsettling discomfort. On the curves, his hands gripped the wheel in an unusual way. This traveller was having a strange effect on him. Of course his smell was repulsive. The old man is a little bit crazy, the way people can be at his age. He drifts like an old boat along the river of his memories. If Robert Martin were honest with himself, he'd have to admit he was irritated because he's white and Charlie Longsong's an Indian. Sitting in the car, they were two individuals, that is, two molecules of the planet's human tissue, both of them no doubt shuddering, burdened with the memory of the ages. An educated man, Robert Martin felt the same age-old reaction as a dog beside a cat. In his car, where all the inventions of human progress were brought together, Robert Martin reacted the way man reacted when he was an ape among other apes. Yet this Indian is simply a pitiful, touching old man who is carried away by the tangle of his memories.

The crowd has climbed onto the flat roofs of the low houses that surround the public square. Robert Martin is the only white man. The little girls are all spruced up in their shiny new shoes and their brightly coloured dresses. The boys aren't dressed for the festivities and they're quarrelling. The mothers are holding their sleeping babies. The fathers are drinking beer. The old people are wrapped in blankets. Down below on the public square, feverish comings and goings announce the festivities. A stranger in a crowd of Indians, perched on a rooftop, without his wife, without his children, Robert Martin is experiencing all the pain of his wound and he feels lonely as he's never felt before. The desert stretches out to the horizon. His life, like that space, has been emptied of everything he loved.

When he was en route to Colorado, Farmer Dubois, too, must have felt abandoned by everyone. Travelling across America on horseback towards his dream, he must have encountered Indians in his roaming. Indians probably guided him along the paths with which they'd marked the continent. Did he fight them? Did they attack him? Did he attack them? On some stormy or winter nights, did he ask them for hospitality? Had Farmer Dubois loved a young Indian girl in the moonlight? In the depths of Robert Martin's sorrow, life begins again. The unknown farmer, Dubois, is an epic character. Robert Martin will prove to his dean that his historian's flame has never been doused. He will write his next book on Farmer Dubois, unknown and exemplary expatriate. His next book will shake up all those sleepy trained frogs who take themselves for powerful oxen. While they croaked, he was silent. His silence won't have been in vain. He's been waiting for the right opportunity. He'll get that promotion. He'll show them what he can do! He will write history the way people tell a good story, without betraying scholarly principles.

Coming from the public square, a song chanted by deep voices spreads like a growling wind. All eyes turn towards the centre of the square, where heads are emerging from the ground.

(Later on, when Robert Martin is curious enough to read up on the subject, he'll learn that these Indians believe their ancestors emanated from the world underground. The people he sees emerging from the earth are coming out of a *kiva*, a circular underground chamber where for days now they have been performing age-old rituals so that rain will come to quench the thirst of the corn that will feed the tribe. Elders, who know how to interpret the silence of the sky and to speak to those who live on the other side of the night, have poured symbolic water onto stones gathered from the four points of the compass. They have smoked magic leaves. The dense smoke filling the *kiva,* and everything it has touched, is now endowed with beneficent power. With long dances and endlessly repeated sacred formulas, they have consecrated the black, white and red sand that will be spread on the earth to fertilize it for the next harvest. He will learn, too, that before the ceremony, the men of the tribe collected snakes from the four corners of their domain and that the snakes too took part in the secret rites of the *kiva.*)

For the time being, Robert Martin observes the costumed characters who are emerging from the earth like a dense and multicoloured harvest. They make their way to the public square, chanting a repetitive tune punctuated by drumbeats that the dance obeys. Their faces are painted to imitate the features of animals. The dancers are of all ages. In the procession are mixed the lightness of youth and the weightiness of accumulated years. Feet beat out the rhythm, stamping the soil in a single cadence and stirring up the dust. Little bells tied to their ankles mark their movements. Some voices are low, others strident. Together, voices, bells, drums and pounding feet form a chorus that seems to be singing deep in the bowels of the earth. Bedecked with the masks of eagles, crows, antelopes or coyotes, the dancers follow, two by two, in line. Some imitate the animal that runs, others the animal that flies. They form a circle in the middle of the square, then another. The dancers in the first circle turn in one direction, those in the second circle the opposite way. Then the circles come undone and form again amid a riot of feathers and coloured ribbons.

Clustered on the rooftops, families clap their hands. The intensity of their gazes convinces Robert Martin that these Indians see something he doesn't see. It goes on interminably. The same movements. The same song. On the rooftops, all the bodies are motionless, except for the hands that accompany the rhythm of the drums. The souls are with the dancers' souls.

The historian feels as if he's on the edge of a high cliff. He is gripped by a kind of vertigo. He moves back a few steps. He feels hypnotized. It goes on. The dancers don't want to stop. They are dancing the way people swim to keep from drowning. Their feet seem not to touch the ground. It's as if they are dancing on the dust. Their energy is never spent. The sun is blazing hot. Its rays set fire to the coloured robes, the feather necklaces. And still they go on dancing. Gradually, the incantation whose words he wishes he could understand is pitched low, like thunder growling in a heavy sky.

Men bring tall earthenware jars and spill their contents into the middle of the square. They had been filled with snakes, which now uncoil and coil up again, untangle and tangle in the blazing light. Without slowing their movements, without supressing their song, the dancers come close to the crowd of snakes, pick one up—each of them in turn—and, still marking the rhythm, they form circles that turn in opposite directions. They dance and dance and the snakes stir restlessly at the ends of outstretched arms. All at once, each dancer brings the head of his snake to his mouth and grips it between his teeth. Trapped, the poisonous little head thrashes and flails at the dancer. Endlessly, they dance and dance around the square. The snakes writhe between the clenched teeth. They dance and dance as if they are trying to fall from exhaustion.

(Robert Martin wants to know more. When he reads up on the subject it will be revealed to him that after the ceremony the snakes will be set free and will go off to the four points of the compass bearing messages to the gods from the tribe that sorely needs water for its corn and for its wells. The people hope that big black clouds will soon advance across the desert.)

Now, though, Robert Martin knows nothing about that. Turning around because someone has touched his shoulder, he spies Charlie Longsong with a snake between his teeth. His legs wobble. His heart stops. His throat is knotted. He has never seen a snake up so close. His face is burning. He feels himself go white. The roof is pitching like the deck of a ship. Is he going to faint? He doesn't want to do that. Charlie Longsong takes the snake from his mouth and allows it to wrap itself around his arm.

"My lord Snake will carry my message to Blanche Larivière, 33 Grande Allée, Quebec, Canada."

7 Charlie Longsong's recollections had been erased from his memory like his youth from his body. They had left him, along with the young man he had been. The recollections of youth had mingled with the dust of the desert and been carried away by the wind. All it took was some rain on the desert and the small white lilies emerged from the soil where they had hidden to escape the drought. All it took was the appearance of a car with Quebec plates and he was able to rediscover images from his past.

Charlie Longsong had retained just one memory. It was from the time before he became a man. He hadn't forgotten his father's anxiety. Other adults he talked to looked anxious as well. Little Tornado Man couldn't understand why. The adults talked to each other in the way they exchanged secrets the children weren't supposed to know. In the evening, his father would gaze at the distant horizon for a long time, but Little Tornado Man couldn't see anything coming. He noticed that his father no longer left his rifle near the door but took it with him to his pallet. His father had told him two or three times, as if he'd forgotten what he'd said:

"If you see anyone coming near, be ready to bring me my rifle if I don't already have it in my hand."

One night the *bohanas* came. Little Tornado Man spied them before his father, who was bent over the corn. To get to the moisture you must plant very deep, and then you're liable to encounter hungry little rodents that tunnel in the earth so they can eat the growing plants. Little Tornado Man, with his slingshot, was on the lookout. The sun was setting. That is the time of day when rodents dare to come out because the sun doesn't burn them. He was very adept with his slingshot. He rarely missed his target. The rats rolled onto their backs when he struck them on the head. In the setting sun he saw five men coming forward. Suddenly he understood why his father had asked him to stand ready to bring his rifle. The *bohanas* were advancing, and at their backs the sun made a great wound in the sky from which blood was pouring. So then he shouted to his father:

"They're coming!"

His father raised his head. Waited for them. There were five. They were walking one behind the other like a ten-legged beast. That was what Charlie Longsong remembered. That was how his memory laid out the facts. They're inscribed there like those signs the ancestor left on the wall of the cliff near the stream. It was the only thing he remembered. He'd even forgotten the war on the other side of the ocean, in spite of his lost hand and the pain it caused him. That was how matters were before he spotted the car that had come from Quebec. It was a memory as vast as the desert. As vast as the night. Little Tornado Man had rushed towards the *hogan* and snatched up his father's rifle. Outside— this he will never forget—the great bleeding wound of the sun had closed. The night was pitch-black like the heart of a *bohana*.

That night, what happened had happened. And it was as important as the day of his birth.

Yesterday, he saw the car that had come from the country of Blanche Larivière. After that, he couldn't sleep. He could only think about the time of his youth and about everything that had happened with Blanche Larivière on rue Gît-le-coeur in Paris. He'd forgotten that. From year to year he had been drifting away from that time. The rue Gît-le-coeur was so far from Arizona. And yet it was all buried in his soul.

The memories of youth made his old baked skin shiver. He was restless. Little Tornado Man had just awakened inside the wrinkled body of an old man. And so to find calm he drank bourbon. He felt strong enough to travel across Arizona, the United States and Canada to find Blanche Larivière. He wished he could sleep, forget all that, but his memories no longer wanted to be merely memories. The young man who'd been wakened wanted to experience what the old man was remembering. Now both the young man and the old man were drunk. Old Charlie Longsong was crying because he now had only his memory. Little Tornado Man was crying because he didn't want to become old. Together, they cried to the stars:

"Blanche Larivière!"

Very early, at dawn, the sun pierced the eyelids of the Indian asleep against his *hogan*. He got up. He must leave his desert now and find Blanche Larivière. Charlie Longsong had heard that the traveller from Quebec had gone to the Universal Motel to sleep. He would find the man's car and get himself driven to Quebec, Canada.

Many other memories have flooded the present. Long, long ago soldiers had come to the trading post to announce that war was about to break out on the other side of the ocean. The United States Army needed strong young men, good marksmen, able to fight. "Write your name on the dotted line at the bottom of the form if you're not afraid of fighting," said the soldiers. Charlie Longsong observed the young *bohanas* who were signing the form. He didn't dare step into their midst, but he wanted to go and fight like them. Suddenly the words sprang from his mouth:

"I can shoot a pebble if you throw it in the air!"

"We need you!" replied one of the uniformed men.

Charlie Longsong hadn't thought about that for so long. He recalled how his feet had suffered in his boots. He had to keep his shoes clean and shiny even if he was marching through mud. He saw himself again, asleep during an endless bus trip that brought him to a group of at least a thousand men. When they marched they were all supposed to lift the same foot at the same time. They were all supposed to carry their rifles on the same shoulder. That's what you had to learn to become a soldier.

After that they boarded a giant boat. He had never seen a boat before. And then they went to sea for several days. It was like riding a horse as big as a mountain whose strides could bring your heart to your mouth. Luckily you could play cards. At the beginning of the journey Charlie didn't know the games. He observed, he learned, not daring to play. Luckily, there was rum to drink. And rum, people said, catches hold of your heart. It was true. His own heart grew numb. Some of the men played music. Others repeated the same song a hundred times a day. No one liked the boat. The beds were arranged like the shelves in the trading post. There were no other Indians like him. He'd seen Blacks on deck— where were they hiding? On the first day his companions didn't want to sleep beside an Indian. Someone told him an Indian's place is on a reservation. Another asked him if he'd brought his bow and arrows. Each time there was much laughter. And there was more when someone said:

"Hey, Chief, show us how to scalp a Nazi!"

Charlie Longsong went up to the man. His white skin turned green when he saw the knife. Charlie grabbed the man by the hair and slipped the blade of his knife onto his Adam's apple.

The sergeant shouted an order. All the *bohanas* stood at attention, even the one with the knife at his throat. Charlie didn't let go.

"Attention! You're fighting your fellow Americans," the sergeant reprimanded them. "Don't you know there's a war on? We're going to fight the enemy, not each other."

Slowly, Charlie obeyed.

"Do you know the enemy is all around our boat?"

Like the others, he realized later that the sea was infested with floating bombs and German submarines. At that moment, though, none of the soldiers suspected any danger. They were floating in their boat the way they'd floated in their mothers' bellies, not knowing what lay ahead of them when they came out. They played cards, sang, slept. Now and then they were given a tot of rum. They spent hours lying on their beds, dreaming about their small towns. In this sombre place Charlie Longsong was still able to recall the sun's warmth on his skin and the scent of sage in the air. He saw there a cactus, here the tracks of a rat, far away the blue mountains, on the right the leaves of a yucca and, in the distance, a leaping cholla with its plump, hairy fingers.

He hadn't thought about that for such a long time. The war he fought seems as remote now as the stories about the ancestors recounted by the Elders of the mesa. Charlie Longsong had fallen into the great black hole of time past.

Blanche Larivière's skin was as white as milk. He still remembers very clearly: when he opened his eyes in the hospital he didn't know where he was. He'd been asleep (he didn't know how long), like the dead. He didn't know what had happened to him. Pain burned his arm. It hurt so badly. He cried out like a suffering dog. A young woman with a white face was bending over him. She was smiling sweetly, as if she hadn't heard his cries.

8 The ceremony has ended. The old Indian wants to introduce Robert Martin to the whole tribe. At each introduction, Charlie Longsong shows off his knowledge of the French language, then asks Robert Martin to confirm his mastery of the language of that country he'd gone to in his youth, to fight a war. He announces to everybody that he's going north with this stranger who will take him to 33 Grande Allée, Quebec, Canada. At first Robert Martin protests feebly. He explains that he's not heading back to Canada right away, that he intends to explore Arizona and then New Mexico and probably California. Most likely he'll come back this way.

"I could pick you up then..."

He's not afraid to lie.

"I'll come to New Mexico with you! You'll learn to like my bourbon, you'll see..."

Robert Martin doesn't want this Indian or anyone else. He needs to be alone. He has no obligation towards this old man. The longer he stays with him, the more sure Charlie Longsong becomes that he'll make the journey. He decides this is enough.

"See you later, Monsieur Longsong! I'll be back in three weeks.... Thank you for the celebration. What incredible dancing!"

He walks to his car. The old Indian catches up with him, grabs Martin's shoulder with his one hand and pleads.

"Take me to 33 Grande Allée, Quebec, Canada."

"I can't!" Robert Martin snaps, impatient. "I'm not going to Canada right now."

"Take me with you!"

With his one arm the old Indian grabs Robert Martin around the waist. What power! The intellectual is worried. How is this going to end? The old man is clutching him very tightly. He's drunk. He's angry. Robert Martin is the only white man on the mesa.

"No," he declares in what he thinks is an authoritative tone, "I'm not taking you to Canada because you haven't got a passport. You need a passport."

"If I stay, you stay."

The old man tightens his hold. Robert Martin doesn't dare struggle. He's too afraid. Afraid of being weak. Afraid because he's alone.

"Call the police!"

He can't take back these ridiculous words that escaped from him in his terror. The onlookers guffaw. He's behaved like a good little well-educated white man who has confidence in his police. He's ashamed. He sees all the white teeth shining in their mocking smiles.

"I want to find Blanche Larivière . . ."

"When I come back this way I'll take you where you want to go . . ."

"You won't come back. There's never a next time."

With wild enjoyment, the bystanders are following this altercation with a *bohana*.

"I can't take you. Make him understand," pleads the historian, gasping for breath. "The United States is a free country. I can take whoever I want in my car. And I don't want to take him! I don't want to pick up every old drunk I see along the road. What would he do in Canada? Could he live with snow up to his armpits? Blanche Larivière's probably been in the graveyard for ages. He's strangling me. Help!"

Laughing and shoving, the men extricate the historian from Charlie Longsong's steely grip. Robert Martin dashes to his car. The old Indian pleads:

"I want to see Blanche Larivière..."

Why did his parents make him a puny intellectual? In America, a man needs hard fists. Why must the sweet moments in life turn sour? His love... his marriage... Attending this ceremonial dance on the rooftop of a house, the only White in an Indian crowd, with that family singing the insistent lament whose words stretched out into the blue sky like a heavy wind: it was a unique privilege. Centuries ago, no doubt, in this very place, Indians danced in the same way, pounding the earth and their drums in the same rhythm. The words of their endless incantation must be the echo across the centuries of the words of the first inhabitants of the American continent. If he had lived a thousand years ago, Robert Martin would no doubt have seen the same shimmering costumes with their fringes, feathers, ribbons and fur to suggest the shapes of the bear, raven, eagle, coyote. And all those snakes... A white man cannot understand. Especially not him; he has a pathological fear of anything that crawls. The ritual he attended is a testimony to the time when man was not yet divorced from nature. The snake couldn't be an enemy then. What an amazing day! It's as if he were living through a day in the time of Hernando Cortes. He owes this privileged moment to Charlie Longsong. "Thanks, old Charlie!" But Charlie Longsong has also ruined this exceptional day for him. Every time he tries to recall this snake dance in Arizona, a bitter memory will surface of the old Indian on the mesa, clinging to him.

Did Charlie Longsong really live that incredible love story? If so, Robert Martin was too stingy to let him finish it. For a long time the old man will continue to call to his beloved. Whenever he thinks about it, Robert Martin knows he'll feel uncomfortable, slightly guilty. How could he not help someone who wants to love? Has he hated love since the end of his own love story? His behaviour was petty. He didn't want to allow someone else's destiny to be fulfilled. He's behaved like one of those comfortably well-off people who won't let anything disturb their routine. He has no reason to be proud of himself. Could he have acted otherwise? He himself is a wounded man. He no longer has his wife or his children or his house, his chalet, his boat.... He's a man whose love has been amputated.

All of that seethes in his head while he's driving towards Colorado. He has decided to go back to that town in the mountains where he discovered the notebook containing the signature of Farmer Dubois. He wants to reread the contents, make a photocopy. Why did that adventurer choose to plough the earth rather than dig under the mountains in search of wealth? So many mysteries in a man's life!

When you drive your car for two days, alone in a region whose inhabitants don't seem to have arrived yet, you have time for daydreams. Here is a gas station in the midst of some shacks plastered over with advertising posters. Across from it, there is fruit for sale. Robert Martin is hungry, thirsty; above all, he's hungry to talk with somebody. There, a junk shop. Someone has gathered up everything the inhabitants of the region might have thrown out, if there were any. In one corner sits a pile of several hundred books, grey with dust. Might there be something about Arizona? Colorado? The Indians? Even if he didn't let that drunken old Indian in his car, Robert Martin respects the culture of the first peoples who inhabited America. He knows he lacked courage. Historians are not courageous people. They only venture into the past, where everything has already happened. Robert Martin is being tortured by his own grief. The old Indian called out the name of a woman as if he'd been suffering for a century. Robert Martin couldn't bear Charlie Longsong's grief on top of his own.

He leaves with a bag full of old books that recount the story of the West, with its cowboys, Indians, bandits, mines, saloons: the entire culture with which Farmer Dubois must have been familiar.

Over the past two or three years, Robert Martin has lost his appetite for reading. When he opens a book he always has the impression he's already read it. He has lost his appetite for discovery. The dean was right: his career has become sterile. The old books he's just tossed onto the seat smell musty.

The stones glitter in the sunlight. The asphalt is so hot his tires seem to be melting. A motel appears. A swimming pool along the dusty road, behind a fence. The water will feel good when he dives into it. And maybe some pretty traveller will be lost in the desert too. He has his old books on the West.... If it weren't for his grief, this would be a dream: palm trees, books, a pool. He turns the car towards the motel.

Robert Martin swims for a while in the water that is too blue, he goes to buy some white California wine and opens one of his yellowed old books, leafing through it without reading until his eyes light on the words "French Canadians." He stops. He reads. The Valley of the Rio de las Animas perdides—which means "The Valley of the River of Lost Souls"—was very rich land. French Canadians came there to hunt beaver. Their market was the top hat industry in England. Over-hunted, the species disappeared. Then the French Canadians became importers of whiskey. They diluted it. They sold it at high prices to Indians, who paid with furs. In those days, it was said that the mountains of Colorado shone because they were made of gold. They also contained silver, coal, everything.... There was a rush of adventurers from all over: Canada, Italy, Russia, France, China. To accommodate the railway, work got under way to dig out a shelf in the red granite cliff. To smash the rock, to dynamite and dig, workers were sometimes suspended by cables hundreds of metres above the river in the gorge. The Chinese were responsible for the dynamite. Generally, they weren't liked. Once, a noisy group was going to lynch a poor Chinese man who was walking peacefully down the street. A strapping fellow intervened, brandishing his revolver: "If you wipe out my Chinaman, who'll wash my shirt?" he worried. At that time, the Chinese ran laundries. In a saloon one evening, a Chinese man was forced to stretch out on the floor. A dancer performed her show on his back. They played hard. It was not uncommon for a man to enter a nightclub on horseback and knock back a drink without dismounting.... Another time, someone found the skeleton of a gold digger near his claim, murdered by a jealous colleague no doubt. Some jokers invited the skeleton to the saloon and gave him a drink. The manners of these rough men weren't very refined. A famous missionary preacher was in the habit of storming into the saloon; then he'd take out his revolver and force the customers, the girls, the drunks and the killers to their knees for a prayer. After everyone had asked God's forgiveness, he'd put his revolver back in the holster and continue his evangelizing mission in some other gin joint. Before becoming a farmer, had Dubois been a gold digger, a smuggler, a cowboy, a bandit, a dynamiter?

The great red ball of the sun has rolled to the edge of the desert. The earth has become a dark page where characters are printed in black on black. Robert Martin continues to read and drink white wine.

He opens another book. Turns the pages. Geronimo. An Indian warrior. The most hardened American soldiers blanched, says the author, at the sound of his name. And yet, he adds ironically, his name meant "he who yawns." In Geronimo's day, Farmer Dubois sought adventure. Those were troubled times. After the Civil War, the government began to limit the movement of Indians. They were confined to reservations. The government forced them to give up their nomadic way of life and converted them to agriculture and Christianity. Geronimo was the greatest of the rebel chiefs. Undernourished, humiliated, starving, longing for their land and their endless freedom, his brother Apaches followed the furious Geronimo. The Arizona soil became red with all the blood that was shed. Geronimo's raging troops attacked the military convoys and encampments. Never had Arizona been swept by a hurricane so cruel. Had Farmer Dubois witnessed these deeds? Had he suffered from them? In the end, the great Geronimo had to cave in to the Whites. They sentenced him to harsh labour. Soon he was converted to Christianity and turned himself into a farmer. Unfortunately, he had learned from the Whites how to play cards. He became such a keen gambler that the church expelled him. His vice was deemed incurable. Exiled to Oklahoma, Geronimo survived by selling photos of himself at local fairs. The great Geronimo finally looked like what the Whites wanted him to be. In one photo, the man who had been a great Indian warrior is sitting at the wheel of a car of the time, dressed in European clothes like a tourist. The historian is intrigued by the signature on the photograph: Dooboy. Could this name be hiding a Dubois in disguise? Many French Canadians changed their names in the United States. Dubois, Photographer: is it possible? The historian wants to find his subject so badly, he imagines him everywhere.

Even though he was condemned to wander from day to day along American paths, Dubois had the unique privilege of existing at a time when a man could win the freedom to live like a pagan, unconstrained by the conventions of an assembly-line society.

Robert Martin closes his book. Is it the white wine? Is it the anecdotes from those wild times? He feels woozy. He looks at the sky. "Where's the Big Dipper?" He looks up: he can't remember. "A man can imagine that every star is a letter and that those letters form words, but who can read the messages God has written?" Even if he is no longer a believer, he senses eternity in the sky, and it makes him tremble. A little because of the wine, a little because of the stories he's just read, a little because of his vertigo in the face of the night, he feels some affection for what he believed in as a child.

Everything's not over just because his wife abandoned him. Writing Farmer Dubois's biography will help him through the painful process of divorce. The account of a life lived during a century of violent colonization will demonstrate his intellectual rebirth. The dean will drop his dentures in his soup! Robert Martin can't read any more. His eyes are burning his eyelids. He will eat and sleep. He is so lonely. He wishes he were home.

What's going on in Canada right now? He goes to his room and dials his lawyer's number.

"Your ex-wife is afraid you've been hiding out in the States to escape your obligations as father and husband. She wants to initiate a demand for extradition."

Robert Martin says nothing. He's sorry he is too civilized to deliver a punch to the greenish wall that has received many others.

9 Charlie Longsong has fire in his eyes. He was unable to stop the car from Quebec from driving away without him. Out there, it is descending towards the plain, wrapped in the dust it stirs up. He howls. Held down by ten men, he struggles, kicks like a wild horse. His one arm is as strong as the two arms of a young man. His body is as straight as an aspen on the green hills in the distance. He is lashing out as if he had five arms. He cries out in another language.

"Blanche Larivière!"

Each cry seems to rip out his heart. The old man's face is awash in tears. His grief is filled with anger.

"Where does he get all that strength?" wonders one of the men who is holding him. "He's as old as my old grandpa's father."

Robert Martin's car has turned into the dunes and the wind has scattered the cloud of dust it stirred up. Vanquished, Charlie Longsong drops his head and closes his eyes.

"Let go of him!"

"Let him cry all the tears of his sorrow."

The men loosen their hold. They step back. Charlie Longsong is free. Looking lost, he gazes all around him. What does he see that the others do not? Lifting his eyes to the sky he cries out:

"I'm talking to you, Blanche Larivière. Can you hear me?"

The men and women gathered there wonder: "Who is he talking to?"

"Blanche Larivière, where is the rue Gît-le-coeur?"

Is he speaking magic words? A secret incantation? Diabolical curses like the ones the *bohanas* say? Is he casting a spell on the mesa? The dogs bark and stir restlessly at Charlie Longsong's cries.

The *bohana* from the north was right to disappear. He should never have come to this territory. Nothing good happens on the day an Indian meets a *bohana*.

When the war was over, Charlie Longsong appeared on the mesa to show off his military uniform. He boasted that he knew words in a foreign language. He was proud. Others laughed at him.

"A woman, a foreign woman taught me those words."

They laughed even harder.

"Is it because the women here don't want you? Is that why you had to learn a special language to talk to *bohana* women?"

That was a long time ago. Do people as old as Charlie Longsong still remember? Everyone was glad Charlie Longsong wasn't killed in the war. Indians have always known how not to die in a war. A man who comes back from the other side of the ocean can tell whatever stories he wants to those who didn't go. And they had every right to doubt him. They didn't want to believe Charlie Longsong had had a white woman in the Old Countries where all their troubles had come from.

For a long time he didn't go back to the mesa. He lay low in his desert. He never talked again about how the war had eaten one of his arms. He never mentioned again the name of the woman who'd taught him the words in that foreign language. On the mesa, his story flew away with the seasons. The old people forgot it. The young aren't interested in the past.

This morning, there are those who wonder if Charlie Longsong has been bitten by the serpent of madness. The men slowly shrink back and abandon him in the middle of the plaza. He can't see that all around him, perched on the rooftops as if the dance had never been interrupted, the crowd has gathered again to observe his pain. He lies there as if he's fallen asleep. Is he dead? Some fear that he is. An Elder recalls:

"When he was young he left here to fight in the war. He came back alive. That Indian knows how to stay alive."

Another remembers:

"Little Tornado Man has guarded his father's land the way a young eagle guards its nest."

A quietly wise man says reassuringly:

"Even when he comes to the final acre of his walk on Earth, a man can still go crazy because of a woman."

The old Indian doesn't hear these remarks. He stirs a little in the middle of the plaza. He gets up. He sits down. He gropes inside his jacket for his flask. Ceremoniously, he opens it. Drinks. After wiping his lips on the back of his sleeve he lets the flask fall onto the gravel, he gets up, and just as if he weren't drunk, he heads for the road that runs down to the desert. Very far ahead of him, the horizon line wavers. The grey earth turns around the mesa like a great wheel. The old man sways on his legs and crumples and nobody sees it, he himself doesn't realize he's fallen. He rolls down the length of the arid slope where a few tufts of silvery shrubs have sprung up.

Because of the whiskey and because of his grief, he sleeps. He will sleep for a long time. All at once a shadow stirs in the night. It has wakened him. He opens his eyes. He peers into the intense darkness. The wind is blowing in his direction. It brings no sound. The shadow is silent. It moves rapidly. It grows bigger against the sky, it draws near. A horse. He trembles. Someone is coming this way on horseback. He listens. The hooves are silent. Charlie Longsong recognizes this animal that is passing in the night like a cloud in the sky. It's his father's mare. The beautiful black animal. He recognizes his father's way of holding himself so straight that nothing could make him bend. A child is sitting on the animal, holding on to his father. Charlie Longsong can't be mistaken: the child is Little Tornado Man. It is Charlie Longsong when he was a child. He'd like to get up, but his body is so heavy, as if roots were holding it to the ground. He can't move. The black mare comes to a standstill beside him, Little Tornado Man lets himself slip down her flank, then he bends over old Charlie Longsong, who is lying flat in the desert.

"Where are you going, Charlie Longsong?" asks the child.

"I'm going to see Blanche Larivière, at 33 Grande Allée, Quebec, Canada."

The child grabs Charlie Longsong's hand and helps him get to his feet. He is as strong as a man. His father is as silent as the desert night.

All at once the light is so bright it blinds him, even though his eyes are closed. He's as thirsty as if he were about to die. Where is he? Where is his *hogan*? Where is his land? Didn't his father bring him back on horseback? Where has Little Tornado Man gone?

Several hours later, tired, thirsty, still drunk because of what he's had to drink, because of his long walk under the sun, he arrives at the trading post and asks for water. The woman who runs it is amused: it's not often that Charlie Longsong wants to drink water.

10 Robert Martin's wife claims he took off like a criminal. "A failed marriage isn't a crime," he thinks. She is threatening to demand his extradition. He's an honest man. He doesn't refuse to pay what he owes. In our modern democracies, a man now enjoys

only one right: the right to pay alimony to his wife. He doesn't intend to neglect the exercise of that fundamental right. If she insists that he be forced to return to Canada, he could transform himself into an outlaw like the famous Frank and Jesse James, who held up banks and robbed passengers on trains across California, Nevada, Kentucky, Missouri, Arkansas and New Mexico. A historian can turn vicious and fierce. And yet it's his wife, his too-pretty hairdresser, who's behaving like a bandit. After robbing him of his love and his property, she threw him off the train of married life.

Robert Martin has decided to stop for a few days in the Colorado Valley where Farmer Dubois bought his herd. He'll study the terrain in hopes of picking up the farmer's trail. All he has now is time. He is reading the story of Frank and Jesse James in the old hotel that was a temporary home to mine owners, engineers, traffickers, bandits, contractors, performers, ladies of the night— the whole flock of people drawn to the cities that were born amid the fever of quickly made fortunes. In his hotel room, bullets have made holes in the tin engraved with tracery that covers the ceiling. Like a genuine hunter, the historian will move around his subject to encircle it. Following the Jameses across the United States, from south to north and from east to west, will let him get to know the space in which Farmer Dubois moved. In those days, when the veins of the mountains were so full of riches they burst, rumours of quick and miraculous fortunes composed a music that could be picked up by adventurers from Russia, China and Scandinavia. It's a sure thing that Farmer Dubois was interested in other things besides his cows and bulls. How did he manage to amass the money necessary to buy, with cash—according to the records—fifty-nine head of cattle? Did he sleep in this hotel where beautiful plump girls with pale complexions and low-cut dresses danced around the piano that still stands in the same place today, silent now behind a velvet rope?

Robert Martin is dreaming. He has to dream if he's to understand Farmer Dubois. An adventurer is not a man of action; he is first and foremost a dreamer. The historian must reinvent Farmer Dubois's dream because without it he won't be able to track down his soul. He burrows away for hours with his books. Wouldn't anyone regret not having lived at a time when the American continent was throbbing like a heart on the very morning of Creation? No matter how much he dreams, he knows he has always been and will always be a mere turner of pages.

Because his spirit of adventure is so weak, he ran away from the Indian who could have guided him along the paths of an America that's invisible to Whites. He, the historian, refused to listen to Charlie Longsong, through whom the past wanted to tell him its story. He took off like those tourists in exotic countries who are annoyed by the natives. He's not very proud of himself. Robert Martin is a poor, lonely man, a weird customer in an old hotel washed up on the shores of the present day. He doesn't leave his room, he stays shut up there with the scattered books that are so old the chambermaid doesn't dare touch them. She opened one and the pages drifted across the floor.

Robert Martin is no adventurer. He's stingy, fearful, selfish. He's everything his wife accuses him of being. And on top of that he's just as racist as the next guy. And that is why he wouldn't let Charlie Longsong get in his car. He wasn't interested in the Indian's story. The rue Gît-le-coeur in Paris doesn't need an Indian from Arizona. The rue Gît-le-coeur is Robert Martin's turf. When he was young and free, Robert Martin was happy on that street. He was annoyed to see the Indian invade his turf.

There was something else, too: a wound that has never healed, a pain that is trivial, deep, throbbing. Back when the enthusiastic historian was cranking out articles, papers and volumes to enrich his cv and impress his dean, he'd spent a dozen weeks writing up a paper to deliver in western Canada. Was it in Saskatchewan or Manitoba? He remembers only the fields that marked out the prairie in squares. From the plane, it looked like a checkered tablecloth spread on a giant's table. He had accumulated a lot of information about Hi-nu, the beneficent Thunder god of the Iroquois, to whom it's advisable to offer tobacco he can smoke, to thank the god for destroying the monsters that poison the water. He had situated Hi-nu in Iroquois mythology, above his brother Wind-from-the west-who-brings-rain and his other brother, Wind-from-the-north-who-distributes-disasters, like frost on the corn and ice on the rivers. Hi-nu also reigns over Echo, the god who repeats from hill to hill the Iroquois war cry: *"Goweh!"*

As he walked through town, Robert Martin went over his paper in his head. At the university the next day he would try to deliver it without notes. Too often, he'd been condemned to listen to laboured lectures delivered by people who were talking only to themselves. Walking relaxed through this town where there was nothing to look at, where the surrounding boredom offered nothing to distract him, he recited his text and rehearsed the gestures for emphasizing the important parts. It was raining softly. His brand-new raincoat was still as stiff as a coat on a hanger in a store.

"Grab a look at the fancy raincoat on this guy!"

Wrenched from his solitary rehearsal, Robert Martin saw himself surrounded by four laughing Indians who smelled of booze. Their long hair was dripping with rain. Their clothes were soaked.

"Must've paid a lot for this coat . . ."

"Good waterproof cloth, eh . . ."

The four Indians' big fingers felt the fabric.

"It's imported. Betcha it's from London . . ."

"Betcha it cost him more than my welfare cheque!"

"Please," Robert Martin protested, annoyed, "let me get on with my work."

"So he works, does he?"

"Sure. He walks down the street and calls that work."

"Maybe we're working too, since we're walking down the street."

"But he's got his fancy raincoat and us poor Indians are soaking wet."

Robert Martin went back to the hotel without his raincoat. He filed a complaint with the police. In his hotel room he lay on his bed, eyes filled with tears. To have lost his raincoat was annoying. To have been robbed was annoying. He'd felt powerless and that was frustrating. What good did it do to regret not having the strength of Superman? He was crying now because he felt betrayed. For months, he'd taken pains to understand the arcana of this great culture, translated into a mythology as captivating as the greatest mythologies in the world. And now he'd just been stripped by some two-bit street pirates, delinquent descendants of the noble souls who'd created great legends to explain the Universe. Shortly after that episode, he withdrew his paper and went home with a heavy heart.

Was it because of those thugs in a small town in western Canada that he'd been unable to accommodate old Charlie Longsong? Did he want vengeance? Was he afraid of him? Is he a racist? Robert Martin knows that he's an ordinary man. Like ordinary men, he's afraid of the unexpected and of strangers.

11 Charlie Longsong no longer dares to speak the name of Blanche Larivière. It was all just a daydream. He thought there were recollections floating in his memory, but they were only the daydreams of a man who is advancing, alone, down the path of old age. His life is a tent made of daydreams. He picks pods

from among the delicate leaves of a mesquite. His entire life is nothing but a daydream. When he walks in his desert or when he cuts a cactus to take a cup of water from its trunk, he himself is perhaps only a daydream of his ancestors.

The war over there, so long ago, was a bad dream that ripped off his arm as it passed by. And the stories about the ancestors who built cities and villages on this territory, who traded and knew the secrets of the daytime and the night, were they only dreams? And childhood, when he followed his father and helped him do his work, is that too only a dream?

When he came back from the war, as he was putting his ruined *hogan* to rights, he screamed himself hoarse crying out the name of Blanche Larivière. Was she too just a dream? He had seen too many lightning flashes, too many explosions, too many ruined bodies, too many houses torn apart by fire, too many broken machines, too many men in tears. He felt pain in his missing arm, an invisible beast biting him and never letting go. He had seen too many days that were like the nightmares of his sleep.

To forget all that, he repeated the name of Blanche Larivière over and over. Her name resembled peace. She had appeared amid peace. When he said her name and the foreign words she'd taught him, the relentless beast that was biting his arm went to sleep as it did when he drank bourbon. The words of old songs from England would dance in his memory when he became a little drunk. Then he would sing and, with tears in his eyes, he'd wait for the return of his father, who he knew was awake in the depths of the night on his fine black mare with the silent hooves.

Sometimes Charlie Longsong would cry out the name of Blanche Larivière as if he were trying with his lament to split open the starry sky. Charlie Longsong who had fought in the war became again a terrified little Indian lad prostrating himself before his gods and their immense silence.

It was long before the war. He was a small child. His father had taught Little Tornado Man the lightning ceremony. In the summer the sky gods hold a party. At a party there is drinking, breaking, shattering, smashing, brawling and violence dealt out and received. The gods' parties are like those given by men. When the gods brawl they knock each other out and shatter the sky. Sparks burst out and fall to Earth. When they lash out at one another, a heavy, muffled sound rumbles and echoes across the sky. When they tear the sky as if it were a shirt, rain falls in rivers or hail crackles on the ground. The poor inhabitants of Earth don't know what's going on in heaven. Only the missionary is fool enough, his father used to say, to maintain that he knows. No one has ever gone to heaven.

Because it's impossible to know, the ancestors got into the habit of making an offering to the gods whenever they squabbled. When you don't understand, you can't go wrong if you make an offering to those you fear.

Sometimes the black sky would shatter like a window and the gods would fire shots. At those times, under the thunder and between the lightning flashes that hissed and darted towards the ground, the members of his tribe followed the custom of going outside to make their offerings.

Charlie Longsong remembers. His father was still alive. The voice of the angry gods rumbled in the storm. Lightning flashes lashed the desert. Little Tornado Man stepped up, imperturbable, between the flashes. Fearlessly he walked among the cactuses. Above the rain, above the hail, the gods were watching him. He brought them a bowl filled with corn to appease them.

Another day, one he'll remember even after he dies, the air was as black as soot. Thunder was roaring and lightning was ringing out as if all the storms in the world were battling one another. It was not the gods who were angry now but men, who were destroying what the gods had created. On that day, between the flashes, the soldier Charlie Longsong considered making an offering, but he remembers, he was too afraid. A feverish young man in his soaking uniform, Little Tornado Man had wandered into a kind of violence that neither the gods nor the Indians know how to create. That day he had no corn to offer. He had only his rifle and the grenades on his belt and the bullets in a pocket on his thigh. He had nothing to appease the *bohanas* who were sending this blazing confusion over his Indian head. All he could do was add flames to the fire that turned iron into something as frail as men's skin and made it bleed.

Why had Charlie Longsong left the peace of his Arizona? He had obeyed the *bohanas'* law. Often, Little Tornado Man had heard the story of the wars his tribe had fought against the *bohanas*. It had been a long time since the Indians had waged war. They'd forgotten how to fight. Little Tornado Man wanted to learn and so he joined the *bohanas*. He learned how to fight the way they did. He learned how to march the way they march when they go to war.

There, Charlie Longsong was not alone. Thousands of young men piled onto barges. They were white, they were black. He noticed some Indian brothers. They all looked away. Were they ashamed to be taking part in the *bohanas'* war? Waves crashed against the walls. The water fell on them like winter rain. His stomach tried to come out through his mouth, like a woodchuck emerging from its burrow. They'd been told that the Normandy coast was very near. Yet this crossing seemed more interminable than the crossing from America to Europe. He was cold. He was sick. Like the others, he vomited. He was drunk from this sea that was making him giddy. Had the barge drifted off course? Had they lost their way in the middle of the sea? Their feet were soaked. Endless waves assailed the steel. Collisions hurled the soldiers into one another. Their steel helmets squeezed their heads and amplified the sounds. Then all at once fire poured from the sky. The order was shouted not to move, to remain seated, not to fire but to give in, to let themselves be shaken by the sea that was as furious as if it were taking part in the war. The morning sky was ablaze. All the stars seemed to have exploded simultaneously. Suddenly, there was no more light. It was night even though it was day. Thick dark smoke was mixed in with the fog and the air had become black mud. Their barge struck bottom. The soldiers rolled on top of each other in the rising water. The gangplank was lowered. They had to run towards the cliff. The sea was strangling them. Feeling solid ground beneath their boots revived their desire to not die. To live! Live!

In the dark smoke shot through with lightning flashes, they had to advance. Without stopping. The sea still prodded you. You made your way past tanks that had been disembowelled or drowned, landing craft that were crumpled in the blood-tinged waves. Rifles still floated next to men who'd been torn to pieces, who were screaming all around him. Charlie Longsong was silent. Holding his rifle in his upraised arms, in water that had risen to his neck, he headed for the Normandy cliff that was being bombarded with arrows of fire. Beneath the black cloud he could make out the base. Little Tornado Man had made no offering to appease the gods. How could he still be alive?

The army recruiters had promised him he'd see the Old Countries on the other side of the sea and that he'd be given a very powerful rifle. Little Tornado Man wasn't interested in seeing the Old Countries on the other side of the sea. Too much harm had come to the Indians from those countries. A powerful rifle: that's what he wanted. Under the thunder and lightning, instead of holding a dish of corn in his upraised arms to appease the gods, he was holding on tightly to his weapon. Brave Little Tornado Man had learned one of the *bohanas'* warrior principles: "Your rifle is like your wife. You're going to live with her. If you die, she'll be there at your side. Caress her. Cuddle her. Let no one else touch her. She's your wife. The only one you've got." That's what the sergeant said.

Little Tornado Man had grown up in a land of canyons and mesas. He was cut out for climbing. He was urged to hold on to his Indian ways. Once he'd reached the cliff, still alive, he found the rope that was hanging where it was supposed to hang. He slipped his rifle onto his back, his hands gripped the rope and he began to climb. With all the strength in his hands and arms with their quivering muscles, with his heart pounding, charged with so much fear, he hoisted himself up and was no longer able to see the ground or the summit. He was coughing. The smoke burned his eyes. He felt like an insect about to be squashed by a boot.

Up above, the enemy was waiting. Grenades began to fly like wasps when their nest is threatened. They passed close to him. They were exploding, above, below. Suddenly, a sound like a blow from a giant scythe whistled above his head. The destroyers in the rear were firing to clear the summit. Enemy bodies were falling like ripe fruit. Briefly, one of them grabbed hold of his neck, then his hands let go and he tumbled down, screaming.

In the bushes at the summit of the cliff, disembowelled bodies had emptied out where they'd fallen. There were more corpses than ground. Frequently they had to walk on soldiers who were not completely dead. A little farther away stood a house that had been destroyed by a shell. All that was left was a door with a lace curtain floating in the wind. Flashes from shells scratched your eyes. Explosions shattered your eardrums and slammed you to the ground. Little Tornado Man cried and ran between the muddy craters. The grand chief of England had prophesied: "Blood, sweat and tears." The grand chief knew the future. What was Little Tornado Man doing there? Was he attacking? Was he fleeing? A brass bed pitched into the middle of a field resembled a gleaming skeleton. Elsewhere, a dead soldier was folded over the breech of his rifle. Ahead of him, flames like red flags burst out above the black fog. It was a village on fire.

The mud was red with blood. There, a soldier lay on his back, headless, a grenade in each hand. Charlie Longsong rushed into the fire that was crackling under the grass. Where was he going? Why had he left his desert? Here, no one would ask Charlie Longsong for a song. A song? But he'd forgotten them all. He no longer remembered anything.

All at once a great bubble of fire enveloped him, then burst. His rifle was snatched away. He watched it swirl through the air. He saw his hand still clutching the rifle and he saw his arm and his rifle explode, high in the air. After that he saw his Arizona desert where everything was peaceful between the cactuses.

It had been so long since Charlie Longsong had thought about all that. He'd forgotten he had once had two arms, like a man. The stranger's car had driven by and stirred up memories like the dust of the road.

12 "Where is the rue Gît-le-coeur?" Robert Martin repeats the old Indian's refrain. "Where is the rue Gît-le-coeur?" He remembers.

The artist, on her knees, was drawing flowers on the sidewalk with chalk. At one corner of the drawing was a little basket. Passersby stopped and dropped in a franc. She never quit working. She kept adding colours, petals, leaves, more flowers. The passersby who lingered saw the garden being transformed as it is during the growing season. Her flowers were alive. They were as beautiful as flowers from a magical jungle still unknown. The artist was stationed at the corner of rue Gît-le-coeur in Paris.

Robert Martin was a student at the time. When he was going to the university he went that way. A few times he'd dropped a franc into the basket. A few times he'd been moved by the flowers that were born and blossomed beneath the chalk.

Robert Martin had noticed the pretty face with its black eyes. She was always alone. Like other street artists, she had no assistant to watch over the basket for contributions. She wasn't pale like Frenchwomen; she must be a foreigner.

"Do you draw your country's flowers?" he ventured to ask.

"No, I draw flowers that are in my head."

"What country are you from?" asked another bystander.

"Brazil."

"Your country must produce the most beautiful flowers in the world, Mademoiselle, or you couldn't invent such pretty ones with your chalk."

Robert Martin was jealous of this fine talker with the white hair. Why is it that these cold old men know how to tell women what they like to hear, while young men, in the presence of the women they desire, find themselves as mute as a cemetery gate? The old man walked away after he'd tossed some jingling francs into the basket. Robert Martin was alone with the artist. He wished he could say something to her. But he didn't dare. The flower she was drawing resembled a bird with open wings that wouldn't fly very long because, under her chalk, the wings had metamorphosed into the petals of a flower so fabulous that God must have created it somewhere, he thought. To disguise his lack of composure, he tossed a handful of francs into the basket even though he couldn't afford such generosity. When the coins clinked she looked up. He had to say something.

"There's a region in France where you find lots of flowers."

She lowered her head and went on drawing.

"In Provence."

"I don't know Provence."

"You've never seen the fields of lavender, of sunflowers?"

"I've never been to Provence."

"What a coincidence! I'm going there tomorrow. Why don't you come along? I don't drive a Mercedes. I've got a little thoroughbred Citroën *deux-chevaux*. Those two horses are faster than a bike. I could pick you up at eight tomorrow morning."

Robert Martin was surprised by what he'd said. He hadn't planned such a trip. He didn't own a *deux-chevaux*. She stared at him without surprise and replied with her pretty accent:

"I noticed you before. No one else looks at my flowers the way you do. I knew you were going to talk to me."

She went back to her drawing. There are moments when it's important to be bold. Sometimes a young man has to leap into the unknown.

"Where shall I pick you up?" he ventured.

"Here," she said simply, "on rue Gît-le-coeur. I won't have much baggage, but I take my chalks wherever I go."

Robert Martin just had to finish an essay for his professor, then figure out how to borrow a car and some money. All his friends seemed to have fled Paris. The next day he headed for rue Gît-le-coeur on a scooter, a Vespa that was a little rusty and very battered. Would she be waiting for him? No, she wouldn't be there. She would have changed her mind. When your head is brimming over with all those flowers, how can you remember an appointment? She wouldn't go with him. He would stay in Paris. It's not worth travelling to Provence if you're going to be alone.

She was waiting at the corner of rue Gît-le-coeur, with her bag, ready for the land of lavender and tamarisk. He launched into an explanation; he had to tell her why he couldn't use his car. She didn't want to listen.

"Let's go. Things will be better in Provence."

They took isolated roads through the countryside. They visited churches whose ancient simplicity moved them deeply. They slept on hay in barns and under the stars. Then all at once the air was different. They could make out the scent of fruits mixed with the perfume of the sea.

"There's a hint of thyme," said Gabriella.

That was her name.

"I'd say rosemary . . ."

They decided to head for a spot on the map whose poetic name appealed to them. The road, which was as narrow as a path, ate into the flank of the mountain. They began to climb. The valley was covered with sunflowers. The slope was steep. They were climbing towards the sky. The scooter wasn't strong enough, it hiccupped, choked. In the end they had to push it up to a place where, at the end of an apricot orchard, a hamlet built up around an old manor was waiting for them.

"This is paradise," she said.

"Look, those are the good Lord's vines."

"I won't need to draw flowers here . . ."

They slept in a room with walls as thick as those of a fortress. The too-narrow window framed the beautiful blue sky of Provence. People had climbed up and down the stairs since the Middle Ages, wearing away the stone steps. Light streamed into the hamlet. The goats bleated. When the inhabitants spoke, they made music with their words. The cicadas chirred as if this season was to be their last.

They lazed around in Provence for a few days. They drove between hills where olive trees with gnarled branches seemed to suffer from rheumatism. They slowed down to gaze out at valleys where merely looking at the vines made their heads spin. Sometimes they would stop by the roadside in the shade of a cypress simply to enjoy the happiness of breathing. The air carried the scents of grapes and melons, apricots and peaches. Elsewhere, lavender painted the meadows purple.

Too soon it was time to return to Paris. They had found happiness, but they still had to do some schoolwork if they wanted their grants renewed. When Robert Martin stopped his scooter at the corner of rue Gît-le-coeur, he knew he would never leave Gabriella. She told him:

"My place is small but it will be too big if I'm alone there."

Robert Martin has brought together so many memories of the rue Gît-le-coeur. Because he loved there, he'd become a man. And it was there he'd learned that love is a season that passes like the others.

The other day, in the Arizona desert, when he'd heard the old Indian utter the name of that street, he had felt a twinge in his heart.

13 From Colorado, the historian heads north towards Kansas. Spread before him are infinite plains broken by a few tall oaks. This luxuriant earth is among the most fertile in the world, he read in a tourist leaflet. The soil is made up of sediments from the sea that covered it millions of years ago. The wheat that spreads in amber waves was imported here by Mennonite immigrants. They found here their Promised Land. They were able to sow this wheat they'd brought from Europe because the Government had driven the Indians from these lands.

The mind is free when the gas tank is full. The historian is speeding down the highway that crosses the dry seabed. History is invisible and memories can't be read in the movement of the wheat As for the suffering of the Indians, the generous earth seems not to remember. Robert Martin lets his gaze glide over the peaceful farms that file past. The earth refuses to tell what it knows.

The trip to Provence with Gabriella is one memory he has tried hard to forget. He's gone to great pains to erase those days of sun and flowers and cicadas as if he'd never lived them. His wife, his ex-wife, the too-pretty hairdresser, loathed that trip to Provence. She didn't allow him to have taken it. She didn't forgive him for having enjoyed the delight of being young in a country that gives you everything while it asks for nothing in return. As soon as he had told the too-pretty hairdresser about that expedition, she began to hate Gabriella and perhaps to hate him, too. During the inevitable quarrels, his wife, his ex-wife, would say:

"How do you expect me to believe a man who picks up girls on the sidewalk?"

Back when he was still publishing numerous articles and books, Robert Martin was invited to a conference of historians at Montpellier, in France. Wasn't that a fine opportunity to introduce Provence to his too-pretty hairdresser? She shot back:

"I don't want to go on a trip with that Brazilian between us."

Today, free, flayed and miserable, Robert Martin still savours the taste of the bountiful Provence he'd once crossed as a man who was free because he was in love. His dream and the reality both bear the name Gabriella. And she lived on rue Gît-le-coeur, in Paris.

He stops to stretch his legs. He should resist the urge to phone his lawyer. There's bad news waiting to pounce on him, he knows it. He'd be better off not knowing. Why can't he simply run away?

Flight is often the wisest course; he once read a thick book on the subject. He, though, is drawn to this war being waged by his wife. He can't escape. He phones the lawyer. He listens. Amazed. He hunches over as if it were raining bricks. He concedes:

"I'd never have thought she'd do that to me." He hangs up. His wife, his ex-wife, is demanding a written guarantee that the entire amount of her ex-husband's life insurance policy will be paid to her in full after his death. On top of that, she demands undivided ownership of the family plot in the graveyard.

Robert Martin could weep but he doesn't want to give in to that particular pain. He refuses to think about the new problem. He starts the car. He does his best instead to recall what he read in his motel room yesterday. One after another come the still, furrowed Kansas plains—the endless plains, the fascinating plains, the farms, their outbuildings clustered together for protection from the wind, and the cramped towns whose rooftops seem to float above the wheat.

"What's become of you, Gabriella? Do you remember the rue Gît-le-coeur?"

His wife, his ex-wife, wouldn't accept the fact that Robert Martin had lived a life before he'd met her. She'd have liked him to have been unborn until the day they met. . . . He'd better think about something else. . . . About the book he'll soon be starting. He's glad to feel the passion for history vibrating in him once again. For some years now he's been indifferent to history. Too many things have left him indifferent. The too-pretty hairdresser often used to reproach him for his lack of enthusiasm. Robert Martin had lost the feeling of desire. One of his old teachers noticed it and told him:

"The day you open your files and your heart doesn't stir like a child's on Christmas morning is the day it will be time to give up history."

Thanks to Farmer Dubois, he has regained the ardour of his youth. His passion for discovery has returned. The past is throbbing all around him. He will cause it to be born again in a way that will change our perception of the future. French Canadians have forgotten that their exiled ancestors gave French names to mountains, valleys, rivers, torrents and towns in the United States. They no longer know that their forefathers opened hunting paths and trade networks all across the surface of North America. He'll suggest to his people—that small people with no memory—a myth that will inspire their everyday lives. This book will have style. People will say: "Here's a historian who writes with the breath of his soul!" Scientific rigour, yes! Objective research, yes! A style, but also phrases that crackle like the lightning in the Arizona sky.

The highway splits the plains and the Kansas sky is peaceful and blue. The dean at the university chides Robert Martin for no longer being the historian he once was. He'll come back in force with Farmer Dubois. The dean will have to apologize for his subtle invitations to resign. *Farmer Dubois Triumphs Over Savage America*: he can already see his book in bookstore windows. Rational analyses, new, indisputable documents, innovative research: yes! But characters too! And action! It will be written the way a film moves along! With rhythm!

Yesterday he bought a shopworn book, *The Oregon Trail*. The account is populated with French Canadians whose names are Sorel, Labonté, Chatillon, Rouville, Bissonnette, Lerouge. "They are," writes the author, "half-white, half-Indian and half-devil." They can imitate the cries of animals. They would rather swim in the rapids than stay on a raft. When Chatillon sets off on an expedition, he doesn't want to be separated from his squaw. Most are famous buffalo hunters. Hunters of women, too. There was one who wasn't afraid to attack another convoy and kidnap an immigrant woman who'd caught his eye. And what name has Robert Martin spotted among those adventurers in search of paradise? Dubois! It happened in 1846. Can it be that the trapper who guided the author along the Oregon Trail is the same man who later on settled down and became a farmer in Colorado? Robert Martin will follow that vein like a prospector following his vein of gold.

14 Charlie Longsong hates these tears that linger in the fissures of his skin that's as dry as the Arizona desert. So he becomes impatient and wipes his face with the back of his left hand as if he were slapping himself. He never cried as a child. Even that night when his father was killed by a bullet, his eyes were dry. Instead of crying he fired at the bandits. To stay dry-eyed in spite of your sorrow, to fearlessly follow your path and preserve your territory: that's what Little Tornado Man was able to do. An Indian must live through his span of days with no one able to read his thoughts or the pain on his face. An old Indian must pass through the end of those days as impassive as an old cactus.

When the war took away his arm, he wailed, he screamed. Inside the tent were many soldiers wrapped in blood-stained bandages. Some were crying. Soldier Longsong's eyes were dry, despite the fire inside his eyelids. Ever since the stranger in the car from Quebec passed through, Charlie Longsong has been feeling the need to sob like an abandoned child. He knows what it is to be abandoned. On his father's death he found himself alone in the great black hole of the night you fall into again and again, alone in the blazing day where the light is even more frightening than the dark. Little Tornado Man did not whimper. Today, old Charlie Longsong cannot hold back his tears. Too many memories are rising to his eyes. Looking around, he sees nothing but his past. Blanche Larivière has been reawakened in his drowsy memory. Drinking bourbon doesn't lessen the pain in his soul.

After he left the hospital, drinking would still the invisible wolf that gnawed at his arm. He wants to drink some more. The world is too vast. The past is too remote. His solitude is too profound. His memory is too full. His sorrow is too persistent. His body is too heavy. His thirst is inordinate. His comprehension is too weak. He knows too many things. He does not know too many things. His hand shakes. His heart is startled. He is so remote from everything, so remote from his dead father, from the time when he went back to his mother's house, from the youth he believed he'd never had. He even feels remote from his Arizona, where his feet make the gravel crunch and the dry brushwood crackle. He even feels remote from the old man he's become. So he drinks bourbon, and the pebbles of the desert become as soft as if the soles of his old boots were alighting on the blue sky.

"Blanche Larivière, 33 Grande Allée, Quebec, Canada."

He has drunk so much in the past few hours. The sky sways like a lampshade at the end of a cord. The sky pitches and tosses as it did when a barge was transporting the soldier Charlie Longsong towards the cliff where the enemy was nesting. . . . Ah! that torn-off arm makes him suffer as if it were alive, far away from him. The arm he lost in the mud of a country on the other side of the sea has always refused to die.

Over there, is that a lizard? Charlie Longsong's gaze is confused. He has seen too many days. His eyes are worn out. The lizard has sensed the old man's footsteps. He runs in search of a place to hide. That's a chuckwalla trick. He senses you coming from a distance. You mustn't let yourself be distracted, because he'll disappear very quickly. He's heading towards the rock that is arching its back to the sun. There's no tastier meat, because the chuckwalla feeds on fresh flowers. Charlie Longsong guesses precisely where the animal has taken refuge. He's not staggering now. He steps prudently, precisely, silently across the gravel. He peers off in the direction where his shadow is cast. He is no longer thinking of his grief. He is a hunter and he's about to kill. Slowly, he bends down. The animal merits respect because he is going to die. Charlie Longsong knows these lizards. They slink into a crack where they swell up like a balloon. The chuckwalla stays there, wedged into place like a dowel in a hole. The hunter will do as the Elders do. He opens his pocket knife and sharpens the tip of a dry branch. His left hand mustn't tremble, but it has become so old. Once, twice, three times he stabs the skin of the lizard, which, full of holes now, deflates. Now it's easy to grab the little beast. It surrenders. It doesn't even try to run away. He picks it out of the crack like an almond from its shell. He bashes its head against the rock and slits its belly with one stroke of his knife. Using dry grasses and brambles he makes a fire. He threads the lizard onto a thin branch and turns it over the flame while he looks at the sky where time disappears.

The other night the Moon was high. It was the hour when dreams rule the Earth. Charlie Longsong saw his father appear at the end of the desert. He was drawing near the way a tornado approaches. Charlie Longsong waited for him. Even though his father was far away, he could catch a glimpse of the shape of his face despite the shadows masking his features. Soon the galloping black mare came very close to Charlie Longsong. Her silent hooves raised no dust. He remembers the warm breath from the animal's nostrils on his neck. The old Little Tornado Man pleaded with his father:

"Papa, Papa, take me to the Grande Allée, in Quebec, Canada, so I can see the nurse again, who took such good care of me."

His father did not heed his request and continued on his way like a cloud driven by wind that doesn't stop for an old Indian. He didn't turn his head to look at his son. He didn't slow his horse to invite his son to ride along with him. Charlie Longsong remembers this visit very clearly. He feels again the sorrow his father left behind when he passed him by like a stranger, without even turning to look his way. How he would love to see his father come back in the light of day, stop and dismount and crouch by the fire! Charlie Longsong would give him the lizard.

His father saw him born with two arms like a man. He never asked:

"What did you do with your right arm?"

In his soldier's uniform, Little Tornado Man was covered with blood. He cried out for help. He felt as if a shell were exploding with every beat of his heart. Every explosion tore off his arm, then it grew back to be torn away again. What torture! His body was just one gaping wound. There was weeping and moaning all around him. This makeshift hospital in a barn was full of young men like him whose limbs had been torn to bits. They lay against one another in the hay. Their remaining limbs touched. Sometimes they hit each other as if to take revenge on someone else for their pain. White faces came and bent over him. They talked among themselves. They were doctors, nurses. They gave him tablets to swallow, dealt out injections. Their uniforms were spattered with blood. One day a nurse came to clean his face, then his neck and his chest. He was no longer lying in the hay but on a pallet. She had washed his whole body. He had let her do so. He realized he no longer had any pain. He no longer had his right arm but he was as free of pain as he'd been before the war, before the day when there had been as many explosions as there are daisies in the fields of England. He wanted to stay in his bed. He was afraid to stand up.

Little Tornado Man did not know many women. Those he had paid for in England didn't smile like this one. He wanted to touch her hand but he no longer had his right arm. She had noticed his attempt to move.

"You're doing a lot better now!" she observed. "I took care of you when you didn't even realize I was there. You didn't even know you were still alive . . ."

Time passes, and everything passes away along with it. All that remains are the Arizona desert and the saguaros with their arms beseeching heaven. All that remains is an old Indian who is struggling to remember his youth, who remembers so badly . . . His days have been taken away, as when the Santa Ana wind in November drives the sand away. That idea is too sad for an old man. He sips some bourbon. In the cactus near the creosote bush he's spotted a nest of doves. They're intelligent, those lovely little birds. They know how to protect their eggs. They build their nest in a bower of needles, where they're most tightly packed. To gather an egg defended by all those bristling needles is a game. Little Tornado Man often used to have fun doing that. His father had taught him how to do it. Did he tell that to the nurse?

At first he didn't speak. He could only scream. Spasms. Pain. Burning. Such terrible suffering. A wolf was kneading the stump still attached to his shoulder. He could see nothing. The night was red. Was it blood? The fire of the explosions lingered in his eyes. Later on, he noticed the nurse. Her apron was bright with blood. She'd come to help him drink. Later still, she told him:

"If you want me to believe you're a real Indian you have to get better and get out of this bed as fast as you can."

In one abrupt movement, his good arm pushed back the covers and soldier Longsong stood up, only to collapse.

This nurse wasn't like the girls in English pubs who went up to the rooms with the soldiers. Another time, when she was changing his bandage, she asked:

"Where do you live in America?"

"In the desert, in Arizona."

"Arizona!" she repeated, surprised. "Like in the movies, with the dust and sun and the cactuses and canyons?"

She wanted to know everything.

"Do you eat vegetables in the desert?"

"We take a pointed stick and dig a hole a foot deep. At the bottom of the hole we bury grains of corn. That way they can take advantage of the moisture hidden in the earth."

"How do you store your food?"

"We dig a hole in the ground bigger than a bucket. We put the bucket in the hole. We surround the bucket with sand. We find water to wet the sand. Then we put food in the bucket. And we cover the hole with leaves, grass, shrubs. Or else we cut meat into strips and leave it on a branch to dry."

"What else do you eat there?"

"Wherever there's water you find mesquite. That's a tree that produces beans with golden pods. The little beans taste sweet. Then there's the yucca. That's a cactus twice as tall as a man. In the spring it's covered with white flowers. The missionaries called it 'the Lord's candlestick.' They thought the white flowers looked like the drops of wax along a burning candle. The yucca produces a kind of sweet banana. The desert is harsh but generous. Underneath a tuft of innocent little purple flowers you can find a long root that's tender, juicy and sweet. The gods wanted the Indians to live in the desert, so they placed food for them all over. You just have to pick it up."

While he was talking to the nurse, other patients cried out for help as if they were dying. She pulled the covers up to his chin.

"That's what happens when you talk too much. You're tired now, you must rest."

Once she asked him:

"Why did you come to fight in the war?"

"I followed the *bohanas*, the Whites. An Indian should never follow the Whites. . . . And you, who did you follow?"

"No one. I was living in my city in Canada, on the shores of a great river. It was so peaceful. The sparrows and the politicians squawked. I couldn't stand that peace. My ancestors came from France. I wanted to see the country of my ancestors. Then, the war broke out . . . A young girl can't stop the war, but she can ease the suffering of the warriors."

Charlie Longsong can still hear her voice. She spoke words as if she were singing.

After he came home from the war, he went often to the trading post to have someone write letters to Blanche Larivière. So many years have passed since then. The woman who ran the trading post was a *bohana* who'd come from the north. She knew how to talk to people from the north, even though Blanche Larivière lived even farther away than her north. She was kind, the woman who ran the trading post. She said:

"I can't refuse to lend my hand to a young man who gave his away in the war . . ."

As if she were writing letters for herself, she wrote reassuring words to say that Charlie Longsong still thought about Blanche Larivière, that he could never forget her, that he wanted always to think about rue Gît-le-coeur (she didn't know how to spell that name); she declared that he saw her face smiling in the sky, that he dreamed of her day and night, that he wanted to hold her hand for the rest of their lives; she concocted a story that the hand he had lost hadn't died because it dreamed of stroking Blanche's cheek. (Little Tornado Man didn't like that idea but the woman from the trading post was the one who knew how to write.) She wrote a number of letters for him.

He decided to go back to the trading post. He decided not to wait. With long strides, like a young man with all the strength of one who doesn't know yet what he will become, old Charlie Longsong walks towards the hamlet. He's preoccupied by one matter. People now aren't the way they used to be. Nowadays people don't like the old. They don't like to help. For a while now a new cashier has been reigning over the counter. Will she write a letter for him? His uncertainty worries him. Because he's worried he swigs some bourbon. He knows what he wants to write to Blanche Larivière: "I think about you day and night. We must see one another again before we're summoned to the land of the dead. You haven't seen my desert and I haven't seen your snow." That's what has to be written.

He walks into the trading post. The hateful cashier is busy with some visitors who've lost their way. Bulbous watermelons are piled up in the fruit section. He tries to pick up two but they're heavy this year, so heavy. He has only his left hand. Finally, he takes just one and carries it over to the strangers.

"Here, I'm giving you this. This whole store belongs to me. All this land belongs to me . . ."

"Oh, how charming!" exclaims the lady. "Can we have our picture taken with you? Darling, put on your hairpiece for the picture. Will someone take our picture? It's easy. Everything's automatic. We don't have any pictures with a real live native yet."

15 Missouri... Illinois... Robert Martin is driving back north again, towards Chicago, Detroit, Canada and, finally, to the east, the province of Quebec. He's not eager to get there. Yet he is driving very fast. He has lost his wife. Always, he knows, he will feel seared by their separation. It's said that an amputee feels pain in the absent limb. Robert Martin is suffering, but he's a man with an ambitious project. He will recount the epic of America as it was lived by French Canadians. He's sorry he lacked the courage to take on board that Indian he left behind in Arizona. Robert Martin would have seen landscapes, followed roads, through the eyes of the old Indian who has been dispossessed of everything but his ancestral memories. Perhaps that whimpering old man only wanted to take a jaunt, like a tourist? He claimed he knew someone in Quebec City. It's an old trick. Robert Martin isn't that naive . . .

"I'll show that dean what kind of book I can write!"

After the flat fields of Kansas carpeted with lupines, here are the lovely rounded hills of Missouri. A tourist brochure informs him that the first ten thousand settlers of the state were French Canadians. Did Farmer Dubois pass this way?

Yesterday, before he went to sleep, because he wanted to take his mind off his divorce and the too-pretty hairdresser whom he still loves, whom he once adored to the point of giddiness, because he wanted to take his mind off being alone on the roads of America, Robert Martin became engrossed in another old book, which he'd found in Providence. Hundreds of thousands of French Canadians explored the trails of Illinois, Indiana, Wisconsin, Arkansas, California, New Mexico and Louisiana. They invented the occupations needed to survive. A man named Ruelle discovered the gold in Sutter Mills that set off the rush to California by hundreds of thousands of adventurers. In Santa Fe, New Mexico, the first traders were French Canadians like Henri Mercure, a native of Quebec City. The celebrated Frémont, who in 1840 led a scientific expedition to the western United States, was guided by French Canadians. French Canadians fought the Mexicans to consolidate the United States' domination of California. A wealthy French Canadian named Ménard built himself a castle in Galveston, Texas. Chabot, who'd attended school in his Quebec village for only a brief time, became a millionaire when he invented hydraulic systems. It was he who installed the first system to supply water to San Francisco. Aubry set up the first commercial traffic network between California and New Mexico. Born in Maskinongé, Quebec, he died in 1854, at the age of thirty, killed by a man with whom he'd had a heated argument about the most appropriate place to lay out the future railway that would go to Santa Fe. Exasperated by his stubborn arguments, the man had stabbed him in the heart with his knife. Another French Canadian, named Nadeau, transported silver and lead to Arizona, Nevada and California; he owned a hundred mules and a hundred wagons with high wheels circled in steel. Would a Utah town have been named Provo if a trapper called Provost, another French Canadian, hadn't been the first to set his traps in that spot?

Without donning a giant's seven-league boots, those men, like Tom Thumb in the fairy tale, had travelled across vast expanses. Along the way they gave French names to the rivers, valleys, mountains, to the new towns that sprang up. This morning, Robert Martin looked into his maps to pick out the French names these rough men with a beautiful language had left where they passed, names that resembled precious flowers: Nez Percé, Washington; Fort Défiance, Arizona, the Purgatoire River, Colorado; Pomme de Terre Lake, Missouri; the Bon Beurre River, Missouri; the Qui Court River, Missouri; Cache à Poudre, Colorado; Plume Rock, Wyoming; Bruneau Dunes, Oregon; Bellefontaine, Ohio; Bonne Terre, Missouri; Crève-coeur, Illinois; Pigeon, Michigan; Grand Téton, Montana; the Marais de Cygne River, Kansas; Terre Haute, Indiana; Missouri; the Coeur d'Alène mountains, Montana; Belle Vallée, Ohio; Pend Oreille, Idaho; Poteau, Oklahoma; Malheur Lake, Oregon; Racine, Wisconsin; Grande Prairie, Texas; Des Plaines, Illinois; Gros Ventre, Wyoming; Belle Fourche, North Dakota; Eau Claire, Michigan; Des Moines, New Mexico; Ledoux, New Mexico; Bouse, Arizona.... Those French names were assigned by adventurers who were tired, starving, lost and drunk on dreams. And those who repeat them today echo their dead voices. The French names that float across the memory of time are the beautiful pieces of the wreckage of those adventurers, now engulfed in oblivion. Never will Robert Martin be able to report these facts. He knows that his ignorance is as vast as this continent. He hasn't written the story he should have told. So many other French names have been cast onto the land of America by those French Canadians fleeing their own misery. They were not conquerors. They didn't have the ambition to build an empire. They were only passing through. They passed through this territory on their way towards the unknown. Nothing is left of them now but those names scattered across maps and painted on road signs in every corner of North America. A historical society leaflet declares that there are twelve million descendants of those French Canadians in the United States. The historian feels as proud as if he were their father. What a story! That's the one that needs to be told! Farmer Dubois will be the Ulysses of this American epic. How Robert Martin would like to write a letter of resignation to his dean:

My dear Dean,

In the wake of the success of my recent book, which has been confirmed by both academic and popular critics, I wish to advise you that I am resigning from the position of Assistant Professor in your faculty. The mediocrity you have established as the norm is unacceptable to me both morally and professionally. I can therefore no longer serve a sentence of forced labour in your henhouse, where it is considered better to cackle than to think.

Robert Martin applies the brakes. Carried away by his new project, he's been driving too fast. In the blue sky that undulates like the prairie, the wings of a crane, alone in space, wave like the arms of a great orchestra conductor. It's a northern bird. Canada isn't far.

What is he compared with those adventurers, those giants of the past who had the stars for light and who fed themselves to survive as wild animals do? A mere intellectual, a tired historian, a writer who's run out of steam, a civil servant pensioned off before retirement. The dream of those giants of the past invented a continent and filled it with the treasures they'd set out to discover. Who is he? Will his children at least bear his name?

He shouldn't have phoned his lawyer last night. Every time, he knows he'll be struck by some disaster. But he can't stop himself from talking to the man. He is fascinated to know what new problem the lawyer's voice will announce. His wife, his ex-wife, the too-pretty hairdresser is demanding that the children take their mother's name. The reason put forward: the unworthiness of the father.

Why is he heading back to Canada?

His car is full of books. His wife, his ex-wife, liked books, but only if their covers matched the modern painting on the wall, which harmonized with the colour of the furniture, which echoed that of the drapes. She would be deeply disappointed to see the arrival of this cargo of books that are shopworn, dog-eared, falling apart, crumpled, scarred, stained like old clothes.

She didn't really like books. A hairdresser, neither did she like the life of an intellectual. Her clients, she thought, lived like queens. She listened to them tell of their travels to sunny lands and their adventures in expensive boutiques. Their husbands some-times appeared on local television. They were important men. Money was like the air they breathed. The too-pretty hairdresser listened to their confidences. She knew only male hairdressers, and they didn't like girls.

Robert Martin had met her at a bus stop. The street was icy. The cold air rasped their faces. With her red cheeks and her fur hat, she was very pretty. They boarded the same bus. They exchanged looks but not one word. The next day, he arrived at the bus stop a little earlier. She showed up a little earlier too. He hoped to see her again. She hoped to see him again. They said to each other:

"Not so cold today."

"It was colder yesterday."

The bus pulled up. A seat was empty. They sat together. He said:

"I get off at the university."

"Are you a student?"

"No, I've finished my studies."

"Me too."

"I'm just back from Europe. I studied at the University of Paris."

"I'd like to go to Paris . . ."

She had stammered slightly. Would this young man who had studied in Europe forgive her for not having travelled or studied as he had? Her self-confidence came back and she declared:

"I practise the art of aesthetic hairdressing."

"This is where I teach. I'm getting off. Tomorrow my classes are at the same time. I'd like to invite you to the university . . ."

Robert Martin didn't like the university very much. He wished he could write history books without having to endure it. His students seemed to have come to history by mistake. During endless department meetings, his older colleagues argued like old married couples; he had to listen to them squabble over the position of a comma in the minutes of an earlier meeting. The university was a fortress that real life did not penetrate.

Soon, the too-pretty hairdresser moved into Robert Martin's apartment. While he read, wrote notes or revised the manuscript of his first book, she stood at the mirror arranging her curls. She looked at the photos in her fashion magazines. That was fine. Robert Martin's life was nothing but books and reading. The people around him, his colleagues, read too much. It was delightful to live with someone who looked away from printed material as she did from the misery of the world. He worked with people who, before they experienced a feeling, carefully consulted everything that had been written on the subject since Sumer. His too-pretty hairdresser reacted like a bird, a butterfly, a stream, a leaf on a poplar tree. Robert Martin envied her fine ignorance.

She had a simple way of asking essential questions whose naive aspect concealed depths never found in the pointless questions with which minds stuck in their own knowledge torment themselves. Often, he looked at history with the eyes of his too-pretty hairdresser. He did not conceal her worth from anyone. Did he not say: "She is the author of my books. I'm nothing but her devoted secretary . . ."?

What an imbecile he'd been! She cited his words in the divorce papers. She demands his royalties, all arrears and the accumulated compound interest.

Shortly before their marriage, Robert Martin thought he should confess his affair with Gabriella, the Brazilian girl. The too-pretty hairdresser listened to his description of the wonderful garden drawn on the sidewalk with chalk; she listened, tight-lipped, to the account of his first conversation with Gabriella. When he launched into the story of their departure for Provence on the battered scooter, with the tent and the bags, she asked if he hadn't felt a little ashamed to have taken off with a stranger like that. At the point in his account where he mentioned that night was falling and that before nightfall they had to put up the tent, she started leafing through a magazine, turning the pages as if the photos irritated her. He painted the colours of the setting sun. That evening the mountain air, the scents emanating from the earth floated in the blue sky, and the air of the distant sea created invisible veils on which the splendours of the Provençal sky were reflected and multiplied.

"You've never given me a night like that in Canada."

Robert Martin knew he'd been tactless. Why had he talked so much about the beauty of that night?

"Do you want me to be jealous?"

If he was so long-winded, it was because he was trying to be sincere. He loved his too-pretty hairdresser. At the time, he thought that when one loves, one has to say everything. "Where a secret exists between two persons, love cannot flourish." That was a sentence from a marriage preparation handbook they'd had to read at the time. And so he told her everything.

From that moment he was forbidden to say aloud the words "Brazil," "Provence," "scooter" or "tent." That was how his too-pretty hairdresser waged war on the Brazilian who had dared to pass through the life of her man at the end of one summer during his youth. Through that innate capacity women have to read the souls of their men, his too-pretty hairdresser knew that the artist who created flowers with chalk would live in Robert Martin's memory forever and that she would never leave his dreams.

What became of Gabriella? Did she meet an ambassador's son? Did she meet a worker who took her to a suburban high-rise? Can she still create flowers that might have inspired God Himself? Has she become a fat woman surrounded by her brood of children?

Their own children are grown now. His too-pretty hairdresser was bored. She hated university life.

"People won't talk to you unless you sound like an encyclopedia," she complained.

She didn't like her husband's colleagues; she found fault with them for smelling like musty paper. She detested the women in particular, who were proud of their messy hair.

One evening, to raise money for stray cats that were victims of their owners' negligence, an art gallery organized an exhibition of its artists' work. Between the works, inspired by the works, coiffure artists sculpted hairdos for rich women who were generous to cats. His too-pretty hairdresser was chosen to sculpt the hair of the head of an employees' union. The union leader was coming back from dinner, she'd had a little too much to drink, she laughed a little too much, her desires shone in her eyes. She insisted on introducing the too-pretty hairdresser to the man she'd had dinner with, a charming young man who travelled the world and came back with amazing images.

"Look at the wall. Do you see that natural sculpture in the rock? He photographed it. He says that the landscapes of the Grand Canyon in Arizona are music frozen in stone. A delightful boy..."

Robert Martin wanted to forget all that. His too-pretty hairdresser came home very late, at dawn.... Well into dawn.... The next morning.... She wasn't tired. She sang as she prepared the breakfast coffee. She had brought with her some photographs of rocks, cactus, the desert.

"I'd like to see that for real. It's in Arizona," she pointed out.

How could she know that? She confused Australia and Italy. Robert Martin wishes that none of it had happened. He lost his temper. He, an educated man, a man of reflection, a historian who searches discreetly in the past, howled like an animal caught in a trap.

At the end of the day, a bailiff knocked on his office door. He'd brought with him a petition for divorce. He was accused of violence. Yes, he'd shouted very loudly because his pain was agonizing. Yes, he'd wept violently.

And he left. Could he have fled anywhere else but to Arizona?

16 A man knows he is old when he can no longer find his things. The other day, Charlie Longsong spent hours looking for his rifle. He was afraid to spend the night without his weapon. Even a man who knows the desert doesn't know what is hidden in the night. He looked everywhere for it. He was so worn out from worrying that his back was covered in sweat. Some hours later, he found the rifle in its place, held up by the two nails on the wall of his *hogan,* where he always keeps it.

He forgets his words, too. What do you call the vortex of wind that pulls into its eddy fine sand, dry grasses, wisps of straw, pine needles, leaves fallen from thickets that swirl in the wind like a top in the desert? For days now he's been trying to remember the name of that column of light debris that the wind compresses into a skein and spins.

One thing he'd like to remember is the reason why Little Tornado Man left his *hogan* one day and let himself be taken so far away, to the other side of the sea, so he could fight. It wasn't a war against the Indians. It was a war pitting *bohanas* against *bohanas*. Whites wanted to kill other Whites. What was he, an Indian, doing there? There, nothing was as it had been. People wore uniforms. He was no longer allowed to walk the way he'd always walked. He could no longer carry his rifle the way he'd always carried it. Everywhere, the earth was so green it was overwhelming. And he had seen the sea, which he'd never seen before. It was as if the whole desert had been changed into wriggling water. As for the war, it was an enormous black-and-red storm. The Indian gods have never been so wicked as to set off anything like it. What was Little Tornado Man doing there?

The last days were visited by peaceful clouds that passed calmly over his land. Charlie Longsong became very observant. He studied the clouds. He listened to them. Ancestors in the form of clouds come to visit the generation that is now alive. The ancestors' voice told him that, in the territory of light, a man cannot walk against time. A man must carry the burden of his age as far as he can and make his way to the end of his old age. That is his fate. There, he'll arrive at a cave. The entrance to it is so dark that he will hesitate. Only there will he be given the privilege of belonging to all time and of floating in the sky, his soul wrapped in a cloud.

An old prayer rises to his lips:

"*Tunkasila Wakan Tanka, Unci Maka, Tatuye Wiyihpeyata*, Grandfather, Great Spirit, you are the ultimate creative power of the Universe. Grandfather, you have given life to many spirits on this Earth and to each of them you have taught a way of life. I come from the belly of my mother the Earth and you gave me life. You gave me the gift of learning, from my winged brothers and from those who have two feet or four and from those who live in the water, how to live on the right road . . ."

Charlie Longsong can't get to sleep. The rain is drumming on the corrugated tin roof of his *hogan*. In the past, he enjoyed walking in the rain, like his ancestors who had no need of clothing to protect themselves. They were strong enough inside their skin not to feel the cold. Then the *bohanas* came, they brought warm clothing, and the Indians became as frail as they were. Through his door, Charlie Longsong watches the rain fall and he shivers from the cold. The night is beautiful: a great desert without stars. To warm himself, he sips bourbon.

During this season when the *arroyos* fill with water, a little patience is needed. Time will pass like the cars speeding along the road.

A few days later, the angry wind pounds on his tin roof. He can't sleep any longer; he gets up. The earth is completely white. He has never seen snow here. He thinks about what everybody says: because of the harm that's been done to the Earth, she has fallen sick. It's the fault of the *bohanas*, with their cars, their factories and their inventions. Indians do not harm the Earth, who is our mother. Her desert is covered with snow now like Blanche Larivière's native land.

She didn't want to come down to Arizona. She didn't want to see him again. Looking at the ground that gleams like a mirror under the black sky, he remembers very clearly. He had letters written for him at the trading post. A number of letters. He told her he wanted to be near her. He offered to travel to her northern land. She never replied. She didn't want to see him again. He had more letters written. A man his age has forgotten so many things.... But a man will always remember when he's been forgotten.

A shadow stirs. Could it be his father on his black mare? Will the animal's hooves leave marks on the snow this time? The Moon is round and bright. The Earth is sparkling. Little Tornado Man will always remember his horseback rides with his father. The black mare was as proud as the proud horses of olden times, when the ancestors crossed the deserts and the prairies, free as the wind. His father held himself as erect as a man who owns land received from the ancestors to be passed on to his descendants. Little Tornado Man straightened up like the child who is learning to become a man. He was waiting for the glorious moment when his father would hand him the reins. The horse would obey him as she obeys a man.

The gods have a reason for putting desires into the souls of men. Desires announce what is going to happen. One day, Charlie Longsong has no doubt, his father will appear on his black mare to take him riding to the land of clouds where life begins again.

A few hours later, it is raining. His landscape is veiled in gloom. As he can see nothing outside, he looks inside his soul. His thoughts are agitated like the water in the *arroyos*. Long ago, strangers came to drive Little Tornado Man and his father from this land. When Little Tornado Man made a fire, they fled, the way the *bohanas* flee when Indians defend themselves. Today, he owns this land the way his father owned it. Everything on this land is his. Therefore he can give away everything on this land, for a man must share what his land gives him. At the trading post the *bohanas* don't understand that. They don't know how to share, they've only learned how to take. They laugh and their white faces turn red when he offers them watermelons, bottles, lettuces, fruit or shirts. But he has no son. To whom will he bequeath his land?

Unlike his father, Charlie Longsong has no son to seat on the horse that would take him to the limits of his land and make him dream while gazing at the horizons, to teach him to know the perfumes of plants by explaining their names, by telling him when to gather them and how to use them. He has no son whom he would teach how to sniff the scent of the breezes and how to interpret messages from the ancestors who live in the clouds. Charlie Longsong is not a father. He will have only been a son. When a man has a son, does he still wait for his father to carry him away? An old man without a son is a child without a father.

The war grabbed hold of his arm. Something was wrenched from his soul as well. He doesn't know what it was. He has never known. The war took away a part of his soul just as it stripped him of those years that won't return. Had there not been a war, what would have become of him, with his entire soul and his two arms? What would have become of him without the pain that never sleeps, that never forgets the lost arm? What would have become of him without the sadness he caught in battle?

In the springtime, the leaping chollas bloom. These cactuses have many arms with hands that have two or three fingers. Once they've bloomed, the fingers fall to the ground. The wind blows them and makes them leap. Eventually, the fallen segment will take root some distance away. There, a new colony will begin. Maybe his arm that fell on the other side of the sea, his lost arm, will have started a colony of Little Tornado Men? Why is he having such crazy ideas? It's the snow, the rain, the silence of Blanche Larivière, it is his rejection by that traveller from Quebec who shouldn't have come to Arizona. . . . He sips some bourbon as if he were taking a deep breath.

The rain has stopped. The approaching light drives away the night. The morning doves will be happy! They'll find water to drink right next to the cactus where they nest, instead of having to force their way through the winds of heaven all the way to the hidden mountain springs. At this time of day the coyote retreats in search of shelter and cool shade. Little Tornado Man used to see them, proud and satiated, their prey still dangling from their jaws; sometimes they were unsuccessful, condemned to lick the crust of salt that forms over holes where rainwater flows out. Charlie Longsong hasn't seen one for a long time.

There are fewer animals now. In the past, you just had to wait till sunset and you would see them weave their way through the cactuses and shrubs. During the good years, spying a coyote was a sign there was game to hunt. You just had to be more silent than the coyote, more supple than he was, you just had to sniff through your nostrils and you could extort the coyote's prey from him! The Indian is a good hunter when he has learned everything from the animal. Besides, a coyote leg roasted over a fire was delicious. Modern days are not coyote days . . .

Charlie Longsong remembers. . . . His father used to describe the mountain sheep he'd seen at the end of the desert. These weren't lazy, sleepy sheep like his, but fighters that sprang from rock to rock and attacked head on. His father would gesture broadly as he described the horns, the great coiled horns of the mountain sheep. Occasionally, back then, one of the sheep would venture into the desert and lose its way. Instead of its usual grazing land, it would nibble on sage and salt shrubs. It would get drunk. It would go in circles. It wouldn't know where it had come from. It was as big as a young stag. The good taste of its meat was well known. When the hunter approached, the mountain sheep would try to jump, to climb, to clamber in order to escape. There were no rocks or ledges or rough edges in the desert. The sheep would fall onto the flat gravel, ridiculous. The *bohanas* paid very dearly for its wool and above all for the horns. Now they'd been hunted until none were left.

On the mesa the other day, the Elders were talking about everything that has disappeared. They talked about how, up north, the *bohanas* have killed so many buffalo that their bones, bleached by storms and winters, form frightening mountains. That happened in the prairies of Canada, the land of Blanche Larivière, the nurse he met on the other side of the sea, when he no longer had his two arms to embrace her.

Through his door open onto the night, an old man can catch a glimpse of so many things . . .

17 This divorce has given him a shock comparable to the one produced when an asteroid fell on New Quebec. Robert Martin is wrapped in a sombre dust similar to the dust sent up by the asteroid that veiled the light of day for centuries. A poor forlorn dinosaur, Robert Martin believes that he is threatened with extinction.

He tries to reason with himself. He's bought a book, *Anatomy of Love*. The author is interested in the genetic aspect of behaviour in love. In his opinion, infatuation is caused by the production in the brain of a chemical substance called phenylethylamine, or PEA. If the author is right, you shouldn't regret loving someone. How can you regret a chemical reaction in your brain? A chemical reaction made you think you'd met an angel from heaven. The author does not explain divorce, however. Could divorce be a chemical reaction too?

The historian is sad. Often a tear will slip down his lashes even when he tries to smile. He misses his children so much it's as if they were dead. He still can't quite believe that this disaster has swooped down on him. When he wakes up in the morning his eyes discover a room whose walls aren't familiar yet. He's not indifferent to the curtains; he hates them.

When he got back to Quebec, he found a place to live in the student neighborhood near Outremont. When he walks into this room he feels as if he's stepping into a coffin. He spends as little time here as possible. He can't read. Sitting with his open book, the memory of everything he's lost comes back to torment him. So he flees wherever he can, crushed by the weight of everything he no longer has. He thought this student room in a bourgeois basement would be a cocoon from which the abandoned man would emerge metamorphosed into a free man with great butterfly wings.

There are piles of books beside his bed. Whenever he gets up he curses the clutter. He no longer even looks at his notes before giving his lectures at the university. The biography of Farmer Dubois still strikes him as an exciting adventure for a historian, but he doesn't feel ready to start it yet. First he must cure his grief.

One evening after his lectures, a student asks to talk to him about her essay.

"Let's go to my office."

He doesn't have his key. Where did he leave it? In a pocket? On the table inside?

"You won't find that key because what you really want to do is go to the pub for a beer."

He doesn't like it when female students talk to him like an old pal.

"The key's right here. In the lock."

It's not his door, it's a colleague's. This student disturbs him. No doubt she's aware of it. She's not young like the others. He wouldn't go to the pub with one of those adolescents who have barely left behind their teddy bears to come and hunt down a degree.

"I just need some practical advice. I've got too many ideas. The subject I've chosen is the evolution of woman since 1850. Ideas run through my head like the cars on the Jacques Cartier Bridge."

Robert Martin and his student are walking towards the pub. She of course is no longer as young as the other students. She has a fair amount of flesh on her bones. She has wrinkles around her eyes. She walks as if she were late for an appointment. And she dresses in colours that proclaim: "To hell with autumn, I say it's spring!"

"Instead of beer," she says, "wouldn't you rather have a bottle of Beaujolais Nouveau?"

"Actually, I think I'll have a mineral water."

"Don't be afraid. I'm not trying to get a higher grade for my essay.... Let me tell you why I'm taking your history course. It's very simple. I didn't go to school for very long. Now I'm making up for lost time. A person can do whatever she wants. All you need is patience. I wanted to start with history. It's less complicated than chemistry.... Tell me what I have to do so my ideas won't be all tangled together like noodles in a pot."

Robert Martin speaks. She listens. Then suddenly:

"Okay," she cuts in. "I've got enough advice. I'm liable to be like those women who travel with overloaded suitcases.... I want to be able to remember all your advice.... We're drinking wine together.... Since we're doing that, I'm going to ask you something. When you saw me in your class, could you tell that I'm a woman on her own?"

"I try not to make any judgments based on my students' appearance."

"If you didn't realize that I'm a woman on her own, I wonder how you think you can understand people who lived hundreds of years ago . . ."

"I judge my students by their work."

"I'm a widow. My children are at school in the States. My husband left me a small transport business. I'd never been inside one of his trucks. It was his business, not mine. I'd never opened a ledger. I didn't know a thing. I did the best I could. Now, eleven years later, I own a fleet of a hundred and seventeen trucks that travel right across America. When the children were small I enjoyed discovering little things along with them. Now I want to discover big things. After history, I'll study law. And then music, which is a foreign language to me. I want to learn to play the violin. You're on your own too, I can tell."

Even while he resists, he alludes as discreetly as possible to his painful separation. To the sadness that followed. His utter helplessness . . .

"I think we need another bottle. . . . Waiter!"

He tells her about running away to Colorado, to Arizona. He describes the fabulous geological castles in the valley of the gods. He talks about meeting an old Indian who knew the rue Gît-le-coeur in Paris and who wanted to come with him to Quebec. He explains how overwhelmed he was to read the name of a French-Canadian farmer on the first page of the official register of a small mining town in Colorado.

"Have you started writing that farmer's story?"

"No. There's still too much sadness in my head."

"I'm going to tell you something, but not because I've been drinking . . . Mind you, the Beaujolais Nouveau helps, but I've been thinking about this for some time. You must have guessed that I haven't slept with a man for a while now. If you didn't pick that up, there're lots of things you'll miss when you come to write your book. I'm inviting you to sleep with me. And let me remind you, I'm not trying to get a better mark on my essay. I'm not one of those little girls who'll trade their virginity for an A. . . . I'm rich. If that makes you uncomfortable, it's normal. If I'd told you I was poor, you'd still feel uncomfortable and that would be normal too. Together, neither you nor I will be alone. Together, the night won't be so long. Together, we'll have less time to think about the past. . . . I'm looking at your surprised expression. . . . I understand it's been a while since anybody told you you're a very attractive guy. I hope you'll accept my invitation. Living alone makes a person ugly."

A few weeks later, Robert Martin finds himself settled into the building that belongs to his student's company. His room is too bright. A team of research assistants and secretaries will help him with his project to write the story of Farmer Dubois. The transport company has joined forces with the historian. He's also going to study the development of trade and transportation networks in North America. The company's special projects division has signed an agreement in principle with a television network; the biography of Farmer Dubois, an unknown hero, will be adapted for TV.

America is turning around him like a carousel out of control.

"When the U.S. calls," his student assures him, "you have to answer."

This is all too much for Robert Martin. It's all happening too quickly. The more they bustle around him, the slower he becomes. So then he slips away and takes refuge in his student room. As soon as he's shut the door he wishes he were somewhere else. So then he stuffs some books and clothes into his bag and goes back to his student, whom he's christened Miss Camion, because of her trucks. Yesterday she asked him:

"Does it bother you to be loved by a woman who dreams about trucks when she sleeps?"

She is fond of big hats that sail away like kites in the wind. On her, they don't look ridiculous. She could have been one of the plump women Renoir painted. Robert Martin noticed her during the first moment of his first class, even if his eyes could see nothing then except his own brutally shattered life.

Yesterday she said to him:

"I was thinking about that beautiful trip to Provence you described to me. I really hope that Provence was as beautiful then as you remember it. And I hope your Brazilian girl on your scooter with her hair in the wind was as beautiful as the images in your memory. When I was the age of your sweetheart, you wouldn't have looked at me twice. I had one babe in arms and I was pregnant with the second. That's not what attracts romantic boys! My own artist never opened a book. He was afraid of books. He was sure that reading makes you go blind. But he knew the road map of the United States by heart. And all the shortcuts. My own artist was never stirred by the beauty of a shower of stars in the sky, but when he lifted the hood of his truck you'd have thought the Blessed Virgin had appeared to him in person. No, I'm not jealous of your wonderful trip to Provence. All I want is for you and me to have something just as beautiful. By spring, you'll be tired. You'll have finished your book . . ."

"I won't have finished it. It's a long job. You don't make a book the way a hen lays an egg. I want it to be my best book. I'll need time. A book has to ripen like a fruit. I won't be free in the spring."

"By spring you'll be tired. We'll be in Provence at the same time as the flowers. We don't need a tent. I prefer a hotel. I'm going to buy you a motorcycle. Every man dreams of having a motorcycle. . . . Do you think I'm trying to buy your friendship? A person whose soul is as deeply wounded as yours can't be bought. I have wounds too. You and I are both alone, we're both wounded. And I'm rich. So let's go to Provence. . . . I couldn't invite you if I were poor."

This woman who wears a little too much make-up, who wears dresses cut as deep as the Grand Canyon, organizes everything like a general on campaign. Robert Martin doesn't like giving orders and he hates to follow them.

18 In the past, when Robert Martin published a book, a few months later three or four historians would review it for their university bulletins. This time he hasn't written a single line but Farmer Dubois is already famous. Robert Martin, who doesn't know a thing about his hero yet, has been photographed and interviewed by the newspapers; he has appeared on television with thin, dishevelled actresses, artists with AIDS, nationalist rock stars, politicians revealing their human side. He's even been invited to deliver a speech on the theme "The Giants of Our Race" to members of the Confederation of Unified Separatists. None of the books he's written in the past has aroused as much interest as this biography he hasn't started.

This sudden fame bothers his dean at the university, who has written him a note suggesting restraint.

While publicity is a necessary element in this century, when consumer values rule, it threatens the objectivity and the traditional slow progress that are essential to the scientific process, whose goal is not celebrity but truth—in other words, science. The genuine researcher must do his work in the shadows, because it is in the shadows that light appears.

The dean is jealous, of course. Robert Martin won't stop promoting his project. On the other hand, he's well aware that the unexpected interest in his book wouldn't exist without the special projects division of Miss Camion's trucking company. Thanks to it, Farmer Dubois has already been turned into a national hero. The Patriotic Society has asked for documentation on Dubois, the King of Colorado. It intends to "rehabilitate his memory and honour him" on the occasion of its annual parade. Robert Martin has even been invited to join the Academy of Provincial Literature.

Miss Camion is a volcano. It's not surprising that she can send her hundred and seventeen trucks to the four corners of America. Or that she's working on a plan to open restaurants for truckers, to be located at the major crossroads of Canada, the United States and Mexico. This is the woman who came to ask him how to give some order to her ideas . . . This woman, whose energy could power the country's electric turbines, sometimes lays her head on his shoulder and sighs:

"I'm glad I didn't meet you earlier. You'd have wanted me to be like someone else; I'd have wanted to please you and I'd have been unhappy. Today, you let Miss Camion do as she wants, and Miss Camion always wants to come back to her little history professor who's got a great big bandage around his aching heart because his little wifey left him."

That's how Miss Camion talks. The wind gets caught in her hats and sometimes her two hands can't hold them in place. She dresses in fabrics the bees mistake for a flower garden. Her skin is as white as milk but she spreads as many colours onto it as Riopelle does on his canvases. Other ladies exhaust themselves in gyms, trying to lose weight. Miss Camion doesn't want to lose any of the silky waves that roll across her frame. After making love, she declares, as if she's just enjoyed a meal:

"That was so good I must have gained a kilo!"

One night, when she'd affectionately kept him awake until pale glimmers slipped inside the curtains, she chided him:

"You haven't finished your homework, Professor."

He replied:

"I'm dead and I have to give a lecture in a few hours. And you're going to look tired at your board meeting."

She rolled onto him, cooing:

"The best make-up for a woman is a sleepless night devoted to love."

That's the way Miss Camion talks. She is a giantess of America. She also told him:

"You, you're lost in the past. You never try to seduce me. You don't dream about taking control of my company. You don't ask me for anything. You haven't even noticed that I'm crazy enough to give you everything. I love you the way you are. And you have no idea how strong you are."

All that is very hard to understand.

Through her lawyer, his ex-wife, the too-pretty hairdresser, is demanding an advance on the royalties from his biography of Farmer Dubois. According to the lawyer, Robert Martin is only one-half the author of the book. Had it not been for his wife's divorce petition, Robert Martin wouldn't have taken that trip to Colorado where he got the idea for the book. And so, since his ex-wife was behind the project, she has a legal right to a fair share of the revenue, i.e. 50 percent. She could demand a higher percentage, explained the lawyer. The reason the historian has been able to develop his research methodology and improve his talent is that over many years his ex-wife displayed a maternal understanding.

During all those years, she provided an atmosphere conducive to reflection around the historian's work, by accepting responsibilities, tasks and concerns that would normally be the historian's responsibility, which he has been relieved of through his ex-wife's devotion.

Miss Camion said:

"It's high time you saw a good lawyer: mine. I've already called. He's expecting you."

It's been a long time since Robert Martin has stepped inside such a tall building. The clouds stroke the windows. He feels slightly dizzy because of the dimensions of the office, the paintings by well-known artists, the audacious sculptures, the panoramic view spread before him: the city below, the river, the mountains. . . . This lawyer soars in the sky . . .

"You have to understand," the great lawyer explains, "that all lawyers are sharks. There are small sharks and big sharks. To know which kind you're dealing with, look at the aquarium they live in."

"This high up," suggests Robert Martin, "the rent must be impressive . . ."

"What part of town do you live in?" asks the man of law.

"Near Outremont."

"One square metre of my office costs as much as your entire apartment. Now let's talk about your business. It's a divorce? How old are you?"

"Thirty-nine."

"Fifty-two percent of couples in your age category have divorced. You're normal. We're going to squeeze your wife dry. Here, we win our cases."

Once he's left that place, Robert Martin needs air. He needs to walk for a while, at ground level, with ordinary people who aren't parasites feeding on other people's suffering. His too-pretty hairdresser has ruthlessly declared war on him. He has decided not to defend himself. After she's taken everything from him, maybe then she'll make peace.

"To take our minds off that, let's think about Farmer Dubois."

Aside from the mention of Dubois's name in *The Oregon Trail*, he has picked up no new traces of the farmer. Yet he's gone over the entire history of the one thousand, nine hundred and eighty miles of the Oregon Trail and that of the three thousand, five hundred miles of rivers, forest, prairies, mountains, torrents, precipices, famine, snow, ice, rain and deserts of the expedition from St. Louis, Missouri, to Astoria.

Rather than persist in looking for the unknown Dubois, why not follow William Frederick Cody, the future Buffalo Bill, who killed four thousand, two hundred and eighty-one buffalo to feed the men who built the railway in Kansas? Why not talk about those poor men Jones, Vallée and Leclerc? Lost for months in a blizzard in the snow-covered western plains, starving and frozen, they haven't slept for three days, haven't eaten for three days. Suddenly they see the brown shadow of the buffalo charging into the storm. Jones, Vallée and Leclerc bring down thirty-two buffalo, twenty-eight mountain sheep lost on the prairie and a dozen stags. They'll provide enough meat for the winter, enough skins to cover the cabin they put up and plenty of fur for clothing.

Robert Martin could spend hours with those convoys advancing towards the limits of America, with carts or travois laden with dried fruit, corn, ploughs, beans, hogs, weapons and utensils, with women and children. At night, the convoys form a circle. Some keep watch over the Indians skulking in the night, others dance to fiddle music, still others pray. These convoys are made up not only of farmers but also of promoters, braggarts, swindlers, extortionists, embalmers, coffin-sellers, insurance agents and travel agents who rent carts, wagons, rafts, canoes, wheelbarrows and mules. In 1846, one of these travel agents invents a wagon with sails that can travel fifteen miles an hour when the prairie wind is favourable. In 1849, another agent offers clients a thousand-foot balloon that will take them from St. Louis, Missouri, to California in three days, at a cost of fifty dollars, wine included. In the convoys there are also preachers whose voices are often drowned out by howling coyotes, missionaries whose role is to pacify the Indians by promising the Kingdom of Heaven while the Whites seize their kingdom here on earth. Murderers are hanged as soon as they've been judged, from a tree or from the upturned shaft of a wagon if there's no tree nearby. Rapists are punished with thirty-nine strokes of the lash over three consecutive days. The convoys also carry thugs who frighten the Indians by showing them a flask that they claim contains the devil who spreads the pox and peddlers who trade the Indians a tin kettle for a horse. With their turkeys, hens, cows, goats, dogs, geese and cats, members of the convoy always strive to travel faster, farther, despite the Indians who defend their territory and who have a tremendous need for the horses, weapons, gunpowder and food the wagons and carts are loaded down with; they make progress despite the black wall of whining mosquitoes that eat you alive, despite attacks by grizzly bears that leave more victims than the Indians, despite the cholera so violent that a man can come down with it in the morning and be buried that same evening, despite the frequent drownings when they cross waterways or the accidents caused by stray bullets fired by immigrants who are clumsy with firearms. The poor animals that pull the wagons and carts die of exhaustion. They are unhitched, the leather shoes that protect their hooves from stones and cactus spines are removed, they're replaced with other animals and the convoy sets off again. Every one of them hopes that his story will be told in the future. At mile 814 of the Oregon Trail, on a long rock that resembles a whale washed up on the prairie, the adventurers put down their names, written in tar or carved in the stone. Dubois didn't bother inscribing his. Did he know how to write? At the time, the vast majority of French Canadians were illiterate. He'll have to look further.

Farmer Dubois was probably an ordinary man like the millions of individuals nobody talks about. Why has Robert Martin decided to write the life story of an ordinary man? Can an ordinary man's life be interesting? Wouldn't it be more fascinating to write a book about the germs spread across North America by the Whites, which, more than the might of their weapons, ensured the conquest of the continent? Unfortunately, that significant contribution to the understanding of the past has already been presented. Just one principle prevails: historians shouldn't visit the past like nuns visiting a shop filled with fragile, pious objects.

Why not simply tell the story of a caribou that, as he has learned, travels a distance of two thousand, seven hundred miles across the tundra between his birth and his death? He could describe the landscapes crossed, itemize the dangers lying in wait for the herd, depict the seasons, recreate the course of his migration, establish the laws of the group . . .

Why not write instead the life story of Duffault, a French Canadian in love with horses? As an adolescent, he broke away from his Catholic family in Quebec; from farm job to farm job, he walks to the Canadian west, learns English which he'll embellish later when, after making up a new name for himself, he invents a new existence. He becomes the historian of his own imaginary life; he also becomes the architect of his imagined adventures. Will James is celebrated in magazines and films. The real man, the man who is not imaginary, the unknown Duffault, wanders and drinks like any poor devil. When Will James dies, he leaves all his possessions to poor Duffault. Isn't the story of that man who lived in the mirage he created, the story of America as well?

Why shouldn't he undertake a biography of Mrs. Chadwick, a poor girl from Ontario who later on, in the great cities of the United States, would become the intimate friend of wealthy bankers, passing herself off as the daughter of a contemporary billionaire? She borrows millions of dollars. The bankers would never dare be so discourteous as to check the wily crook's claims or her credit. If you were among her friends, Mrs. Chadwick would have a grand piano delivered to your house the way someone else might send flowers, or she'd invite your young daughter, along with nineteen other young daughters of her wealthy friends, on a cruise around the world. Isn't America also this way of running behind a dream? When dream becomes reality, isn't that gigantic schizophrenia really America, hypnotized by her own dreams?

Would it be better to recount the life of Pierre Dorion, voyageur, guide, hunter, coureur de bois, multilingual interpreter, half Indian? With his white father and his Indian mother he always lived in a tent, among the various tribes that took them in. He doesn't know what a roof is, or solid walls. One night, when he's been drinking with his father all day, Pierre Dorion gets into a terrible fight with him. The old man fights back with all the strength of his experience as a coureur de bois. In the end, exhausted, he must surrender. Following the Indian custom of the time, Pierre Dorion takes out his knife and grabs hold of his father's hair to scalp him. At this tragic moment, the father remembers that his son is also a White and cries:

"Son, I've educated you too well; you aren't going to behave like a savage!"

The impulsive Pierre Dorion stops his move, puts back his knife and wipes away his sweat.

"I'm sorry, Papa."

Then he gives his old father the last drop of whiskey.

Instead of Farmer Dubois, wouldn't it be more interesting to follow the Indian princess who married a European trader in Quebec City? He spoils her with luxurious gowns, jewels and perfumes from Paris. One fall, the trader is called back to England on urgent business. He leaves his Indian princess in tears on the pier. He will return in the spring. She waits during the long winter. When spring arrives, she goes repeatedly to the wharf to inquire about the ships that are due. In June his ship returns. The Indian takes her newborn in her arms and runs to greet her husband. At last she sees him. He descends the gangplank. She recognizes him right away, even though he's changed a little. He recognizes her, too. She holds up her son. He waves. He is coming. On his arm is a white woman in a wedding gown. The trader is kind. He doesn't send the Indian woman away. He takes her as a servant. She will give him other children.

Robert Martin could also talk about Jean Beauséjour, who called himself John Day. One winter he was travelling in the Rockies. A group of Indians was watching the lone adventurer. They ambush him. They take his horses, his provisions, his weapons, even his clothes. They beat him and abandon him, naked, in the snow. How does he survive with no weapons and no clothes, in the icy wind, surrounded by enemy tribes, in a region devoid of game? A group of adventurers passes that way some months later, in the spring. They find him, gaunt but alive. He even has the strength to carry his share of the baggage. He walks as quickly as his new companions. He even joins in their songs. All at once, a band of Indians looms deep in a valley. John Day, who has suffered too much, has undoubtedly come to the end of his psychological resistance. In him are unleashed all the fear accumulated over the winter, all the terrors of his nights, all the suffering, all the frustrations of having been alone to face the immense white menace. He is trembling as if his body were going to be torn apart. He starts to scream. He throws himself at his companions. He is so dangerously mad he has to be shot down. . . . As he wandered through the United States, could Farmer Dubois have survived such trying seasons?

With all these heroes waiting for their stories to be written, Robert Martin is lost in America. His memories of what he has read swirl around him as if he were in a birchbark canoe, riding torrents, tossed about between two cliffs. Wanting to relate the birth of America, Robert Martin is as confused as when he discusses the history of the beginning of the world . . . Why has he taken such an interest in Farmer Dubois? Let his wife, his ex-wife, take 100 percent of the royalties on Farmer Dubois's biography if she wants! It will never be anything but a project. To hell with his lawyer, the shark! You step out of his office with a nauseating idea about justice. To hell with Miss Camion's company that turned the cretinous Dubois into a hero like Davy Crockett! To hell with Miss Camion! He wants to be alone and free. He doesn't want to find himself in a tête-à-tête with an amorous locomotive. He goes back to his student room.

A delicious perfume greets him. A huge pot of azaleas sits on his work table amid the open books and sheaves of notes. A card bears a message:

My little love, I thought you might be a bit upset after meeting your lawyer and you'd prefer not to see me right away. . . . I understand. . . . Here are some flowers so you won't forget me. Come back when you want, when you're ready. . . . Solitude is bad for you. And it's just as bad for me . . .

Robert Martin lets the card fall into an open book. It has pictures of ornamented garments. The French, he reads, taught the Huron how to embroider with glass beads. The art later spread to all the Indian tribes in North America.

19 With flowers adorning the saguaros, a new springtime is beginning in Arizona. It's been a good nine or ten years since Charlie Longsong has seen so many flowers in his desert. Last fall, the rain lasted into December. After that the weather was mild. Only on a few nights did hoarfrost turn the gravel white. In February, the rain was abundant again and the *arroyos* overflowed. After that no clouds disturbed the sun. That explains the abundance of flowers. Towards the west, between the plain and the mountain, the *bajada* gleams with everything that's growing in its rocky soil. The ground is covered with tiny purple and white flowers. Garlands of flowers hang from the rocks. There are narrow red ribbons dangling from the tips of the ocotillo branches. Everywhere the sage is covered with red stars, packed very tightly together. At the end of the afternoon, white flowers open on the yuccas. In the evening, clouds of moths come and lay their eggs in nests of flowers. In May, the chollas produce their fruit. The paloverdes blossom into glorious golden bouquets. It's a celebration in the desert. Bats come in the evening to feed on insects in the agave blossoms. In the distance a stag cries like a child. Probably he gathered some of the sweet fruit of the cholla and now his muzzle is bristling with cactus thorns.

Charlie Longsong's snake, his friend, is happy. For many years now he has been sharing his *hogan*. Every morning the cascabel emerges from his shelter under the cabin, crawls in his own way—sideways, always towards the same dip in the ground—and warms himself in the sun. When the heat is too strong, he goes back to his shelter. Never has Charlie Longsong seen him hunt. How does he feed himself?

In the morning, there's nothing more wonderful than a visit to his saguaros. Straight as soldiers bedecked with flowers, they are celebrating a victory. And doves pirouette all around them.

That was what Charlie Longsong reported to the people of the mesa. They listened, but they want a story from the time of his youth . . .

"This happened nearly fifty years ago. The war was over but there were still minor flare-ups. Everywhere, there was havoc. And me, I was thinking about a beautiful white nurse who'd taken care of me. The war was over and I'd lost my arm."

They listen to him. The old man relishes seeing the young people discover how little they have lived. All at once, Charlie Longsong is enjoying his own old age. He doesn't want to stop telling his story.

He remembers a hotel. Only one wall was still standing. The roof, the other walls had been destroyed. It was the Hôtel de la Victoire. Everyone thought the name was funny. It was written on the wall. The wounded with their crutches, the sick who weren't feverish and those who weren't sleepy from drugs were transported to the city of Paris for a big parade. Many houses had been gutted. The girls were wearing thin new dresses with delicate flowers. The soldiers' souls were older now but their bodies were as wild as they were young. Those dresses were too light. The war was over. The soldiers were worn out from hating. They wanted to love. Soldier Longsong had that searing pain in his stump. He drank to numb his suffering. The girls' dresses were as delicate as the dew. The soldiers were thinking about what they barely concealed. The street was as wide as the whole mesa.

People were gathered there as if for a day of dancing. Waving flags and singing songs, the crowd joined the parade along with the soldiers, the tanks, the jeeps, the trucks. No one was afraid of the war now. No one was afraid of dying.

The girls in bright dresses climbed into the jeeps, clambered on board the trucks. They hopped onto car fenders, they perched on the tanks. They had flowers in their hair. Everywhere flags were waving. The soldiers tried to maintain a military pace but this was a civilians' party. They joined the troops. Girls threw themselves into the soldiers' arms. The crowd sang, wept. Bells rang. The people applauded, danced, skipped, unfurled banners. Everywhere, it was raining flowers. War doesn't stop flowers from growing. Celebrating, people had climbed onto roofs, cars, lampposts. All had tears in their eyes. Charlie Longsong was marching with his regiment, but he had only one arm to swing.

Someone was brandishing a blood-stained enemy uniform at the end of a stick. An Indian doesn't cry like the *bohanas*, who are soft and sensitive, but Little Tornado Man's heart was pounding hard. His tears stayed behind his eyes. He wished he were home, in the peace of his Arizona. He wished he were a child again, when his father used to lift him onto his black mare. He wished he hadn't gone to war. A number of those who had climbed the Normandy cliff with him had been torn to pieces or had fallen into the sea. Little Tornado Man was marching down a broad street in Paris to celebrate the victory. He had lost only an arm, while others had lost everything. He was standing while others no longer even had a body to house their souls.

He thought: "I've lived with the *bohanas*, I've fought with the *bohanas*. When I go back to Arizona, when I come to the mesa with just one arm, they won't recognize me."

"Soldier Longsong!"

In this foreign city, no one knew his name. Because he was alone at this celebration that was too happy for a man who was sad, because his head still echoed with the sounds of the war and the cries of his own suffering, because he was also thinking of his desert that was waiting for him on the other side of the sea, he had imagined there was someone calling him.

"Soldier Longsong!"

He wasn't the one being called. A woman's voice insisted:

"Soldier Longsong!"

No woman in this foreign country knew his name. He didn't even turn his head. He kept marching. She took him in her arms. She smelled of perfume. He could feel the swellings of her body under her dress. He was ill at ease. At his age, when a woman walks by you catch fire. She was talking to him but he couldn't hear: too much crying, too much singing, too much music, too many heels on the paving stones. His blood was pounding at his temples. She took his hand and led him away from the parade. He followed her. Feeling a woman's hand in his made his legs go limp.

"My you-know-what was getting hard in my pants," he pointed out to his listeners, who understood the comical aspect of the situation.

"So that was peace, was it? Sounds a lot better than war!"

"Do you remember me, Soldier Longsong?" she asked in her mannered way of speaking English.

He answered:

"No."

He was sorry he'd said no. She went on:

"I looked after you when you were suffering."

"I hate suffering . . ."

"You'll always have a little. A little too much. . . . But isn't that better than much too much?"

That was what she said to him with a beautiful smile that made him feel good, as if she'd stroked his forehead. She continued tugging him by the hand. He did not resist. They walked. They stopped at a café. She ordered red wine. She was beautiful. Blue eyes. Skin so white. A way of talking that put music in the words. She said to him:

"Soldier Longsong, I looked after hundreds of boys like you who were bleeding and in pain. They died or went away. And you, Soldier Longsong, I find you again here, in this city where millions of people are dancing in the streets. Why is it that I'm seeing you again? . . . It's a sign. . . . My name is Blanche. Blanche Larivière."

She taught him how to pronounce her name the way she said it in her language, French. It wasn't easy. He made an effort. She laughed.

"Life is full of signs that we must understand. Humans weren't just flung onto Earth like a handful of pebbles. There are ties between them, invisible threads. . . . I am white; you're Indian. And we're not strangers."

Blanche Larivière spoke with a kind of wisdom, as if she'd heard the Elders of the mesa. She also said:

"We met in the country of my ancestors who left Europe to build their new country in the land of your ancestors. Isn't that a sign? My ancestors brought harm to yours, but then I helped you lessen your pain. Isn't that a sign? You see, we're united, you and I, by many ties."

Then they walked along the great river that runs through Paris. He doesn't remember its name. They crossed a bridge and they realized that night had fallen. They sat in a restaurant. He had told her he hunted wild rabbits. She advised him:

"Order the *lapin à la moutarde*: it will remind you of your country."

She was from Canada, land of snow. Why had she come to the war?

"It's not fair for the boys to go away to fight if the women don't go to nurse their wounds."

He talked to her about the desert, the cactus, the ancestors and his father. They drank more wine. When they got up from their table the street was filled with music. They just had to let themselves float. He had never danced. With her on his arm he hadn't even realized he was dancing. She said to him:

"You and I have come from the New World to dance in the Old World. That's a sign . . ."

They'd drunk too much wine. Little Tornado Man was holding the body of this beautiful white woman with all the strength he had in his good arm. His flesh must have been burning her, his desire was so great. His body had become too narrow to contain all his desire for her. They danced for a long time. After that they walked down some narrow streets crowded with dancers. Then she stopped in front of a big green door. She announced:

"This is where I live."

It was dark. They climbed up a long, winding staircase. She lived in a little room that had a bed and some flowers on a table. She opened the window.

"We'll let the starlight come in. . . . There are so many stars tonight. It's a sign . . ."

She let her dress slip off and she offered herself on the bed. They gave themselves to one another the way youth gives itself to the present. Little Tornado Man became so sad he couldn't say a word. It was good to have a nurse to console him.

When they woke up in the morning, she said:

"You have to learn the name of my street. Repeat after me . . ."

He repeated the name of rue Gît-le-coeur so many times he still remembers it.

The winter winds were fierce on the mesa. They carried away the souls of a number of Elders. With them gone, it is Charlie Longsong who possesses the memory of what has been. It is he whom they ask to recount the past.

He does not tell everything. An old man is entitled to his silences.

The room on rue Gît-le-coeur was so tiny there was hardly room for the light to come in. The young Indian and the young white woman touched their bodies as if to reassure themselves they really did exist. They touched one another as if they were afraid of disappearing a moment later. They touched one another as if they had touched fire. They touched one another the way they'd have drunk water in a burning desert. They caressed one another as if morning would never come again. They loved one another as if each of them was going to die at dawn. Blanche Larivière said:

"You and I are two new stars in the night."

She sometimes talked like the Elders, did Blanche Larivière.... But Charlie Longsong can't tell the people of the mesa any of that.

Nor does he tell them that he went to the trading post and asked the cashier to phone Blanche Larivière, 33 Grande Allée, Quebec, Canada. The old man still remembers the embarrassment that burned his face when he dared to ask the cashier to find the number that would let him hear the voice of Blanche Larivière. He'd tried several times to phone her himself. He'd never heard anything but that electric silence in his ear. Maybe the cashier would have better luck.... There are some things that women do better than men. A hot feeling of feebleness spread to his very bones when the cashier stared at him as if to say:

"You're a sorry sight, Charlie Longsong.... You came back from the war a little crazy. That's why I'm going to help you . . ."

Little Tornado Man had faced up to the fire of war, but now he was trembling as he asked for help to telephone Blanche Larivière.

And up there in the north, Blanche Larivière did not reply. In Quebec, Canada, no one knew the name of Blanche Larivière. So Charlie Longsong went back to his desert and drank bourbon. He knew that Blanche Larivière existed.

Nor does he tell them about the days when he sat outside his *hogan* waiting for her as if she were going to come and visit him. He waited, his gaze fixed on the horizon, as if Blanche Larivière were going to appear between the cactuses, like those whirlwinds that rise up in a gust of wind and form one body with the dust, sand, twigs, the wisps of straw, turning, dancing, breaking up when the breeze has blown itself out.

Nor does he tell them about his desire like a hunger, a thirst, to have a son. A man who has no son is a man who has not really arrived on the Earth. That man has not passed on the legacy of the Elders. The blood of the Elders has curdled in him like milk in the sun.

There are so many things an old man cannot tell . . .

20 Robert Martin is surrounded by piles of books, by stacks of magazines. The computers are full of data. Maps are pinned to the walls. File folders overflow with notes. His documentation is becoming as vast as the landscapes of America, as abundant as her rivers, as unpredictable as her mountains, as long as her plains, as abundant as her game. The historian no longer knows if he ought to advance, retreat, turn left or right. Though he has not yet written the first word, this book is already more famous than all the books he's published to date. A distinguished lady stopped him in the street.

"I have cousins by marriage who still live in the country, and on their side of the family there's a Lamothe who married a Dubreuil whose grandmother was married to a Dubois. That Dubois's daughter, who was married to a Pélerin, died in the United States. That's a trail you shouldn't neglect if you want to work your way back to Farmer Dubois."

The fury of his wife, his ex-wife, the too-pretty hairdresser, has subsided. Instead of making him happy, this respite has him worried. This fine weather must be hiding an upcoming storm. Events provoked by Miss Camion's special projects division are moving quickly. Today, the author of Farmer Dubois's biography is the guest speaker at the annual luncheon of the Association of Black and White Cattle Breeders. This organization wants to promote better understanding of the beneficial role of milk in the settling of America. It's providing significant financial support for his research on Farmer Dubois. In return, he's had to agree that his book will be subtitled *Milk, Gold and Silver*. He hates such obligations, but he couldn't refuse this concession to the special projects division. Nor did he hesitate to declare as the conclusion to his speech: "We will demonstrate most eloquently that the conquest of America is nothing but the victory of milk, whose empire spread across the territory more solidly than any religious doctrine, any economic force, any political ideology!" He was stunned to hear himself make that statement. "Well," he decided, "it's a new historical theory."

Before he was a farmer, Dubois must have been a hunter, at a time when there was an unrestricted market and fur was valuable. The historian has come across the inventory of a trading post from the end of the winter of 1857: seventeen thousand, seven hundred and five pounds of beaver skins, four hundred and sixty-five beaver pelts, nine hundred and seven otter pelts, ninety-eight sea-otter pelts, one hundred and seventy-nine mink pelts, twenty-two raccoon pelts, twenty-eight lynx pelts, one hundred and twenty-four fox pelts, seventy-one black bear pelts and sixteen grizzly bear pelts. Farmer Dubois must have taken part in this kind of carnage. Was it carnage in those days?

Someone brings him the newspaper. The headlines.... The same news.... Didn't he already read that yesterday or the day before?

Here, there's something about his book. An attack on his book! This is too much. He hasn't even bought the paper to write it on! "Once again, once too often," protests the letter-writer,

a male historian wants to reduce the history of America to the simplistic dimension of one of those sorry men who carted their peckers and their rifles in one direction or another, depending on which way the wind blew. Once again, once too often, a male historian is going to relate history as if this continent contained nothing but horses, oxen, hogs and men. Once again, once too often, a male historian hasn't taken into account the fact that women were needed to populate North America and to knit a few values into its civilization. Mister History Professor, who wants to borrow your hero's historical balls because your own are little and soft, I'll have you know that without woman there would be no life. If you were honest and objective, it's the story of Farmer Dubois's wife that you'd be writing. But can we expect objectivity from a man? It is public knowledge that the author of Farmer Dubois's life story has just forced his wife and children to undergo a painful divorce. Mister History Professor, your problems with your wife don't give you the right to take your revenge on the history of America. Mister History Professor, history is either true or it isn't. And it will never be true if people claim it came about without women.

This attack hurts. He hasn't done anything yet but he's been found guilty and sentenced. He's not the one who asked for a divorce. That bare-chinned ink-slinger has no right to attack him in public because he's suffered. Oh, he'll find the words to assassinate this bluestocking who takes her headaches for ideas. A number of women think like her, no doubt. It's true though that history written by men has seriously neglected women. That's a fair criticism and one he cannot evade. Robert Martin will never forget his first history lecture at university. The great professor had entered the lecture hall in his gown, with more books than he could carry. He'd tossed them disdainfully onto the desk, looked his students up and down with a contemptuous expression and declared enigmatically, in the voice of one who knows everything and doubts nothing:

"History is made in bedrooms."

And as if with that he had said everything, he departed the lecture hall, leaving his books behind.

The lady who is attacking him in the newspaper is not altogether wrong. History is made by women too. He must insert into his book the story of a courageous Indian woman he's made note of. That will give his book a female perspective. He must admit he's never thought about the role of women in the history of America. What is a man without a woman?

A squaw accompanied her husband, a French-Canadian voyageur who was exploring passages through the Rockies. The group was attacked by a fierce tribe. Her husband's throat is cut, then he's scalped. She has been able to hide. Their devastation completed, the attackers move on to pursue their gruesome combat elsewhere. Now she can flee. They haven't taken everything. She picks up some pelts, some beaver meat, some dried salmon. She ties her bundle to a horse's back. She settles her two children on the back of another horse and charges into some mountainous territory she doesn't know. To avoid being spotted they go to sleep without lighting a fire. It is January. In the Rockies in January, the cold saws your bones. The snow is deep. The horses are tired. She spies an abandoned cabin. Could it be that the God of her Christian husband has prepared a shelter for his children? She pushes open the door. The floor and walls are spattered with blood. It froze before it dried. Enemies are lurking. They're not far away. They mustn't stop here. They must flee even deeper into the mountains. Looking around, she finds a ravine and rides into it. Here no one will see the smoke when she lights a fire to warm her children, who are chilled to the bone. In this spot she builds a wigwam with some branches and the pelts she's brought with her. Her stock of meat is soon exhausted. She kills a horse. Smokes the meat. There is peace. In March, winter still rages. She must kill the second horse. Wolves are approaching. The squaw picks up her two children and for days, through snow so deep she sinks into it, over patches of ice where she slips and falls, she walks, not knowing where she's going. In the end, she collapses, exhausted. Horsemen from a friendly tribe find her asleep in the snow, her children in her arms. They are saved. Perhaps Farmer Dubois's wife had such courage. He'll have to look, have to find out.

Thanks to Miss Camion's special projects division, this book is creating a storm. It's not that he wants to criticize Miss Camion. She takes what is disorganized and organizes it. What strength she has, in those dazzling dresses that resemble wild gardens in the Amazonian jungle! He loves her in the way one can love a locomotive, a bulldozer, a mountain or Niagara Falls. Her strength doesn't crush him; little by little it becomes his own, it settles into his soul, it feeds his former weakness.

Robert Martin admits that he loves her. She holds him tight against her, she holds him for a long time against her body which vibrates as if her heart were big enough to fill it. This woman is like a beautiful summer day. After a moment of that warm carnal silence, she says to him:

"I've never asked you if you love me. Sometimes you seem to

be in such pain. . . . I know that someone who's been wounded finds it hard to love. I told myself you must love me a little because you take me as I am, you've never tried to change me. I've loved you from the very start. Because of the way I'm made, my grief can't last very long. There's joy flowing in my veins. That's the way I am. But I think a woman always needs a little grief. You're mine, and I try to console you. You and I are going to straighten out that business of your divorce. We'll be generous with your ex-wife. Your children will remember their father's generosity. And then, later on, when time has cooled everyone's emotions, your ex-wife will realize that she left a generous man. We're going to finish your book about Farmer Dubois. And then you'll be free for another project. You'll have become North America's greatest historian. I hope you'll still love me a little then."

"I often feel like an old book," he admits, "with yellow pages filled with old ideas. I can see life passing by while I'm stuck there in my dust."

"Since I first met you you've put on some weight. An unhappy man gets thinner. . . . We've already come through three seasons together. It's already spring."

Three or four days later, he's wanted urgently on the phone while he is teaching a course on the evolution of the notion of property as defined by Montesquieu. His heart gives out. The telephone is so far away, at the end of a number of corridors. His legs are numb. At last he picks up the receiver.

"Professor," says Miss Camion's familiar voice, "forgive me for disturbing you. . . . I'll never do it again. I'll never call you again and say it's an emergency. It's wrong to interrupt your lecture, Professor. But I wanted to so badly, just this once. . . . Just once. For the fun of it. . . . Professor, I can hear you panting the way you do when you make love to me. You've been running. I shouldn't have made you run just to listen to me. I'll never do it again. I'm in a meeting with my accountant. I'm going to buy twenty new trucks. While I was talking about my capital depreciation I was thinking about how much I love you. That thought grew so big, I couldn't keep it to myself. So I called you on an urgent matter because I had an urgent need to tell you that. At my age I shouldn't behave like this. I love you because you give me a past. I love you because you give me the power of thinking."

Robert Martin is very annoyed at being interrupted. Her avalanche of warm-hearted words soothes his irritation, though. In a world in which so many people wither away amid indifference and solitude, isn't it pleasant to be called away urgently to be told that someone loves you? He searches for the right words. He doesn't know how to put his feelings into words. Finally, he declares:

"With your great wings you're a butterfly as big as a truck!"

"Those words give me tickles up and down my back. . . . Did you get my flowers, Professor?"

"Now listen to me, please don't send any more flowers. There are so many in my office I can't get in."

He has to admit, he's not entirely unhappy. In co-operation with the special projects division of Miss Camion's company, a travel agency has started massive distribution of a tourist brochure.

Stop being an ordinary tourist. Discover cultural tourism. Follow in the footsteps of Farmer Dubois, the brave French Canadian whose adventures led him to conquer America! To discover your itinerary, read his story in the book by our national historian, Robert Martin. Our comfortable, fully air-conditioned buses will leave from the simple house where Dubois was born, a humble peasant, and end up in Colorado, in the graveyard where he lies beneath a modest stone. He'd have been neglected forever if our great national historian hadn't recognized his trail as the footsteps of a great man: Dubois, Father of America.

This is not an easy book to write. His central character is one of those people who leave no traces . . . But wasn't America built by those who leave no traces? True history, penetrating history, is the story of desire, of thoughts, of dreams, of joys and sorrows. These don't produce official documents, signed and counter-signed. Was Farmer Dubois the kind of man who never goes back to the place he came from?

Since last summer, Robert Martin has described so many times the grandiose state of Arizona while others listened to him around a table, incredulous and enraptured. He has often declared that the rocks carved by time are as sacred as the famous cathedrals. On several occasions he has professed that human architectural genius seems limited compared with the genius of time, which, long before humans, invented every known shape. Dozens of times, too, he has explained how, in a Colorado ghost town, he discovered the notebook on whose first page he read the name of Farmer Dubois, the first man to buy a herd of fifty-nine head of cattle in a town where gold fever was dying down. The final chapter of his Arizona adventures would inevitably end with the account of his meeting with an old Indian, a little crazy and a little drunk, who kept repeating the names of the rue Gît-le-coeur in Paris and the Grande Allée in Quebec.

One evening during dinner with Miss Camion, the phone rings:

"I apologize for disturbing a busy historian like you. I haven't had a chance to look at your other books, but I'm very anxious to read the one about Farmer Dubois. I congratulate you for writing history as it was lived by the people. There's no more democratic way to write the history of the world's greatest democracy."

"Do you have some information for me?" asks Robert Martin impatiently.

"I'm sorry.... I had to tell you of my interest in your work.... Here is the reason for my intrusion. Friends have told other friends who've told me about your meeting with an old Indian who knew the rue Gît-le-coeur in Paris. As soon as I heard your anecdote, some lines from a poem stirred in my memory. I'm a professor of literature. Your story is amazing. I could send you the poem. I'm taking too much of your time.... Perhaps you're not interested. Excuse me. I shouldn't have disturbed you."

Robert Martin loathes the telephone. The instrument is a skeleton key that lets anyone into your house like a thief. He says nothing.

"I'm disturbing you, I can tell. Excuse me. The poem talks about an Indian and the rue Gît-le-coeur. Would you like to hear it?"

"The poem says something about Farmer Dubois?"

"I realize I just have a photocopy of the first page."

"Read me the first page then."

"Here it is:

> *O my young Indian brother*
> *You have left your desert*
> *For the great ritual of fire*
> *And you took my heart*
> *On rue Gît-le-coeur*
> *And you gave me yours*
> *O my young Indian brother*
> *We made peace*
> *In the month of August*
> *On rue Gît-le-coeur*

In Paris
Far from your desert
O my young Indian brother. . . .

"The poem is taken from a chapbook entitled *Shivering Flowers*. And the forgotten poetess, who influenced Anne Hébert, was called Blanche Larivière."

"Blanche Larivière!" exclaims the historian. "That's amazing!"

"Are you familiar with Blanche Larivière?"

"No. Thank you for the information. Give me your phone number."

"I'm so sorry I took so much of your time. Excuse me."

Robert Martin puts down the receiver. He feels a strong urge to move. "If chance is the first principle in the creation of the world, it's not impossible that it's also the historical principle," he thinks. He is overwhelmed. The old Indian he abandoned by the roadside last summer has reached him. He can no longer run away, sending up gravel under his tires. He repeats the lines he remembers:

You took my heart
On rue Gît-le-coeur

Quickly, before he forgets them, he jots the lines on a file card. Feverishly, he also notes the title of the book of poems. Who is this poetess? Before he forgets, he should also write the note on the barehanded boxing matches organized by saloon managers to get their clients out of the brothels and keep them in their own establishments as long as possible. Like all poor people, Farmer Dubois must have been a boxing fan.

The next day, an assistant at the National Library very delicately hands Robert Martin a copy of *Shivering Flowers*. The author's name appears in letters decorated with very fine flourishes. He opens the thin chapbook. The glue in the binding cracks. Has it ever been opened before? Has even one reader gazed at the words of the poetess? The poem on rue Gît-le-coeur is on page nineteen.

"Do you have any information about this author?"

The assistant slides the *Biographical Dictionary* across the counter.

Larivière, Blanche. (Born Quebec City, 1919, died there 1964.) Married to René Goupil, notary, devoted her life to Catholic charities. Particularly involved with education of young Indians in Ancienne-Lorette, near Quebec City. Also dabbled in poetry, producing five books including *Life Goes On, The Star in Your Eyes* and *Shivering Flowers*. Born into a bourgeois family, brought up with traditional values that enriched both her poetry and her life. Also gave birth to a son who followed in his father's footsteps and became a notary. Blanche Larivière died after a long battle with cancer. At the time of their publication some of her poems were praised by Father Lévesque, O.D. Regrettably, her work has been neglected by the younger generation. During the final days of the disease that would kill her, she often said: "I have not said everything." This sense of leaving behind an unfinished work is the mark of a genuine writer.

"Is there a file on Blanche Larivière in the archives?" inquires the historian.

The assistant taps away on his computer.

"Definitely," he replies with the certitude of those who know their institution is perfect.

"Then I can consult the Blanche Larivière file?"

The assistant taps away again.

"The Blanche Larivière file cannot be opened before the death of her husband, René Goupil, notary."

"And is the husband dead or alive?"

Again the assistant taps away, and again, and again, then all at once he looks as sad as if someone has just given him some bad news.

"The computer doesn't know," he whispers.

21 Who is coming? A cloud of dust is rolling towards his *hogan*. Charlie Longsong no longer has eyes to see. He goes inside to make sure his rifle is where it's supposed to be. In the past, he could see as well at night as in the daytime. A van skids to a halt on the gravel. The dust blows over it and past it. Three, four young men jump out of the vehicle. What do they want? He is just an old man. He steps back to be closer to his weapon. One of the men is carrying a case of beer.

"Hi there, old man Charlie Longsong! We've come to talk to you."

What is in the wind to make young men want to hear an old man's stories? In his day, those who would soon become men wanted to learn what they needed to know from those who had been men. In the old days, the Elders recounted and the young didn't forget what they said. There was continuity in time as there was in blood. But today's young don't want to listen to anyone. They're so ignorant they think they know all there is to know.

"I've got nothing to tell you," he says slyly. "A man always talks too much, even if he keeps quiet."

"If the old people let themselves go to their graves without telling the young what they've learned, the young won't learn anything."

Is there a new voice in the wind, advising the young to listen to their Elders? Is there a special taste in the water that makes them want to hear an old man who's been silent for so long? Is there some weakness in the corn that is making the young people need an old man's words? Charlie Longsong knows that he will speak. He also knows that he must postpone the moment so they'll be really ready to listen to him. He remembers how in his youth the Elders unfurled their remarks slowly, letting time select the words along with them. It is very empty, a time of youth in which the words of the Elders do not fall. It is very sad, the life of an Elder whose words do not sow youth.

The visitors have uncapped their beer. They offer one to Charlie Longsong.

"Tell us about white women."

"Are they white all over?"

That's very funny. They laugh. Charlie Longsong looks far away, towards the horizon, as if his memory were at the end of the desert.

"White women are white, white as snow. They're even whiter when they take off their dresses. You mustn't think about that. It's not good for an old Indian to dream about white women. It's not good for young Indians to listen to an old Indian talk to them about white women."

The bottles are already empty. Quickly, they hand out more.

"Is it true that white women do things our Indian women don't know about?"

They burst out in that noisy laughter of the young when they're declaring they are eternal on this Earth.

Behind his face that's creased like an ancient cliff, Charlie Longsong seems to have heard nothing.

"White women," he goes on, "are very happy when a war is over. They're as white as snow. And they melt like the snow."

The seething light flattens the desert. In the distance, the mountains seem to be gasping. Heat rolls in waves that bounce off their faces. The sun pours blazing fire onto the arid plain. In the shade of their pen, the sheep lack even the strength to bleat. Words soften and become sticky on dry lips.

After his father's death, Little Tornado Man went back to live on the mesa. There were many men in his mother's house. To avoid blows he stayed outside as much as possible. He liked listening to the Elders. That's what he wants to tell his young visitors today. He was only a child, he didn't understand everything the Elders said, but he remembers all of it.

"The Indian mustn't be a man who has nothing. The Indian mustn't be a man who possesses only the stories of his Elders. The Indian must go where there is fine grass, sweet water. There, he must buy himself an animal. In every animal there are a thousand. In one sheep there are a thousand sheep. But to have a thousand sheep you first need two. In a horse, there are a thousand horses. An Indian should want to own a thousand sheep, a thousand horses and a dozen children. To take care of his animals he must rise before the sun and go to sleep after the sun. He mustn't sleep during the day. The Indian mustn't curse the fatigue that comes from caring for his animals and his children. The Indian mustn't say, 'I'm tired because of you and I hope lightning strikes you.' The Indian mustn't say, 'I hope a snake bites you.' If the Indian calls down these afflictions they will come, like obedient dogs. The Indian must not lose a child or a horse or a sheep or a single grain of corn. Each of them contains a thousand."

So the Elders had said that autumn, when he was a lonely, sad child . . .

Charlie Longsong did not heed their advice. Instead of heading for a place where there was fine grass, where there was sweet water, he went to the other side of the ocean to fight in a war. Instead of buying one sheep in which there were a thousand, he gave away his best arm in the *bohanas'* war.

"That's what happened. We can't change anything that has been. But we can change what will be."

Young people no longer listen to the Elders. They're only interested in the noise from their radios. And so they don't understand what's happening in their tribe or in the world. Yet they've come here to offer him beer and ask him to tell them things. So he must tell them. He has become an Elder. And the young will understand life better if they don't forget his stories.

On the mesa, Little Tornado Man could hear the men complain that no rain was falling. The desert was dead earth. The *arroyos* stayed dry. The sheep could find nothing to feed on but twigs. And the corn was stunted. So the master of the snakes explained:

"Ever since the *bohanas* came to the land they've been killing every snake they see. They think snakes are enemies of the human race. Killing a snake is a very wicked deed. Snakes are the friends of the Indian race. The snake is our brother. After the dance, the snakes go home, back to their dark hole under the earth, and they tell the spirits: 'Kachinas, send rain to the poor Indians for their corn and their sheep.' The Indians dance with snakes, while the *bohanas* kill snakes. When the snake is dead he cannot go and tell the Kachinas, 'Send rain to the good Indians who dance with the snakes.' And that is why the desert no longer receives showers as it did in the old times when the killers of snakes had not yet invaded the desert."

His visitors have run out of beer but they're not leaving. Charlie Longsong has fallen silent. They want to hear more. And then he remembers another story.

It was in a cold land, very far north, where lived the ancestors of his ancestors. The land was so cold that no fire could warm the ice-covered cabins. After some very long discussions, half the people decided they could no longer suffer like this from the cold that would eventually freeze their blood. The other half decided to stay in the ice. The one group began to follow the sun towards the south. With their children and grandchildren, this new people walked for more than a hundred years and then a hundred years again. They crossed steep mountains and plains as long as eternity, they forded turbulent rivers, they walked through deep canyons until finally they came to a sunny valley where the earth was smooth and fertile along a river. Those people were never cold again. And until the *bohanas* appeared they were happy. Those invaders made them suffer more than all the winters in the distant northern land.

Was Blanche Larivière cold in her northern land? Charlie Longsong wouldn't want his visitors to know that he's thinking about her. There has been no more beer for some time now. They've heard enough stories. They leave.

Night falls and mingles with the alkaline dust. The earth is so dry the mere weight of a shadow makes it crack. On the horizon at the end of the chalky soil, tree-covered mountains offer the cool shelter of the northern side of the vales, of crevasses, breaches and transverse valleys. Under the dried-out heather, a mouse advances on the tips of its paws. The silence is so intense that Charlie Longsong can hear its minute claws scrape at the gravel. A grey fox cub has smelled it. He's waiting between the burdocks that his fur dares not brush against. This will be an easy prey. While the peoples of the light are asleep, the peoples of the night take possession of the desert. A bewhiskered shrew gorges himself on insects. His erect little ears spy on the silence. Bats that have come from the canyons rush at the insects too. The shrew recognizes their wingbeats. He scowls. Reassured, he continues his feast. Some snakes that have slept all day also leave to go hunting. The shrew must be careful. It's an ordinary night, with its hunting and its wars. Each needs the other so the species can continue. For Charlie Longsong, this is the hour for sleep.

Now the curtain of shadows is opening. A dark man materializes, astride a black mare that advances on silent hooves. She comes to a standstill in front of the *hogan*.

"Little Tornado Man . . ."

His father called him by his childhood name. Charlie Longsong has always preferred his child's name to the name he was given when he became a man. Is a man always a child to his father?

"Little Tornado Man, long ago, before your birth, I was a young man and I noticed a young girl. She had noticed me too. She desired me as I desired her. I wanted to take her as my wife and she wanted me for her husband. So she followed the custom of our tribe. She was pretty, Little Tornado Man. I had no urge to look at the other girls beside her. Following the custom, she came to bring my mother some corn she'd ground as fine as the dust of the dew. My mother said, 'No one has ever ground corn so fine.' She agreed to take her into her house. My mother agreed to become the mother-in-law of this pretty girl who knew how to grind corn so fine. My mother agreed to give the girl her son for her husband. I had an older brother. Our tribe's custom gave my older brother the privilege of marrying before me. It was to him that my mother gave the pretty girl as her husband. She took him. So I fled to the desert, my eyes red, my heart raging, my blood boiling. I stayed there for a long time and didn't go back to the mesa. I lived like a furious animal. But all beings go back to the place of their birth. I finally returned to the mesa with the idea of making peace with my brother. At the foot of the mesa, in the corn field, I spied the pretty girl who had brought my mother corn so finely ground. We did not speak. But we loved one another. We loved one another. Nine months later you were born. Her husband, my brother, had doubts. Someone had noticed us. He fired at me. We did not make peace. I went back to the desert. The wind brought me rumours that my brother was beating you. He wanted nothing to do with a false son, a son his brother had made with his pretty wife. So I took my rifle and I set out to get you. My brother didn't fire. I took you with me and I called you Little Tornado Man. In the desert, you had no mother. So I taught you what the mothers in our tribe teach: how to sow corn deep in the sand; how to plant squash; how to care for the peach tree so it will yield fruit even if it's standing in soil that's too dry. I taught you how to grind corn and how to cook *pikis* and *pikamis*. I taught you to put the right quantity of sugar into cakes. I taught you how to make mutton stew, to put in plenty of fat and dried peaches. I showed you where to put the sheep to graze, how to milk the goat. And so, Little Tornado Man, you knew everything you needed to know. Now you only had to become a man."

Is Charlie Longsong dreaming? He stands up. The door of his *hogan* is open to the night. The sky is covered with stars and the desert stretches out into the vast darkness.

From the way his heart is pounding, he knows that he's been visited by his father. He longs for him as if he were a child.

22 One of the research assistants has spotted the name Dubois in a bibliography of maritime books. Now this is strange! Hundreds of thousands of French Canadians left their country to work in American factories, on farms, in mines, forests and ranches. What was this Dubois doing on a ship? The bibliography indicates:

Joseph Dubois: *Aventures en mer*, published in Boston in 18——1 [third figure illegible], 32 pages; written in French.

Did this Dubois who was lost at sea come back to terra firma and buy himself a herd in Colorado? According to the records, a single copy of Dubois's pamphlet apparently still exists. It is preserved in the library at New Bedford, Massachusetts.

A special messenger brings a somewhat blurry photocopy of Joseph Dubois's pamphlet. The director of the New Bedford Library apologizes for the poor quality of the document:

> I hasten to send you this photocopy of a photocopy made by a reader who had borrowed the original. A descendant of a French-Canadian immigrant family, he knew French well enough to appreciate the story of Joseph Dubois. He took the pamphlet to read on his ship when he was at sea. A hurricane swept the boat away, even though it was moored at the wharf. That was how the original was lost forever. Fortunately the reader, a civil servant cautious by training, was in the habit of making copies of every document that came into his possession. That was how Joseph Dubois's pamphlet was saved from the shipwreck. Already, the print quality of the original left something to be desired. It was a very modest pamphlet, the printing cost probably assumed by the author himself...

As Robert Martin's hands hold these precious pages, they are shaking. He reads:

> I was not yet sixteen years old, I had left my family far behind me, I had not a penny in my pocket and I was boarding a ship with a very tall mast. I had never seen a ship until

that day. A bearded man who had an arm with no hand gave me a canvas bag, a mattress, two wool blankets, some denim pants for work, low leather boots, high rubber boots, an undergarment, two flannel shirts, a knife, a coat made of waterproof skin, a belt, a tin cup and plate. Another bearded man with a scar slashed across his cheek and his nose toted up the cost of all those items I would need to undertake the journey:

"You owe me fifty-three dollars. Your advance on your wages is just fifty dollars. What are you going to do?"

I checked his addition against the price of the goods.

"There's no mistake. What are you going to do?"

The bearded man's gaze was so powerful I felt I'd been thrown off the ship. I did not want to leave it because I had decided I would travel on the sea. I was big and strong for my age. I wanted to see the sea because I had seen a lot of land. I did not want to disembark from this sailing ship because I had nothing left to eat or to smoke. The man who had the arm without a hand started to take back what he had piled up in front of me on the counter.

"I know what I'll do. I'm used to sleeping rough. I have no need of a mattress."

The historian's eyes can't read any more. Is he too sad? Is he too excited? This young Dubois could be the man whose name he found in the old notebook in Colorado. Nervously, Robert Martin goes on reading.

What an adventure! Young Dubois, who didn't go to school very long because his "father alone could not earn enough to feed a family of fifteen," finds himself at the age of sixteen on the seas of Moby Dick. (The historian regrets having never tried to read that novel.)

For two years, young Dubois sailed the seas on a whaling ship that hunted down the leviathans. He had never "climbed any higher than the roof of my father's barn to replace the shingles blown off by the wind." He learned how to scale the main mast where "when the wind is up it seems as if the deck is rolling beneath your feet, then swaying above your head." He tells how he melted whale blubber in huge cauldrons chained to the deck, how he rolled and stacked the barrels of oil in the hold. At first his hands, though work-hardened, would bleed on the cables that hauled in the whales.

Two years later, young Dubois disembarked from his sailing ship. He knew that a single whale can yield eighty barrels of oil and two hundred and forty pounds of whalebone, for use in corsets and for making umbrella spokes. He had also learned not to tremble when Captain Thomas brandished at him the arm that had lost its hand when the rocket on his harpoon exploded. He had also hardened his heart so he no longer missed his father's house when the ship sailed under what the sailors called the watery northern skies because the sea was reflected in them.

By the light of a candle made from whale oil using the method invented by a Jew named Rivera, Joseph Dubois practised reading in the Bible the captain had lent him. To improve his writing, he copied out passages again and again, assigning himself dictations. Finally he understood that everywhere he'd gone, the sea moved as if humans didn't exist. It moved as it did before the reign of man and as it will continue to move when that has ended.

Wearing boots burned by the salt, dressed in rags, his pants and shirt faded and torn, he turned up at the town newspaper to apply for work. He told his story to the editor, who took him to a tailor. In front of a mirror, young Dubois held himself erect. From his eyes came a cold light, a powerful self-confidence. He had seen all those storms go by. The editor told him:

"You have to stay at the paper long enough to reimburse me for that suit. I know you're not made to take root behind a desk. If you stayed on your whaling ship for two years, it's probably because you can't swim."

"No, sir. I can't swim."

The phone rings. The copy of the death certificate he requested is now available. He need only turn up at the office in person.

Robert Martin is annoyed at the interruption.

"What death certificate?"

"The certificate attesting to the death of René Goupil, who died on October 6, 1975."

"There must be some mistake. I've never heard of that individual."

"Are you Robert Martin the historian? Didn't you ask for the death certificate of René Goupil, husband of Blanche Larivière?"

"Yes, of course."

Robert Martin knows he's preoccupied, impatient and tired. Where will Farmer Dubois take him now? This book is starting to resemble a recalcitrant whale. If he weren't a scholar accustomed to the discipline of objectivity, he'd be cursing those French-Canadian Catholics who named all their sons Joseph and whose big families begot even bigger ones. In the end, everybody was called Joseph Dubois. "It's pointless to force nature," Miss Camion said, "Farmer Dubois's season will arrive when his time comes." A team of assistants is supporting him. "Let them work." As for Robert Martin, shouldn't he relax a little? The death certificate of René Goupil will open the door to the secrets of an unknown poetess who once composed an ode to the rue Gît-le-coeur.

At the Bibliothèque Nationale he heads for his usual table. He likes that table by a window from which, if he looks up from his documents, he can watch the pigeons perched on the ledge. As if he were presenting his own heart in his hands for an operation, the assistant finally appears with a big sealed envelope. The historian's fingers start to untie the string.

"No, Monsieur Martin, not yet. You have to show me some identification. And I need a witness."

Now that all the formalities have been observed, he can open the envelope. He spreads the contents on the table. He checks to see if the number of pieces included corresponds to the inventory inscribed on the slip that's stuck to the main envelope: three chapbooks of poems, three clippings from the *Revue dominicaine* of Quebec City which comment on each of the chapbooks, a thick envelope that contains, according to the inscription, the "Diary, unpublished and incomplete, of a young French-Canadian woman in Paris, in the early days of the Second World War," another envelope from which he takes three short stories by Blanche Larivière: two were published in the *Revue populaire et moderne* in 1947 and 1953; the other appeared in 1963, in *Femmes-Québec*. Another envelope bears the careful title *A Bottle in the Sea*.

Robert Martin looks at the first story. Blanche Larivière presents a woman painter who is exploring the savage landscapes of Arizona in search of inspiration, "worn out from having rubbed too much against the rock of life." She meets a hundred-year-old Indian who tells her about ancient vanished cities and about the sun their inhabitants worshipped. After being invited to his humble village, the painter doesn't want to leave "the age-old wisdom of these modest cabins to go back to the deafening madness of our concrete jungles." These words appear in the last line of the story.

The hero of the second story is "a well-brought-up young man from Quebec City, where he feels as much an outsider as if he'd come from some distant land." One day he receives a mysterious package in the mail. It was sent from Arizona and contains a tiny leather pouch decorated with coloured beads and filled with some polished stones, a few small bones and bits of dried twigs. The young man, who often questions heaven, convinced that he's being observed from on high, knows these are sacred objects shamans use to cure disease and prevent misfortune. The young man will never know from whom he has received these precious objects. He will never know who has sent them. For the rest of his days, in the beautiful city of Quebec, "he will be convinced that he has come from somewhere else. Every night he observes the stars as if they were mysterious traces of his own unknown past."

The third story, too, is set in Arizona. What an intriguing obsession the Quebec City poetess had with that arid region! A beautiful Indian, writes Blanche Larivière, lived in a cabin surrounded by cactus. A cowboy passed through "like a gust of wind blowing over the desert sand." The beautiful Indian had a child. She looked after him, giving him all her love. The beautiful Indian grows old, but her wrinkled skin still shivers when she thinks about the handsome cowboy. He too has grown old and lives in a hamlet where "every gust of wind made it disappear into a sky of dust." When he was drunk—and he got drunk every day—the old cowboy would spy at the end of his ranch a beautiful Indian he had loved long ago, in his youth. The old drunken cowboy would rush headlong towards her, staggering, but as the last paragraph puts it, "life flies before you like a butterfly that refuses to let itself be caught."

Robert Martin takes a notebook from another envelope. The label on the cover bears the title, carefully inscribed: "Diary, unpublished and incomplete, of a young French-Canadian woman in Paris, in the early days of the Second World War." Robert Martin won't go through the diary today. He flips some pages, picks out a few lines at random. Here, the poetess talks about a black curtain she has sewn and hung at the window of her little room to block the light during curfew. She lives on rue Gît-le-coeur, "an adorable little street where nothing happens but the arrival of the morning sun, the afternoon shade and the darkness of night." The poetess mentions the cry of the alarm sirens ordering her to run, "gas mask in hand, towards the underground shelter as cold as the catacombs," where a lounge chair was placed for her by her concierge when he learned she was in mourning for her fiancé, Tony, "sacrificed to the unbearable tragedy." The Nazis tighten their stranglehold on Paris. Germans "disguised as women or Frenchmen" infiltrate and mingle with the crowd. While working for the cultural service of the Canadian delegation, Blanche Larivière did not neglect her appearance. She continued to go to the hairdresser so that "the sorrow of my lost love cannot be seen except in my soul." She even went to Bordeaux to buy herself some trinkets. The poetess reports that she'd been fined because her blackout curtain let out a thread of light. Later, she is befriended by some women in the underground bomb shelter; they "spread honey on my aching heart." On another page she notes that "members of the Gestapo have been captured who were carrying passports taken from the corpses of Belgian soldiers. In addition to losing their lives, those Belgians, hardly more than children, had to suffer another unbearable humiliation: their passports helped the enemy to accomplish a cowardly betrayal." Final page: June 16, 1940. One last entry.

German newspapers were thrown from a plane onto the Place de la Concorde. German troops parade down the Champs Élysées. The Nazis entered the city tonight. I am leaving.

A letter from the Quebec City publisher Garneau is attached to the manuscript:

We regret we are unable to publish your diary account of a painful period in recent history. Unfortunately, too few of our contemporaries are inter-

*ested in knowing our master, the past. For that reason it would be fool-
hardy for us to publish your diary. However, our house is always interested
in your very sensitive poetry. The author of* The Indian of the rue Gît-le-
coeur *will always be welcome here.*

There remains the envelope bearing the title *A Bottle in the Sea*.
It is sealed in three places, in the old way, with a wax seal
stamped with the letters BLG, for Blanche Larivière-Goupil no
doubt. Without breaking the seals, Robert Martin tears open the
envelope. A few sheets of paper fall onto the table. Elegant paper.
The handwriting is very careful. No hesitation. The calligraphy
is disciplined.

*O unknown passerby, fraternal reader, you are gazing now upon a secret
that will be unveiled as the day unfurls into the night. I hope you will
listen to my voice like an affectionate soul. As you enter into the heart
of the life of a dead poetess, you will understand that behind the face
of a woman who had to wear a perpetual smile, she was suffering such
pain that the face of her soul was constantly bathed in tears. Unknown
passerby, you have left the chaos of the street to explore the marvellous
countries that reach into these documents. To you I shall confess what
I have kept hidden. My silence has been a death I have inhabited during all these years. So many times the words of my confession have come
to my lips.*

 *I held them back. I buried my despair in a smile. Is it possible to drown
a sea of suffering in a breath of false joy? Sometimes the first syllables of
a confession would slip into what I was writing. I held them back. I was a
faithful and devoted wife. A woman can be a good wife and still carry in
her heart a sin that is bigger than the Earth. Was it a sin? Perhaps only
one sin is possible: to cause grief. A poet addresses not family, but posterity.
That is why, unknown passerby, you are the first to whom I confess my
responsibility for the unhappiness of three men. One of them has suffered*

nothing yet. His pain will begin at the moment you reveal to him what I am about to confess to you. The other has probably suffered more than I can know; his race is accustomed to pain and does not abandon it easily. As for my poor husband, he has not received the happiness he hoped for from me. His poor bones in his grave will feel a pang when you read the confession of my sin, which was as great as the most beautiful love story.

Someone touches the historian's shoulder respectfully.

"Excuse me. You're wanted on the phone. It's about someone who's been found."

He pushes aside the page he's been reading.

"So the woman cheated on her notary husband," he sums up. "Hello."

"I've dug up a Dubois in the Yukon," announces the research assistant. "But there's something odd. At the time there were only thirty-four Whites in the North West and Yukon Territories, but I've identified two named Joseph Dubois. One was a fur trader for the Alaska Commercial Company. The other one first appears in the early days of the Klondike gold rush. He was in love with a French singer named Emma Lamour. She'd come to seek her fortune in the new cabarets being hastily put up in Dawson City. Do you know how Joseph Dubois met her?"

"How should I know?"

"You're the boss. . . . From the photos, Emma Lamour was a pretty girl with just enough to properly fill a dress. One day she was standing on the shore of the Yukon River, dressed in the latest Paris fashion, her twenty suitcases all around her, her fancy shoes stuck in the mud. The men had no time to look after the women. They would run as fast as they could to get hold of a piece of land to prospect. Joseph Dubois, though, stopped when he noticed Emma Lamour. He introduced himself. He apologized for having a beard like a bear. He offered to pick her up and carry her to his own canoe. He also piled in some of her suitcases. He made some other adventurers take Emma Lamour's other suitcases in their canoes. He warned them: 'Be careful with the baggage, the little lady doesn't like wearing wet dresses.' Between cliffs forty metres high, Joseph Dubois, Emma Lamour and her suitcases travelled up the Yukon River to Dawson City. On the white water eddies of the Chilkoot Pass, where the canoe took the bit between its teeth like a bolting horse, they sensed that they loved one another . . ."

"I found Joseph Dubois in Colorado," Robert Martin reminds him. "How could he be in the Yukon too?"

"Nobody stayed in one place in those days. The new Americans were crazy about space."

"I need dates, precise dates," the historian orders. "I'd like to know why you young people detest dates. Why are you so suspicious of precision? Time's not as elastic as you seem to think."

He goes back to *A Bottle in the Sea*.

I was young then. When we're young we believe that we're eternal. We conduct ourselves like gods, as if there will never be an end. I was a goddess. A wounded goddess. The war took my fiancé, Tony, from me. I had come to France to work for the cultural services of the Canadian delegation in Paris. A young man at a reception pleased me because of his elegant manners and way of speaking. Listening to him, it seemed as if the dark clouds weighing down on the sky of Europe at that time were lightening, that the thunder of weapons at the borders was suddenly fading. Only one thing worried me. He was too handsome. I learned that he was the only son of a very famous novelist. While Tony didn't write, he had inherited his brilliant mama's way with words. We saw one another again. Very soon I became his "little savage from Canada." I depicted for Antoine de———, whom I called Tony, the unbridled power of Canadian snowstorms, the multi-coloured symphony of our forests in autumn when a small rainbow adorns every leaf, and the dizzying flights of snow geese that stitch the sky when they go north in the spring or south in the fall. One evening he confided to me: "I want to leave this old Europe; I want to live where I can be free as a bird." Listening to him, I thought again: "You're too handsome." The Nazis entered Paris. Tony went into his kitchen, he sent the maid home and he turned on the gas. In his own way he was a deserter. He was too handsome to go into battle. I cried so much. I'm crying again as I write these words. Without ever marrying my fiancé, I had become a war widow.

"Professor Martin, you're wanted on the phone."

It was Miss Camion.

"My little love, I know I'm disturbing you.... Excuse me. I just heard that you've discovered Farmer Dubois in the Yukon. You must go there and see what it was like. And you'll need some distractions! Let's go to the Yukon together! We'll go canoeing on the river!"

"I'm extremely busy. I'll call you later. We'll have plenty of trips to take, to take together ..."

23 Separated from my fiancé, Tony, who hadn't wanted to hear the iron heels of Nazi boots strike against the paving stones of Paris, I found myself plunged into the tragedy that was spreading blood and tears across Europe. I was a mere stranger alone in the storm. But what was the solitude of Blanche Larivière compared with that of Tony, lost in the black forest of death? I was wounded. The war had deprived me of my love. I was suffering.

I often went to pray in Notre Dame Cathedral. One day at noon I was kneeling in a ray of sunlight that fell through a stained-glass window. It seemed to me that this sacred light was murmuring in my ear. Tony and I had enjoyed moments of great happiness while pain and suffering were spreading across Europe like black and red snow. God had lent me Tony. He was an angel who had been delegated to Earth. He could not long remain on a planet whose inhabitants were condemning one another to death. That same day I left my office at the Canadian delegation and signed up with the Red Cross as a volunteer.

Could I be available the next day? "I'm available right now," I replied, determined to forget my sorrow. In the blue-flowered dress I'd bought during the weekend in Bordeaux with my dear friends from the delegation, the Roquebrunes, I clambered into a van.

And so, far from Paris, I travelled a road as painful as the Stations of the Cross. Some wretched little baby soldiers who hadn't finished growing looked me up and down, their eyes shining with the desire that consumes young men. Then their eyes went back to their plates. They seemed to have eaten nothing for days. Some, still clean, were heading for the combat zones, bearing on their shoulders, along with their weapons and kitbags, a tragic silence that weighed heavily despite their vulgar songs. Others were returning from the front, muddy, covered with blood, limping, limbs wrapped in dressings, faces covered with bandages, lying in trucks, carts, even wheelbarrows. Deep in their eyes there were still memories of hell. My love had flown away like a bird that would never come back to unfurl the joyous trills of his laughter. My grief was so slight compared with that of those poor little soldiers.

First I served the soup, I handed out the bread, I poured water. At times I had to feed as if they were babies the young men whose hands had been burned in the fire of war or whose arms were imprisoned in dressings. A number of them were still children. They made silly remarks, vulgar jokes. They laughed crudely. Like children, they made noises to lessen their fear. After working in the canteen, I became a nurses' aide. The hospital was sometimes in a tent, sometimes in a bar, a field or the *back of a truck. Just as the sea casts flotsam onto its shores, the war was sending back its wounded. I was despondent because I couldn't help all of them. One morning I collapsed, exhausted, between two pallets. When I came back to myself, a white-haired doctor told me: "We don't ask you to cry, we ask you to smile at them. They haven't seen a human face for so long." I forced myself to smile.*

When I slept I had horrible nightmares. So much blood was flowing before my eyes, as if the St. Lawrence River had turned crimson. From slashed stomachs avalanches of slimy entrails fell onto me. Broken limbs, the flesh pierced by splinters of bone, advanced towards me like a limping crowd. Faces torn off like masks bent over me to give me a kiss. By day, I smiled . . . No, I was not insensitive, but I smiled.

My wounded took the place of Tony in my heart. It seemed to me I'd met him a very long time ago, during a previous existence, when blood did not redden the rivers, when humans were still innocent.

For a long time I tried to remember every soldier I looked after. I will speak here only about the young man lying on some straw in a barn in Normandy. One of his arms had been torn to bits. His face was covered with a mask of dried blood. I took water and a cloth and started to clean off his forehead. It turned out to be not white and pale like those of the other soldiers. His eyelids were shaped differently. The others begged me to numb their pain. This one was silent. His eyes were impassive. I changed the bandage on his stump. He was in pain. Suffering. He told me that in his country, in Arizona, there was no war.

What a monstrous irony is war. One must travel the road of horrors to arrive at peace. Could we not take a shortcut and attain peace right away? And why had a young Indian been thrown into the midst of that horrible madness of the peoples of Europe?

Chance is a pseudonym God uses when he doesn't want to sign his name. My meeting with the young Indian was a sign. He belonged, I reasoned, to a race that the white man tried to eradicate from America. I, a White woman whose name actually means "white," belonged to the race of those who continued to convert, to assimilate and wipe out his people. Had God wanted to give me a chance to right some wrongs? A French-Canadian Catholic in English-speaking, Protestant North America, I too belonged to a people that others had attempted to drown. And now, centuries later, the Indian and I had both survived. We were in Europe. Our peoples were not extinct. Were both of us together to proclaim that those who refuse to die do not die?

He had two names, he told me, his soldier's name and his Indian name. I preferred his Indian name: Little Tornado Man. One morning, he wasn't there. I was told he'd been transferred to a clinic outside Paris.

I have always maintained that when humans meet it's for a reason. We are atoms of a single body. Our trajectories obey precise laws whose mystery science has not yet solved.

The Indian had not yet shared any confidence with me. Not one tear had run down his cheek. He had not exhaled a single moan. No contraction had creased his brown face. Why was I more obsessed by Little Tornado Man than by the other patients who had recounted their brief lives to me, in tears? I didn't understand. I was confused.

(I could not then guess the future: so many tears would furrow my face, which I'd have to keep serene even as my heart poured out so many sobs. You, the passerby, the friend, who are crossing the path that was followed by a young poetess who became an ageing woman, wasted by cancer, forgive me if "now as I write these words / My heart is close to breaking." Centuries before me, the poet François Villon also wept as he was composing his last will and testament.)

The war dragged on. Every day I could see its horrible grimace on the faces of the soldiers who were brought to the clinic. "Tony was right to leave this world," I thought at times, "he who was only joy."

After long seasons when nothing had flowered but turmoil, peace was restored. Paris was liberated. Beneath her, a volcano of elation awakened. The earth trembled, but it was because of the dancing. Paris was marrying peace. Paris was insisting on a glorious wedding! And I, a simple

Canadian nurse on the Champs Élysées, far from my own country, widow of my fiancé who had refused to take part in the war and by so doing had excluded himself from the celebration of peace, I was alone. I wanted to sing, to dance, but I was alone. I watched the parade. I applauded. I heard cheerful songs, but it seemed to me that the happy soldiers filing past us were heading for another war. I would no longer be there to care for their wounds. I would return to Canada. My family was worried about me. Now that peace was restored, they wouldn't have allowed me not to come home.

To my amazement, I caught sight of my Indian patient. He was marching, swinging his one arm. I recognized him as if he were my brother. I was holding flowers. Tearing through the crowd, I ran to give them to him. He continued his rhythmical march. He didn't recognize his nurse. I was seeing the young Indian again: wasn't that an astonishing sign? I pulled him away from the parade and I told him:

"Peace has come back to France; you see, you were right to go to war."

He was perplexed by this strange woman who'd grabbed hold of him. I told him that I knew he'd come from Arizona. At these words, he followed me. We made our way towards the Seine. We stopped in a café and drank red wine. With the third glass, he began to smile. Later, he couldn't stop laughing. I, Blanche, the White woman returned to the land of my ancestors, and he, the Indian stripped bare by them, we were as happy as two children who have not yet learned that hatred exists. When we arrived at the Seine we stood for some time gazing at the water flowing towards the sea that separated us from America.

In the streets, everywhere, Parisians were dancing. They needed to hold one another to assure themselves they weren't dreaming. On the Pont des Arts I said to Little Tornado Man:

"You won't need your rifle any more; throw it into the Seine! We have peace."

"We have peace!" he repeated, "so I'm throwing my rifle in the water . . ."

We walked some more. People were dancing to the music of accordions.

We had drunk more red wine. Overhead, the sky was pinned with stars that glittered over the peace on Earth. The open air beneath "The Wandering Moon" was no doubt too vast for us. I, Blanche, from the Grande Allée in the city of Quebec, educated by the Ursulines, I led to my little eighth-floor room the young Indian who was slightly drunk, as I was. I tore from my window the black velvet curtains that were hiding the stars in the Paris sky.

O unknown passerby, friend of poetry, you who are entering my life as I am about to leave it, I confess to you that every time I've thought about that beautiful evening when peace returned to Paris, I've cried as if I'd committed a great sin.

Soldier Longsong, whom I prefer to call Little Tornado Man, stayed with me for a few days. I know the definition of eternity: it is the moment when we forget that time is passing. Seeing those days again on the screen of my memory, I wonder if I didn't imagine them. Only my tears attest that they were real. For three days we did not leave one another. We wandered beneath the plane trees of Paris. We drank wine in those open-air cafés where we could dance what the French call guinguettes. At the window of my little room we worshipped the stars. Little Tornado Man didn't say much. I made him repeat the name of my street: rue Gît-le-coeur. He uttered it a thousand times a day; he forgot it a thousand times. He wanted to know where to find me when I went back to my country in the snow. I taught him how to say: "33 Grande Allée, Quebec, Canada." Those words too he repeated a thousand times a day. But he forgot them anyway.

I no longer thought about my books. I preferred his few words to all the poems in the world. Once, we were dancing under the Chinese lanterns with the people in the neighbourhood. All were pale from mal-nutrition. He said to me: "When I was little, I killed my father. Strangers came. They wanted to take my father's land. I tried to defend him. I fired my gun like a man. I was too small. It was dark. The strangers were beating my father. Yelling insults at him. I fired. I wanted to defend my father. It was dark. I fired. I often hear the sound in my ears. The strangers ran away." I protested: "Children like being frightened and they make up all sorts of nightmares. . . . The strangers killed your father. You were a brave little man. You couldn't chase the strangers away. You were too small. And you thought you killed your father. You're like our Jesus, who took upon his own shoulders the sins of mankind."

He said: "It happened a long time ago. We can't prevent what has already happened. And I stayed by myself in my desert." So then I cried. I wished Soldier Longsong could be small again, as small as the brave little man who had tried to defend his father. I'd have rocked him in my arms.

Then it was time to take him to the station. When the train pulled away, he stood at the window of his car and repeated: "33 Grande Allée, Quebec, Canada."

Two weeks later, I boarded a ship for Canada. The sea, both when it was angry and when it bowed low, docile, offered me an endless mirror in which were tangled the reverberations of the intense moments I had spent with Little Tornado Man. The waves streamed past like the hours, the days, the weeks. I felt fragile, floating across this profound life that was dark because of its unfathomable mysteries. The prodigal child was returning to the paternal home. I had loved. I had been loved. I had not lost my innocence, for I knew that in a powerful Universe I was still fragile.

Six days after our departure, the steamship slipped into the St. Lawrence River, leaving behind the gulf where the ice floes that come down from the Far North resembled ghost ships. There I realized that I'd never again be alone. I had given myself to the young Indian. He had given himself to me. My womb had been sown. I was as frightened as if I'd been thrown into the black water. Since that day, every day I have wept. I was carrying an imperceptible seed in my womb. And yet it was already bigger than I, more boundless than our past, more spacious than the future.

In our house on Grande Allée, the floors had no doubt been waxed, the curtains washed, the mattresses turned, the carpets beaten, the lace cloth spread on the table. I was coming home from Europe, back from the war, alive, I, the reckless girl. My mother would want to know what the ladies on the elegant streets were wearing. She would want to know if I'd placed my hand, in Notre Dame Cathedral, on the pillar near which the famous Catholic poet Paul Claudel had been converted. My father would want to know if I'd met people who weren't Catholics and if I'd seen any dead Nazis. Then, without listening to me, he would tell me what really happened in the war. My father was a well-informed man.

(O you, the stranger, the fraternal friend who is passing through the garden of my memories, I tell you again that as I write these lines, my tears are mingling with the ink.)

The shores of the river were closer together now. Quebec was opening her arms to me. The big family house was waiting for me with its proud turrets, its broad windows looking onto the park behind the house that runs all the way down to the river. I was returning to the Grande Allée, an avenue that dreamed of Europe. I was coming back with a child hidden in my slender body, the body of a nurse who had bandaged the horrors of the war.

My parents were models of the middle class. Pious Roman Catholics, fearing God and what others might say, they were good people. They hated sin. In the homogeneous society of Quebec City at that time, a city of flowered hats for the women and grey fedoras for the men, my parents looked down on the poor, though they supported all manner of charitable works. They feared the few Blacks who sometimes appeared in the Upper Town, though they subscribed to missionary works in Africa. Even though the Jews had condemned Jesus Christ to death, my father would have forgiven them had they not owned several businesses in Quebec City. His newspaper had never been willing to sell advertising space to Jewish merchants. He was more than a little proud of that. Could I tell my parents *that the father of my child was an Indian who had conquered me the way Europe had conquered America?*

I wasn't brave enough to jump over the guardrail into the abyss that was growing more and more peaceful as we came closer to port, but I wished the steamship would sink like the Titanic. *At the same time, I wanted to arrive at the wharf, to come back to Quebec. My child must be free, as free as the summer breeze on the flowers, free as the north wind of winter on the ice. Only I could give him that freedom. To become free, he must be born.*

In Paris, peace had extinguished the war. Dancing had been victorious over boots marching in rhythm. I had met there a young man in whom the ancient heart of America was beating, whereas in me, a French Canadian, the heart of ancestral Europe had never ceased to vibrate. In the past, the people of my ancestors had fought the people of his ancestors. On that festive evening, because of the music, the wine, the peace, because of our young blood and our ecstasy as we faced the future, because of the giddiness we had both experienced on the edge of the abyss of history, we were no longer enemies. The hidden forces that led humans to spread across the planet and to survive misery, curses, disasters, those sacred forces had urged us into one another's arms.

The city of Quebec, her pointed roofs, her stone houses and her chateau came gliding towards the ship that was bringing me home. I was carrying a child whose father had also gone back to his own people, the Indians of Arizona, to his poor house where cactus grew, "taller than a man" he'd told me. He did not know he'd left me with his child. My parents were waiting for me. I had to smile at them as if I hadn't been sown with my secret. Already my mute and microscopic child was drastically changing my own destiny.

With my make-up pencils I drew happiness on my face. The ship berthed. The crowd was fidgeting. I soon spotted my parents because they were placid. The sailors had made fast the ropes around the bollards. I felt as if I were the one being tied to the dock here in Quebec City.

I should have been blissfully happy. I was carrying inside me the seed that would cause a child to blossom in the garden of the world. (Tony, my deceased fiancé, had an eccentric belief: he was certain that because God gave birth to the world, God is a woman, not a bearded old man.) I had no right to be happy.

If they discovered my wonderful secret, my parents would be appalled. Neither my mother, my saintly mother, nor my poor father would be brave enough, in the basilica on Sunday, to make their way towards Jesus Christ dying on the cross like good Christians who have managed to stop sin from being spat into his blood-covered Holy Face. My dear father would never again be able to show up at his newspaper, knowing that his own, well-brought-up daughter had behaved no better than those poor girls in the far-off countryside who, he thought, like animals in stables and pigsties, dispensed with the blessing of the holy sacrament of marriage to beget their offspring. My father knew girls who'd been rejected by their families, big-bellied, thin-faced, eyes darkened by scalding tears, humiliated because they had been beaten as their father would never have dared to beat his unfortunate animals; they were looked after in convents by severe nuns while awaiting the moment when they would be delivered of the fruit of their sin. After depositing the illegal child at the orphanage, they were directed to middle-class families who were Christian enough to give them floors, clothes and dishes to scrub and scour. My parents always helped out these unfortunate girls without thinking twice. We'd had several working for us in the house. My mother forbade them to touch the children we then were. From middle-class families and even from certain clean families in the Lower Town, my father, along with other kind and generous men, collected baskets of groceries for these poor wretches, who, he said, "didn't know any better than the misery they would bequeath to their children." My mother often worried: "What will be the future for a child who even before his birth has been claimed by sin?" The sin I had committed would crush my mother. My father would be so ashamed he would never again dare to express an opinion in his newspaper. I was arriving from Paris after spending days celebrating the victory of life over death. Inside me I was carrying a spark from that celebration. My dear parents thought the way people thought at that time. In those days the city of Quebec was as closed as an old presbytery where the priest can't detect the smell of rancid butter. I was offering my parents a bouquet of shame, sorrow and disappointment.

I descended the gangplank. Quebec had been polished by the luminous winds come down from the Far North. I embraced my father. I embraced my mother. They stiffened when my lips touched their cheeks. I embraced Monsieur and Madame Goupil. I was surprised that they'd come to meet me. I held out my hand to René. His own hand was blazing. He pulled it away quickly. I was surprised to see that he wasn't wearing his seminarian's soutane. When my ship had raised anchor for the Old Country, René had just started studying at the seminary. His Excellency the Archbishop of Quebec was his uncle. René had heard the call of God who was asking him to follow in the footsteps of his uncle. Oh, my mother had told me that René had left the seminary, but I'd hardly paid attention to the news. While I was in Paris, the city of Quebec had seemed very far away. And at that time my heart belonged to Tony.

After all those years and all that travelling, there I was facing René. As an adolescent, he'd seemed to be the reincarnation of his uncle the Archbishop. Everyone thought that God had stamped on René's destiny a resemblance to that of his uncle. Love comes to young girls in springtime, as flowers come to gardens. My soul shuddered when I spied him bent over his missal, in the choir of His Excellency the Archbishop's basilica. I seemed to see heavenly angels flying about him. I loved René, knowing I had no right to love him. God had chosen him and he could love only God. But I, a humble earthly flower, I loved him. While already, in his meditations, René could make out the fragrance of the divine garden.

And now, just a few years later, here was René standing before me, all stiff and starchy in his grey English flannel suit. It was a sign. Hidden behind the stars, in the very depths of the sky, destiny transmits signs to humans. Only the poets know how to decipher those sacred symbols.

René's parents were my own parents' best friends. They practised Christian charity with the same good works. They believed in the same principles, they supported the same ideas, they read the same books, the same newspapers, the same magazines. They never argued. When one of them spoke it was to support the ideas of the other. Their certainty was never troubled by doubt. They were convinced that God thought the way they did. The Goupils had been notaries for generations. Now that he'd left the seminary, René would no doubt follow his father, who was also chairman of the board of my father's newspaper. His Excellency the Archbishop had imposed his brother on the board because the Archbishop's palace was the newspaper's principal shareholder.

"You must be so happy, little girl, to be back among your own people!" my mother began.

"She doesn't need to say it, Mother," my father assured her. "Can't you see it on her face?"

"I can't wait to hear her speak the beautiful language of France!" said Monsieur Goupil. "There's nothing more beautiful than the words that have been gathered from the shores of New France like agates, then polished on the banks of the Seine in Old France."

I addressed my first words to René.

"I missed our Canadian autumn so much. I long for the sight of a forest set ablaze by autumn."

The parents couldn't stop themselves from exchanging a smile of satisfied complicity. After all, hadn't they brought René Goupil here for me? As far as my parents were concerned, my flight to Europe was over. The time had come for their young daughter to become a woman who no longer dreamed about being independent in Paris. René was their bait. They saw me snap it up like the most unthinking char in the river. They were happy. Dear parents, you couldn't guess that I had lost my naiveté in Paris as well as my Quebec accent.

"The maple trees on the Île d'Orléans have started turning," announced René.

"Ah, how unreal the rue Gît-le-coeur seems now," I declared.

"We thought you didn't want to come home," said my mother.

"We had to win the war so we could bring you back to Canada," my father joked.

"Yes, my friend, we won it bravely," Monsieur Goupil went him one better.

I turned towards René.

"I never really got used to the greyness of Paris. The colours of my soul are the colours of autumn."

"You see," said my mother triumphantly, "you don't have to be in Paris to create poetry."

Arm in arm, like one big family, we left the port. I should have been happy.

My soul was weeping, without tears, without sobs, as I would often weep later on, even though my face presented a smile. I was coming back to the Grande Allée in Quebec and I was thinking about an Indian who was as handsome as the son of an Inca emperor, his eyes focused on the horizon in his desert because he was trying to find the shadow of the rue Gît-le-coeur or the profile of the city of Quebec. I was walking beside a childhood playmate. Was he happy that I'd come home? Can someone be happy who once thought he was an angel but has discovered he's a notary? I clung to his arm in the same way I'd have grabbed at a lifebuoy. Maybe I'd been saved.

The next day, René picked me up at the house. We were going to see September redden the maples on the Île d'Orléans. At first, my mother didn't want me to go off with a young man by myself. She decided to come along. In those days, parents knew what a sin was. For the salvation of their souls and ours, they wanted to prevent us from committing it. They knew how easy it is to sin.

"Adam and Eve were left alone in the garden of Eden. And you know what happened to them. . . . They lost their innocence. And the world had to have a redeemer."

My father never contradicted my mother.

"Daughter, you and René should invite both your mothers," he suggested. "You won't always have them. Share your happiness with them. When you lose your mother, it's for a long time . . ."

"Papa!" I protested.

"I'm sure your parents are right," suggested René, who wanted to please my father and mother. "My own parents think that way too."

"No!" I retorted. "In Europe I went through a war without my mother, I nursed the dying without my mother, and I think I can admire the wonderful autumn colours without her, too, even if I love her more than anything else in the world."

"That's the French revolutionary spirit in all its purity," declared my father. "That Jacobin manner is pleasing to descendants of the Normans like us!"

"All the same, children are safer when their parents are keeping an eye on them," said my mother.

"Mama!" I exclaimed. "When I was in Europe I was an adult. I haven't become a babe in arms just because I'm back home."

"Daughter," said my father reproachfully, "if you've learned to distill the spirit of Voltaire, I hope you haven't forgotten the respect you owe your mother. . . . Let's let our darling rebel daughter go now. She's home from Paris. Our friends and neighbours will understand her defiance."

Pulling aside the curtains, my mother watched me get into René's car. She was fretting as much as if I were going away for good. When we left the city, we drove onto the bridge to the Île d'Orléans and I could still feel my mother's worried look on my back. For a number of years I had enjoyed total freedom. Now I was no longer free. I knew I'd never be free again.

I had seen Switzerland, Austria. The trees there don't know how to turn red in the autumn like our Canadian maples. I had visited a number of museums. There is no painter who can make his canvas come alive with the countless rustling of the blazes that set fire to the leaves when a wind passes, laden with the cold perfumes of the snows to come. The trees were coloured even more brightly than my memory of them, ablaze with rubies and diamonds. I was surprised as a poet is surprised who knows that words are powerless in the face of so much intoxicating beauty. René was a little irritated, I think, by my wonderment. He listened to me. He said little. I said too much. The volubility of a Parisian and the silence of a respectful notary were two different ways to express the haunting fear each of us had of the other. In our youth we'd been like brother and sister. Had time made strangers of us?

Our parents' country houses appeared, with their maple-lined lanes in front and the St. Lawrence River behind, on which a boat was gliding. The houses were bright, their gardens lush as they were in my memories. September had killed most of the flowers.

"Our parents have aged so much in such a short time," I remarked.

"And so have we," said René.

When we got out of the car, as we'd done many a time during childhood we headed for the pine tree that stood at attention in the middle of the big stones that we'd used as thrones when we'd look out at the river and decide we were king and queen. How light-hearted and carefree we'd been then and were no longer! Dead leaves covered the path. Our footsteps stirred memories.

Instead of growing, it seemed to me that the pine tree had shrunk.

"I've come back here several times," said René, as if he were making a confession. "Even when I was wearing my seminarian's soutane."

He jumped onto the highest stone and pointed to the trunk of the pine tree.

"Do you remember . . . ?"

"You don't forget something like that," I assured him. When we were children René had carved a heart in the bark, with our initials inside it. Above it he'd written: FOREVER. I came closer. In the scarred bark, the word FOREVER had been erased. Was that a sign? The curves of the heart were nearly intact, our initials still legible.

"Do you remember?" he asked again.

We were adolescents. That day, the rain had caught us by surprise when we were out on our bikes. We'd got soaked. The rain was happiness streaming over us. Instead of going home, we'd made our way to our pine tree and taken shelter under its boughs. Our clothes were sticking to our bodies. I had leaned my back against the pine. René looked at me so oddly then that I felt a warm twinge in my belly. He went and stood on the other side. For a moment, we were silent. Then his hands slipped slowly down either side of the tree trunk and, for the first time, stroked my hair. Then both hands, as if they'd emerged from the trunk of the pine tree, touched my forehead, they glided slowly under my eyes, onto my cheeks, they settled delicately onto my lips and I kissed them, astonished; René's two hands slipped over my chin, they followed my neck, they alighted for a moment on my shoulders and gently, for the first time, brushed against my young breasts which were budding under my rain-soaked dress. That day, René took his pocket knife and carved the heart, then our initials and the word FOREVER.

"I remember that rain very well," I assured him. And as I'd done on that day of our adolescence, I leaned my back against the pine tree. René Goupil stared at me. He was no longer an adolescent keyed up by the attraction between boys and girls. He had become a poor man who does not understand life.

"Children write words like FOREVER," he said, "but it's life that dictates the laws and decides . . ." René felt awkward standing under this pine tree with a girl who had changed so much since that long-ago downpour. Was he, the former seminarian, intimidated to be standing so close to a young woman? Did he who had barely been outside the walls of the city of Quebec feel troubled by a woman who had crossed so many borders? My hands grabbed hold of his and I guided them towards my hair, my forehead, my eyes, my mouth, my neck. . . . As on the day when we'd inscribed our oath in the bark of the pine tree, his hands caressed my breasts. They didn't want to leave them.

After that we walked for a long time, in silence. The dead leaves whispered what we dared not say. Under the majestic pine we had revived our past. We were shaken by the shock of the past and the present which had come to be united in our bodies. What was René thinking about?

Somewhere in the perfume of the pine boughs, the soul of Tony stepped forward, in silence. In the same way, I was brushed by the desire of an Indian from Arizona, who walked through Paris as if he had inhabited that territory before the city was built.

So many times René and I had walked down this path to his parents' house. This time, it seemed to me that I was falling from a high cliff. Could it be that the weight of that small being in my womb was heavy enough to drag me along?

"We've been apart for so long," René whispered.

These were his first words since the pine tree. There were tears in his eyes.

"I thought about you so much. I was sure you'd never come back. The time was so long. . . . I didn't dare . . ."

To me, the time had seemed so short. Even the war, suddenly, seemed to me to have lasted only as long as a nightmare. Time passes in Paris as the wind turns the pages of a magazine. (René, I am weeping as I write these words: I confess I never thought about you when I was in Europe. Paris gave me all I could wish for; I had no need for nostalgia and, most of all, no memory of a backward altarboy who'd been hiding inside a soutane, safe in a seminary.)

Now I was responsible for a child. I had to think about its future. I had to avoid inflicting on my parents a terrible grief that could kill them. I would not go back to Europe.

René took the key from its usual place. A war had torn Europe apart but the key was still hidden on the horizontal decorative panel of the door. The air was damp. The house seemed to be floating on the river *like a boat that was taking us somewhere else. It was a familiar impression; many a time I had felt it in the past. Could it once have stirred my desire to sail for Europe? Everything was in its place, nothing had changed since my departure. I would never sail towards my beloved past. I was condemned to live here.*

René piled some logs in the fireplace. The heavy mist of September had seeped inside the cottage, leaving an odour of seaweed. I had often described the St. Lawrence to my friends in Europe: a river that is a sea. René suggested that I light the fire. I hoped he realized that this action contained a solemn symbol. He was so kind, so "notarial." Fatherly, he wanted to make me happy by giving me permission to play with fire! Oh, René, how could you have suspected you were about to save me? A young woman from the city of Quebec could not go to the Arizona desert to be reunited with an Indian she had loved in a little room on rue Gît-le-coeur in Paris because it was the end of the war, the end of the violence, because it was the beginning of peace, the first day of happiness. Oh, René, how could you have suspected you were going to spare my dear parents a painful blow? You were going to prevent the revealed secret of my Parisian sin from spattering my parents' reputation. You were going to protect me. Thanks to you, I would not have to hide my sin in one of those convents where girls impregnated by their uncle, their father or the parish priest came to seek refuge. René, you would save my child. You would save him from being herded in with those other children who would never be free under the sun because they were marked by the stain of their mothers' sin. At that time it wasn't good to be a child under the dictatorship of the cross my parents worshipped. You, René Goupil, were going to shield me from peril, yet I despised you because you weren't Tony, the son of the great French novelist who was drawn to the little Canadian girl as hummingbirds are drawn to a brightly coloured flower. I disdained you, the notary who kept his gaze lowered to the ground as if you were reading a will or a palimpsest, instead of holding your head high like the handsome Indian who was proud to have emerged from the war alive, proud of holding in his one arm the waist of a White woman from the land of the Whites. You, a pale notary, your footsteps seemed hobbled, still, by your seminarian's soutane. In the city of Quebec, within whose walls reigned a Church that despised our time on earth and was opposed to women having the vote, I had to make an effort not to hate you, the peaceful notary. Today I weep at the thought that, on that day, I did not love you. You deserved my love more than my memories did. They were that which I would never be again; you were that which I would become.

The fire warmed the room. We had taken off our raincoats. In the silence, the flames were crackling. The river streamed by like a long blue afternoon. With no boats, it was beautiful like a leafless tree. The other shore seemed to be moving slowly away from us. We did not speak. We dared not choose any words. Perhaps we had nothing to say to one another. Our souls no doubt exchanged a few silent phrases because suddenly, there we were, we had undressed before the flames. They were "dancing like devils," René said later. "Like angels," I corrected him. Our bodies were united on the black bearskin rug; our adult age was finally joining our adolescence. I am crying like a sinner as I write these words because it wasn't René I was thinking of as he lay on top of me, gasping. At that moment my eyes were filled with tears, but I had to smile at him.

After our fiery caresses, René was ill at ease. He hadn't learned, either in the Grand Séminaire or in the faculty of law, the words a naked woman likes to hear. Disconcerted, troubled, guilty of having loved like an animal, he avoided my eyes. He didn't know this woman who had changed so much since adolescence, when he'd stood with her, silent, under the pine tree, to listen to the voice of the mourning doves. Uncomfortable like Adam in paradise after he'd bitten into the forbidden fruit, René declared all at once:

"Blanche, I want to marry you!"

That evening, we were invited to dinner at the Goupils. Ordinarily, alcohol never touched our parents' lips. Priests who swigged a glass of wine at mass every morning had preached to them that alcohol was distilled by the devil himself over the fires of hell. At dessert, René's father produced a bottle. He couldn't have been prouder had he placed the Holy Grail next to the chocolate cake.

"Let's break open this champagne in honour of your daughter who has come back to us . . ."

"And who will never leave us again," my mother added.

"Let's drink in honour of our children who have been reunited as if they'd never been apart . . ."

"Papa," René broke in, "there's something I want to say . . ."

Our mothers exchanged a smug smile; their maternal intuition had already guessed.

"What is it you want to tell us, son?" asked his mother with syrupy curiosity.

At his newspaper, my father had learned to keep himself above the fray.

"Be patient, we'll soon see."

René's father proved to be not so cautious; he predicted pompously:

"I have a hunch it's news that won't be bad. So, let our cups runneth over!"

"My tablecloth! Be careful of my beautiful Belgian lace tablecloth!" pleaded his wife.

"Madame Larivière, Monsieur Larivière," René began, "I have the honour to ask you for your daught—"

"Though you've taken us by surprise," my father interjected, "you're making us very happy . . ."

"Making us all very happy," his father pointed out.

"God has finally heard my prayers," sighed my mother.

"Our prayers," said his mother.

"God is just," said my mother.

"We've been good parents," declared my father.

"We've brought our daughter up well."

"Our son is a good boy."

Our mothers threw themselves into each other's arms. Both were rather corpulent and large-bosomed and their arms weren't long enough to embrace each other as hard as they'd have liked. They were crying for joy. Our fathers dared not embrace another man. They shook hands. Then they took a sip of champagne and congratulated each other again, forgetting they'd already shaken hands. My father stopped drinking, buttoned his jacket and, after hesitating briefly, decided a speech was in order.

"May our daughter and your son continue the French-Canadian tradition, may they preserve their French and Catholic heritage. May each generation enrich their inheritance! In that way, and only in that way, will the future of our French-Canadian people be guaranteed on this English and Protestant continent. I hope you won't refuse to fulfill the daily duty that God assigns to the couples He has united."

He had to fall silent. He was overcome by a sob.

"My dear daughter!" exclaimed René's mother.

"My dear son!" declared mine.

"Let's drink another glass!" proposed my father.

Placing his hand over his glass, René's father refused.

"We must start discussing plans right away," he advised. "An election's easier to plan than a wedding. We don't have much time: just a few months to plan a beautiful wedding. Perhaps His Excellency our Archbishop will agree to consecrate the union of our children . . ."

"Is there anything more beautiful than a June wedding?" asked my mother.

I interrupted.

"You're quite right, in June it seems the earth is madly in love with summer, but we want to be married in October."

"October?"

"But it's already late September," René's mother pointed out.

"October! That's impossible. You won't even have enough time to pick out a dress."

"And His Excellency our Archbishop will be in Rome for a private audience with our Holy Father the Pope."

"A wedding takes time . . ."

"And the reception . . ."

"October . . ."

"And why in October?"

"I wouldn't know what to wear to an October wedding. . . ."

"June is such a lovely month."

Our parents, who had been so happy, were suddenly furious.

"René, my love," I said, "explain to our dear parents why we insist on being married in October. . . ."

He turned pale. I thought he was going to faint, or run away. He stared at me with a certain terror. Was he going to break the promise he'd made to me as we lay on the bearskin before the fire?

"Why September?" he stammered. "No, I mean, why in October? Because we love each other. Dear parents, Blanche and I have waited so long for each other. Even at the Grande Séminaire, when I was reading my Bible before the crucifix, I couldn't stop dreaming about her."

"There was Paris, the war, all those years. . . . Now we've found one another as we were in our youth."

"We want children."

"We'll marry in October and you'll be grandparents by summer!" I declared.

My father was worried.

"What will our friends think about such a hasty wedding?"

"Will they think our daughter's getting married because she has to?" asked my mother.

René's mother reassured her.

"Our friends know that Blanche came home only yesterday. No one will imagine that our good children have had time to commit the sin that would force them into a hasty wedding."

"May love triumph!" proclaimed my father.

He raised his glass. The champagne was gone and his glass was empty. He brought it to his lips. My poor papa wanted so much to celebrate! He'd waited so long for this event! Even though he wasn't drinking, he choked. We had to lay him down on the carpet. We were afraid his heart would give out.

I could walk along the Grande Allée with my head high. I had found a father for my child. I would be the wife of a notary with a good reputation. I would be a woman who had everything she could wish for. I would have beautiful clothes, a maid. I would have leisure-time activities. I would be free to cultivate my poetry. At that time, a woman didn't ask to be happy; it was enough to appear to be.

The wedding took place in October. It was blessed by His Excellency the Archbishop, our uncle, who had postponed his trip to Rome. During the ceremony I did my best to be radiant. I would have liked to smile. I wept like an April sky! As we were leaving the church an untimely snowfall greeted us, like an avalanche of white flowers. His Excellency the Archbishop was to leave the following day. He would take my wedding ring with him. He would ask His Holiness the Pope for a special blessing.

My son, Jean-René, came into the world in mid-May. When my father first saw him he exclaimed:

"This will be a strong lad! Look at him! He wants to nurse again! Look at him! His eyes, his nose, his skin: like a little Indian! Ah! This one's a Larivière all right!"

My husband was bent over the cradle reciting the multiplication table: two times one is two, two times two is four, two times three . . .

"René, you're going to make your son cry," his mother reproached him.

"The earlier we begin his education, Mama, the more quickly he'll develop," he argued.

"It's true he wants to nurse again!" said my father-in-law, amazed. "Mark my words, this little French Canadian is going to make his way in life!"

"Our son will be named René, like his father: we're calling him Jean-René!" I announced.

I wanted to cry. My son would never be held in the muscular arm where his mother had nestled so snugly. I noticed that René's breath reeked of alcohol. Proud of becoming a father, no doubt he was celebrating the event the way men do. Or so I thought on that remarkable day. The smell of alcohol would never leave his mouth. He never stopped being quietly drunk.

⤫

I've gone back to writing A Bottle in the Sea after a long interruption. Over a number of days, an unbearable headache has kept me in agony, wiping out my thoughts and memories. The white page in front of me seemed to recede, pushed by a raging wind. If I stood up, the floor was lifted by furious waves. The doctor recommended rest. René drove me to our house on the Île d'Orléans. I had him carry me under the big pine tree, that hundred-year-old sage. For one whole week I gazed out at the river where so many images from my past were reflected. And the pain left me, like something one forgets.

On my way back to the house on the Grande Allée, I reread this message. I was a young woman who was hard as bone. I was a little wild animal. I captured René like a prey. At that time society banished young girls who were guilty of the sin of love and punished their children. I wanted my child to have a free and full existence. I was afraid of suffering. Instead of suffering, I chose never again to be happy. Have I been unhappy? When one agrees not to seek happiness, one is never happy and never unhappy.

My son was as beautiful as childhood, as beautiful as adolescence. I love him as I love my memories of childhood. René Goupil loved me. I tried to love him. He was a devoted father to my child. My son loves him as the gentlest of fathers.

My fiancé Tony, who fled into death so as not to die in the war, often came to inhabit my dreams. My handsome Indian from Arizona, who fought in the war, crossed my mind every time I lingered over the little Indian he had entrusted to my womb. Jean-René grew up thinking he was a little White boy like all his friends, who called him the Indian.

Some letters came to me from Arizona. I dared not open the envelopes. Some I burned. Is it possible to burn the past? I received others. I kept them for a few days to look at them, feel their weight in my hands, touch them, smell them. I wasn't tempted to open them. And I sent them back to Arizona, marked "Unknown."

I must act quickly. The doctor has warned me: "This time, if the pain comes back, it won't leave you." Last night the pain reappeared; I recognized it. I'm hurrying now to finish my confession, which I'll cast out like a bottle into the sea. It is the sea that will decide whether to take my confession to my son or drown it in oblivion. I've never found the courage to reveal the whole truth to him. Was it madness or wisdom not to divulge my secret?

My dear Jean-René will have neither the curiosity nor the patience to skim these pages, which I shall entrust to the archives of the National Library. He couldn't bear the fact that I wrote poems. Some day an unknown reader prospecting the past in search of a vein of poetry will look into my modest verbal flourishes. May he listen with respect to this voice of a soul that has died along with the suffering that was her little night music.

24 The magic of history transforms words on paper into human experience. All afternoon Blanche Larivière revealed her secret to Robert Martin. The words she wrote have resurrected her; she will never die again. Her tears will no longer

flow in silence. The historian will give voice to her unfinished symphony. Blanche Larivière will no longer be an unknown woman. Robert Martin has opened the door of the jail to which indifference had consigned her. He asks for a photocopy of every piece of paper in her file.

"Have you found out something about your Farmer Dubois, Professor Martin?" asks the assistant.

"Life is full of discoveries," is the historian's only reply.

The autobiography of Blanche Larivière was broken off in 1963, as indicated by the date at the end of the document. She had banned access to it until the death of her husband, René Goupil, which occurred in 1975. Until today, nearly twenty years later Robert Martin calculates, no one showed any curiosity about the poetess. In Quebec, the oblivion in which poets are buried after their death is identical to the indifference shown them when they're alive, he notes.

Blanche Larivière's next confidant must be her son, Jean-René. And he'll find him!

"As you requested, Professor Martin, we didn't disturb you," says the assistant. "You have three phone messages."

Two messages, one of them described as urgent, are from Miss Camion. The third is from his office: a research assistant. He hurries to dial the number.

"Robert, in the Borrego Valley in California, I've found a monument erected to the memory of Peleg Smith," he announces enthusiastically.

"The man you're looking for is Dubois! I'm not interested in any Smith," says the historian impatiently.

"Peleg Smith discovered extremely rich gold deposits in the Borrego Valley."

"The man I need is Dubois," Martin cuts in, "not Smith!"

"Let me explain. I came across a photo of a group of prospectors who'd put up a monument to Peleg Smith. They wanted him to be remembered in the future. They didn't want Peleg Smith to be forgotten along with his bones in the desert dust."

"I want to hear about Dubois!"

"In the photo, I'm telling you, they look like what they were: genuine bandits. They're sitting on their mules with their packs, their bowls, their frying pans, their picks, their strainers and their sweat-stained hats. The men's names are printed in ink on the back of the photo: Clark, Beatty, Hilton, and Duboi. Duboi without an s. Three of the prospectors are staring at the camera as if it were a revolver pointed at them. The fourth one, Duboi (without an s), is looking away, probably towards his next destination."

"You think your discovery is getting us anywhere?"

"It's a trail . . ."

"A trail. . . . Always trails. . . . Never a Dubois!"

Now, Miss Camion.

"Oh, it's you, my little love. . . . Yes, I only called you twice. . . . But I thought about you at least two hundred times. Have you had a good day?"

"I've discovered an important document."

"You've found Dubois!"

"No, Blanche Larivière."

"Was she Dubois's wife?"

"No. There's no connection between them."

"You were looking for Dubois and you've found Blanche Larivière!"

"No, that's not it!" he says impatiently. "I was looking for Blanche and I found Blanche."

"Then was she Dubois's daughter?"

"No! You don't understand a thing."

"That's what my late husband used to say."

"I've got enough problems with my own ex-wife; I don't want your husband on top of everything else."

"I didn't understand a thing about his trucks. He did, but he's dead. And today I bought truck number two hundred and one."

"I'm sorry. Men say 'You don't understand a thing' when they're impatient. It's a reflex. I'm a little shaken up by what I've just found."

"So you're making progress on Dubois . . . ?"

"I'll tell you all about it."

"With all your knowledge, my little love, it must be annoying to be loved by someone like me who can't understand how you found Blanche Larivière when you were looking for Dubois. All I know is how to keep trucks running. . . . Tonight's your dinner with your old university classmates. Go without me. They're too learned. But I bet not one of them can drive a truck. . . . I have to tell you that my people in the special projects division are getting anxious. They're waiting for your first draft. They need something down on paper."

"Writing history isn't like buttering a slice of bread. Farmer Dubois is the invisible America, the genuine America. Not the America of cannon shots and great fortunes. Dubois is the history of the men and women who left traces that a breeze or a shower can erase from the dust. So don't be surprised if I'm feeling my way. . . . Tell your merchants they have to let the researcher seek and find."

"My little love, I adore it when you talk like that. Do you know what we were doing at the office today? We ordered three hundred dozen tires. . . . I was so proud: I negotiated very well. As a reward, I bought myself a gorgeous negligee you're going to love!

Have fun with your old classmates. As for me, I'm going to forget my trucks and tires. My little love, if I try to read *Moby Dick* will I understand anything at all? I want to christen one of my trucks Moby Dick. Is that a good idea?"

"It's a very novel one. . . . I have to go now. Big kiss. See you later."

Robert Martin bristles if anyone pushes him. For some months now he's been spinning like a kite that's being carried along by huge gusts of wind. He has been abandoned by his wife, flagellated by lawyers, humiliated by his colleagues (didn't one of them write that Robert Martin is the "living dead of history"?), he's lost his house, his car, his children, his finest books, his chalet and his boat. He fled to the United States where he threw himself into the bewildering pursuit of Farmer Dubois. Perhaps this story is no more important than the wattles on a rooster; and yet, he'd decided that, from that point on, it was his reason to go on living, his reason not to die. And then, Miss Camion came charging at him with a truck full of affection. He has been carried away by this sugary cyclone in her frilly flowered dress. His few notes on an unknown farmer have become a company project swarming with lawyers, accountants, agents, salesmen. The historian used to be known by only a few dozen peers; now he's as popular as the singer of this week's hit song. Already his book is being sold, though it hasn't yet been written, about a man who does not yet exist. A runaway into the past, Robert Martin has been snatched up by the present.

His classmates have flabby paunches, bald heads, rolls of flesh under their chins. They shake hands. They slap each other's backs. They laugh at the deposits left on their bodies by the river of time. They repeat old jokes. Robert Martin arrives late. Someone hands him a glass. The political arguments have already started. "They've had time for a drink," judges the historian.

"It's a historical constant: minorities are always accused of the worst faults," declares the actor who lives off the dubbing of American movies into the local patois. "Quebeckers are a people. They want to separate from the federal state so they can administer their affairs like a normal people. We're accused of being racists. Quebeckers are the least racist people in the world. The racists are quite simply those who refuse us the right to be a people."

"I have a Haitian sister-in-law," confides the gossip columnist for *La Presse*. "Her children are brown; they look like delicious little chocolates. I entertain them in my house at Christmas just like my other nephews. Does that make me a racist?"

"I don't see any difference between Yellows, Blacks and Jews. Quebeckers, though, are a fragile people, a minority, a francophone island in an anglophone sea. Any animal, any plant is equipped with a system to protect it. . . . So tell me why we shouldn't have the right to defend ourselves, too."

"As a people, we are fragile," reiterates the actor. "We must allow as few intruders as possible into our race. Those people are different. They don't assimilate. They make huge numbers of children. Will they be strangers among us? Having the courage to state that truth doesn't mean you're a racist, it means you're a realist."

"If there's one thing we can be blamed for, it's for being too broad-minded," alleges the man who has become famous as the workers' lawyer. "We mustn't be blind to the facts. We in Quebec are white, we speak French because we're descended from French people, and traditionally, we're steeped in the Catholic religion. You could call that national homogeneity. If disparate and discordant elements worm their way in, if they infiltrate and multiply, we as a people will lose our homogeneity. We'll no longer be what we are. And we want to remain what we are."

"That's exactly what I preach," says the actor. "Quebeckers have to protect themselves."

"Who is it that's threatening us so seriously?"

Robert Martin has asked his question with a slightly incredulous smile.

He's turned on by his dreams of Dubois and of the other French Canadians he's been accompanying for months now along the new paths in the virgin territory of America.

"Who's threatening us? All those who think we don't need to protect ourselves," retorts the actor.

"There was a time when French Canadians were more adventurous," the historian reminds them. "Between 1850 and 1871, more than six hundred thousand French Canadians set out to conquer America. Beaugrand, Faucher and so many others landed in Mexico at the age of twenty. I've tracked down a blacksmith from Saint-Jean-d'Iberville named Derome in Peru. Our ancestors used a nice expression: '*Courir l'Amérique*.'"

"And all those French Canadians were drowned in the anglophone sea," notes the gossip columnist. "It's impossible to fish one out alive."

"That's what will happen if we as a people don't protect ourselves."

"In the United States," says Robert Martin, "the inhabitants have forgotten the countries they've come from and become citizens of freedom."

"One day, the great-grandchildren of those who have forgotten where they've come from will want to remember," predicts the lawyer. "Widespread amnesia has been this country's strength; it will be the cause of its destruction."

"Already the Indians are recovering the memory of their past," notes the actor.

"And the Blacks . . ."

"And the Latinos . . ."

"All those people will recover their memories . . ."

The discussion is heating up. Robert Martin withdraws. He's incapable of feeling such certainty and conviction. He tells himself that, as usual, his friends have taken up this political discussion because they don't want to talk about themselves: about their dissatisfaction, their family problems, their health worries, their concern about their children's future. Perhaps they really are uncomfortable here in Canada.

"Robert, tell us about this Dubois of yours. You're not just a history prof now; you've become a businessman."

The phone rings. It's for him. Fortunately. What a relief. It's his lawyer. People notice that he's grimacing. Bad news? He listens. He looks unhappy. They try to guess what it's about. His face is like that of Christ on the cross. He says two words, then listens some more. Little by little his friends move towards the bartender who's bustling about, as serious as a university president.

Robert Martin's wife, the too-pretty hairdresser, is asking him to come back. She is prepared to resume life with him. She apologizes. She loves him more than ever. The children can't live without their father. The son has got involved with a gang that robs old ladies. It's his way of protesting the situation.

He hangs up. Then picks up the receiver again. He has to talk to Miss Camion.

"It's you, my little love. Do you miss me already? I'm sorry I won't be in when you come home. . . . I love you so much. . . . You know, you really have to get back to your manuscript. Your Dubois story is the basis of our promotional campaign: 'If Farmer Dubois were alive today, he'd ask us to arrange his move to Colorado. . . .'" Not bad, eh? Someone in the special projects division had the idea we could hire one of his descendants for a TV commercial: 'Our trucks travel all over North America, just like my ancestor, Farmer Dubois.' Not bad, eh?"

His companion's ideas roll over him, as heavy as her powerful trucks.

"I'm sorry, my little love. I won't be home when you come in. Have fun. You work so hard. I have to go to Quebec City. There's a meeting at the Transport Ministry tomorrow. I'm going with the accountant."

"There's something I have to tell you. My wife wants me back."

"Women often change their minds."

"She wants to try again."

"My little love, you mustn't lose any sleep. Don't drink coffee. Make yourself some mulled wine with cloves instead."

Robert Martin will not stay late with his classmates. He's decided to clear out.

25 Clinging to the blazing gravel, lovely white silk flowers glitter among their blue leaves. The brilliance of the day is unbearable, but Charlie Longsong keeps his eyes open. At his age, one closes one's eyes as little as possible. Stepping confidently, he strides up the road to the mesa. He's going to recount the things he hasn't forgotten so the young generations can remember. If he had a son, he would tell him everything he knows . . . He hasn't drunk any bourbon today even though his amputated arm is causing him pain. The war doesn't loosen its angry jaws. Alcohol tangles stories. He doesn't want to pass on tangled stories, with the tail where the head ought to be. Future generations would wonder who the old fool was who made up such senseless stories.

He's an old man and his gait should be exhausted, hesitant, stumbling, but today, in the early-morning clouds, on the sand, on the cactuses, in the bowl of water he drank, he feels new events drawing near. In his old man's body his blood is feverish. Could it be his death that is being foretold?

Ascending the steep slope, Charlie Longsong repeats to himself the drama he is going to relate, a very old story. It was a mesa now vanished because it had known too many woes. It was a mesa that overlooked the desert. So near to the sky, its inhabitants were proud. They were not people who looked towards the ground. Their gaze was always fastened on the future in the sky. This people had never attacked another people. Again and again, enemies had tried to storm the mesa, but never had an enemy been able to set foot on its rock. Never had an enemy arrow struck the mesa. The children grew up without nightmares or fear. Instead of waging war, the men cultivated the fields and hunted. The water reservoirs overflowed. So close to the clouds, it rained abundantly and often. It thundered hard as well, but the thunder gods had never shot their fiery arrows at this peaceful people.

Their ancestors had carved into the cliff the steps of a stairway people used to go down to the fields, then climbed up again with baskets laden with corn or game. The stairway had existed since the oldest generations, and the footsteps of those who had ascended and descended it had worn away the rock.

One day the gods, angry, declared war. They shot fiery arrows. Clouds crashed together. The wind scraped the earth. The inhabitants of the mesa, along with the children and the dogs, huddled together and flattened themselves on the floors of their *hogans*. The wind snatched off the roofs and blew them away like wisps of straw. It sent stones rolling. In a move mad with rage one of the gods brought his tomahawk down on the cliff in which the stairway had been cut. It created a big ball of fire and the stairway caved in amid a shower of pebbles.

Next morning, the sky was peaceful again. As usual, the farmers and hunters wanted to go down into the desert. They discovered the stairway had been destroyed.

The youngest, the bravest, the least sensible thought they could do without the stairway. Some clung to the cliff like spiders and started descending towards the fields far below. Others decided to mimic the mountain goats and sheep and they jumped from bump to ledge. While still others imitated the meandering contortions of the snake through shrubs, bulges, ridges, ledges. One after another all of them, like wingless birds, landed in the desert that was so deep no one saw them crash. Then the people of the mesa understood that it was impossible now to descend into the fields where the water and corn were. They would have to rebuild the stairway.

The most enterprising tackled the rock. The rock was hard. The sun poured onto the workers' backs like boiling water. They were thirsty. The men replaced one another to dig but they quickly realized that they'd never reach the fields. It had taken years and years and whole generations no doubt to carve the stairway into the cliff. They didn't give up. Their supplies were dwindling. Down below the sun was burning the corn. The water level was dropping in the reservoirs.

The day came when the people were hungry and thirsty. All they had to eat were cats and dogs. Birds with long beaks and broad black wings wheeled above the mesa in the sky filled with blue light. The inhabitants were dying one after the other. This people had been abandoned by their ancestors and by their gods. What had they done wrong? No one ever knew, no one will ever know. The black hawks that devoured the remains that had dried in the sun carried all their secrets away with them.

This story was one that Little Tornado Man had received from his father, who had given it to him when he was still alive. Now he will recount it to the children of today. Why was this people punished? It's not always possible to know. He slows down. Hearing the click of gravelly soil underfoot is a privilege only a madman would disdain.

The young people of the mesa should listen to another story, too, one from a very ancient time. The Indians then were free on their own territory. Before the *bohanas* came, no one moved any faster than a walk. You had to walk very far to find the feathers of a parrot. Charlie Longsong himself had gone very far, he'd even crossed the sea. . . . Where he'd gone he hadn't seen any parrots. With all the noises of the war, the birds had gone elsewhere to build their nests.

In the olden days the Indians were a proud people. The Indians walked like people who are showing heaven that they're masters of their land. When they celebrated holidays, their rich and colourful costumes were of a beauty now forgotten. To adorn and embellish their hair, they used rare feathers. Parrots from regions far to the south were clad in sumptuous feathers more precious even than turquoise. To gather these feathers, one had to travel for years. Rare were those who came home from hunting parrots. Often they were taken prisoner by enemy tribes. Or they died of thirst. Some who lost their way in forests as vast as the sea couldn't find the way home. Others were killed by thieves who took the precious feathers for themselves. Still others, too ashamed to come home empty-handed, chose instead to become slaves of a foreign tribe.

In those days the gods had not turned their gaze from the poor Indians who had lost their wars, their territories and even their memories. The Indians were proud. Since the gods were observing them, they had to dress in the finest costumes trimmed with beads, turquoise, gold and priceless feathers.

Sitting on the woven rug, Little Tornado Man had laughed a lot when his father told the story of a feather-hunter who, when he returned to the mesa, was greeted by a gust of wind.

That hunter had travelled through the Arizona desert, he'd scaled mountains, crossed valleys, travelled across other mountains; he'd swum in torrents, been tracked down and captured; he'd fled. Finally, he'd come to the jungle where it was said that parrots as beautiful as the setting sun nested in the giant trees. The huge leaves of these trees covered the earth like green water. Attacked by ants the size of cats, bitten by spiders with legs as thick as a man's arms, the hunter crouched on a branch and kept watch over his prey. More than once he was jostled by the passage of the long cold body of a snake that was hunting too. Not sleeping, not eating, the Indian lay in wait. Eventually his body took on the colours of the leaves and branches. Then the parrots dropped their caution and came and perched close to him.

The brave hunter caught several of the birds. He pulled out their finest feathers, then released them after apologizing:

"Parrot, forgive me. The gods have given you magnificent feathers and they've given me none. They've given you wings and they've given me none. You have received everything and I, nothing. It is just then for you to share your plumage with me."

The hunter wanted to give his chief the most sumptuous feathers he'd ever seen, for he dreamed of marrying the chief's daughter. Finally, his sack was full. He must go home as soon as possible. If he stayed away from his tribe for too long, the chief's daughter would forget his love.

Through jungle, swamps, mud, rivers, deserts, clouds of mosquitoes, plains and mountains, he returned to his home. Along the way, to defend his multicoloured treasure, he fought, he was wounded, several times he killed.

On his arrival at the mesa, the hunter hurried to the tent of the chief, who at that very moment was consulting some old wise men who were helping him interpret the signs in the sky.

"Great chief," interrupted the hunter, "I love your daughter and I want to take her as my wife. Here is the treasure I offer you in exchange."

He opened his sack. The mesa was high. The winds liked to come there and dance. Just as the dauntless hunter who had braved every danger was laying the bag of feathers at the feet of his chief, there rose a gust of wind. The feathers, the most priceless feathers that had ever been seen on the mesa, were carried away in an eddy that sucked them up to the sky. Seeing them fly away like snow in reverse, one of the old wise men consoled the hunter:

"Most likely there's a god who thought your feathers were so beautiful he wanted them for himself. It's no shame to clothe a god."

The chief was more down-to-earth.

"Why should I give my daughter to a madman who offers his feathers to the wind instead of to the father of the one he loves?" he mocked. "Why would I give my daughter to a man who can't even control feathers?"

The brave hunter turned his back and set off for the distant jungle again . . .

This story is very old. Charlie Longsong is glad he hasn't forgotten it. An old man possesses nothing except the stories he hasn't forgotten. Going up towards the mesa in the light that flares as if the night would never return, he knows he's become old. But he is still a man because he has memories. And thoughts. . . . Thoughts have no wings, they have no feet; they travel like the gods. Perhaps the gods are the thoughts of humans? . . . When we think about a person there is always a reason. Recently, he's been thinking a lot about Blanche Larivière. Should he tell the young people on the mesa about that strange swim they took together?

On the other side of the sea, in Paris, near the river whose name he has forgotten, between two big streets, there was a fountain that was like a pond, with statues. . . . Everywhere people were waving flags. They looked like the skirts of girls when they are dancing. Music was pouring into the streets. Songs from far away were rolling over the city like sweet thunder. The soldier who had lost an arm in the war, the Indian who'd come from Arizona, the man from the New World, did not feel lost in the Old World, for he was being guided by a young woman who, like him, had come from the New World. Soldier Longsong was dancing in front of a fountain with the nurse who had taken care of him. Many people were bathing there. Many were dancing. Some still had their rifles on their shoulders. Some were in uniform. Others were as naked as a newborn. Some were holding flowers. All was music and laughter. Finally, Blanche Larivière pushed him and he fell into the fountain. They both rolled in the water. He didn't like the water. The cold on his body reminded him of the morning when he was in the landing craft on the furious sea, blinded by black smoke from the explosions. The cliff they had to conquer was somewhere ahead of them . . .

Blanche and he were soaking wet as after a month of rain. The firm, warm curves of the nurse's body were straining the wet fabric of her dress. Should the old man tell this story? Young people don't know that what they are, this old man has already been. They don't know that they will become what he is now. If he were their age he'd be sceptical too. He has trouble believing this adventure had happened to the young man he once was.

In their battered cars, in their pickup trucks, on their motorbikes, young people today drive around in circles. Leaning against the walls of the *hogans*, they wait for the time to pass. They're sure it will bring them nothing. When they walk, their eyes are seeking something with no hope of ever finding it. When he was their age, Little Tornado Man crossed the ocean. At that age you have to leave for somewhere. Without ever going away, today's young people always seem to be coming back from somewhere else.

Should he reveal to them the secret that the old people in this tribe pass on to the young men when the time has come to do so?

There exists in a hidden place, known to one person only, a cave where, for thousands of years, a fire has been burning that is never extinguished. That fire has been burning since the day the Indians first arrived on this Earth that no human had yet marked with a footprint. Since the very first moment it was lit, the fire has always been alive. Like the Indians, it is never the same yet always the same. As for the *bohanas*, they haven't really despoiled the Indians because they've never been able to capture that eternal fire. As masters of the fire that does not die, the Indians are still masters of their territory. It is a fire that endures, a fire no storm has been able to extinguish. There are those who say that this fire is burning in an inaccessible cave. Others will say that the undying fire is hidden in the heart of the Indians.

And that's what Charlie Longsong will recount today.

26 Robert Martin's wife wants him to come and knock at her door. When she opens it he'll be glad to see her hesitate before his outstretched arms. Then she will push the children towards their father. He knows that his heart will be stirred. He will still think she's too pretty.

It is late in the morning. Miss Camion wants him on the phone again.

"My little love, I've been held up in Quebec City, I can't get home today . . ."

"You know, my wife really wants to get back together. I didn't sleep last night.... I thought..."

"Did you fix yourself some mulled wine with cloves, like I suggested?"

"Mostly I was thinking about Farmer Dubois. He's everywhere and nowhere. He's the invisible man. Dubois has no history. He's like America. He's a memory lapse.... I don't know if I still want to write that book..."

"You have to write it. You've got no choice. You have contracts."

"I want to go back to my children and my wife."

"Go back if you must, my little love..."

"But you and I are together, we've started something..."

"My little love, the only thing you're obliged to finish is the story of your Farmer Dubois."

"With you I've lost the appetite for indifference. I've learned to be passionate again."

"You still love your wife. Her tremendous hostility proves she didn't really want to leave you. And *I* know you were still with her, my little love. You say her name when you're sleeping with me."

"Please forgive me. I'm a historian. In our discipline we don't always distinguish the past from the present."

"Go back to your wife."

"I don't want to hurt you."

"I know what you've given me.... Go back to your wife.... My company will stand by your project."

"I don't know if I should go on with that book..."

"If you don't finish it, my little love, you'll hate me."

"I'm lost..."

"Do you think your Farmer Dubois ever got lost?"

"You're right. The history of America is the history of people who got lost and never found their way home."

"You should put that in your book, my little love."

"There's something different about your voice."

"It's probably the Quebec City air. . . . We'll see each other tomorrow. Tonight, I'm adding up numbers with my accountant. Tomorrow we'll celebrate your return to your wife. I promise I'll wear the most flowery dress you've ever seen."

"With a low neckline, too?"

"You and I are separating, but we're going to celebrate as if we were staying together! In a way, my little love, Farmer Dubois is our son."

"He hasn't been born yet . . ."

Buffeted by the squalls that are disturbing his solitude, Robert Martin ought to be thinking about his own fate. Instead, he's obsessed by the strange biography of Blanche Larivière, the manuscript he discovered on "the shores of oblivion," as she'd written in one of her poems.

The son of Blanche Larivière-Goupil isn't hard to track down. In the Quebec City phone book, under the name Goupil, Robert Martin reads: "Goupil and Son, Notaries." One minute later, Jean-René Goupil is reproaching him:

"Blanche Larivière is a forgotten poetess, which was what she wanted. My mother was a discreet woman. Why don't you let her rest in peace? She deserves that. Dust has accumulated on her little books. I advise you not to stir it up. When my mother was alive, people preferred other poets to her. Her womanly pride suffered from that. My mother was a heroine of the Second World War. Her poetry is unknown, while they've canonized another poetess who discovered she had bones beneath her skin. Holy Mary! Her sycophants heap praise on her as if she'd discovered America. . . . My mother had a good life; let her rest in peace now. . . . Are you Robert Martin the historian, the one who wrote that famous book about Farmer Dubois? I haven't read it yet, but my wife bought it and she's started it."

"Yes," he says simply, deciding not to correct the other man, "I'm the historian."

"My mother was a good mother, a quiet wife. Writing poems was one of her pastimes. Embroidery was the other. She was also involved in various charities, unwed mothers among others. Now please, let her rest in peace."

"Mr. Goupil, I've discovered a document I have to give you."

"I'll give you my fax number."

"Mr. Goupil, I have to deliver this document into your own hands."

Robert Martin hears the notary stop breathing. Now there is only silence. Then, like a slap:

"How much?"

"What?" asks Robert Martin, astonished.

"How much are you asking me for?"

Robert Martin is flabbergasted:

"Mr. Goupil, I'm not an extortionist!"

"You won't get a cent from me."

"This document is very unusual. It's rare for a historian to read a document with tears in his eyes."

"Professor Martin, come to my house on the Île d'Orléans. It's easy to find: a stone house, behind rows of maple trees. The house is historic. My father confessed that the first time he made love to my mother, it was in that house."

A solid, coarse laugh extends from the Île d'Orléans to Montreal.

The next day, Robert Martin discovers the slow tranquillity, the gentle beauty of the Île d'Orléans, which irritate the man accustomed to the speed and disorder of Montreal. Blanche Larivière had described her house in *A Bottle in the Sea*. Robert Martin feels as if he's been here before. He rings the bell, expecting the door to be opened by a pudgy, polite little notary. A big, strapping, broad-shouldered man of fifty fills the doorway. His handshake is powerful.

"Sorry about the left hand," says the notary. "My right arm's been on strike ever since an accident I had a few years ago. When you're a young man on a motorcycle along the roads of America, it's natural to go fast. That ecstasy cost me my right arm. Except for love, though, a man doesn't really need two arms.... Isabelle," he calls out, "come along and bring us a bottle. So, have you brought me that document?"

This man's skin isn't pale like the papers in a notary's office. It's coppery. His hair is black, with no silver threads. His nose and eyes are like an Indian's, he thinks. In his fringed deerskin jacket and his cowboy boots, he doesn't look anything like a notary. Why had Robert Martin expected Blanche Larivière's son to resemble her husband?

"First, let me explain..."

"No, first I'm going to show you around, because as the house is, so is the man, if you'll allow me."

The notary half opens a door. The walls of the room are covered with rifles, shotguns, muskets.... These objects are from every period.... He can make out crossbows, blunderbusses, even a carefully polished halberd...

"I collect firearms. With my left arm, I'm a fairly good shot. Come."

In the living room, which stretches out before a sturdy fireplace, Robert Martin exclaims:

"You have a bearskin!"

"That's right, it's a ... a bearskin," says the notary, who doesn't understand the historian's surprise.

The words in Blanche Larivière's manuscript take on meaning in the present. Such magic stuns him.

"We've always had a bearskin in front of the fireplace. Making love on it is wonderful."

Above the hearth a young Indian reigns. Robert Martin can't look at the painting without feeling a subtle vertigo. All these obvious signs around the notary: has he ever tried to decipher them?

"I collect motorcycles, too. Let me show you."

In the painting, the young Indian's face is hard, like rock. He has accumulated too much wisdom for his age. His expression is sad, as if he could sense the future. His costume is trimmed with multicoloured beads. He has a feather headdress. A sun-shaped pendant hangs around his neck.

"Do you collect paintings?"

"What excites me is reality. Depictions of it leave me cold. I've seen a lot of sculptures, but not one could match the beauty of a simple pebble from the Île d'Orléans. As far back as I can remember, this painting has hung here. Towards the end, when my mother was very sick, she told me: 'Keep this with you. You'll love it more and more, you'll see. The handsome Indian will speak to you.' My mother was weird sometimes, with her poetry.... She was right, though. I don't know why, but I'm hooked by that painting . . ."

A very young woman brings a bottle of wine and some glasses and sets them down on the table in front of the fireplace.

"All French Canadians have a little Indian blood," she adds. "I think my husband has nothing but Indian blood. So it's hardly surprising this painting speaks to him."

"Let me introduce Isabelle. When I met her she was hitchhiking. She came from France. We were in Arizona."

"Arizona!" exclaims Robert Martin.

"I picked her up and never let her go."

"I was a little worried. He was a nice man, but I wanted to know who he was. He told me he was an old notary. I couldn't believe he was old—or a notary."

"Isabelle was spending her holidays in America when she met her Fate, in other words, me ..."

The notary bursts out laughing at the joke he played on Isabelle by changing her life.

"Because of western movies and the books from my childhood, I wanted to see Arizona. . . . I've always been interested in the American Indians," says Isabelle. "With their ancient secrets and their magical rites, perhaps they can help the white man save the planet."

Jean-René Goupil fills their glasses:

"Cheers!"

"Cheers!. . . Your mother wrote about Indians," Robert Martin recalls.

"Yes. I remember a poem about a white woman and an Indian man who met in Paris or something like that. That poem made me hate French literature! My grandfather was a newspaper editor; my father was the Archbishop's nephew. Our family was impor- tant. To show his respect for us, every year our literature teacher would pass one of my mother's poems around the class. And I'd get those poems thrown at me frontwards and backwards! I got a few kicks because of those goddamn poems of hers. But I must admit I delivered a few, too!"

27 Robert Martin goes back to his hotel in Quebec City. He's fond of the elderly Château Frontenac that overlooks the old city and the St. Lawrence. This building that imitates an ancient castle is appropriate for a historian. Without Miss Camion's spe- cial projects division, he couldn't afford to stay under its presti- gious roof. "Thanks, Miss Camion! Thank you, Farmer Dubois!" If

all the plans work out—best-seller lists, translations, a film, a speaking tour, the sale of Dubois dolls and puppets—Robert Martin will turn in his resignation to the dean and he'll be able to bring his wife to hotels even more luxurious than this. Love will be reborn in the soul of the too-pretty hairdresser.

An envelope is slipped under his door. A faxed message.... Does he really love Miss Camion? She's like a beautiful summer day with sunshine and flowers. He'd been so bruised when she came to him. Did Miss Camion love him? She'd taken him far away from his grief. The warm rush of her tenderness healed him. Now he'll go back to the too-pretty hairdresser.

"Latest find," reads the fax. Poorly printed, it's a letter sent on by his research assistant. The handwriting is clumsy but very careful. No doubt the writer had a worker's hands. The letter is dated 28 September 1881.

My dear mother and father, I am in a place called Santa Fe. There are a number of Indians and a post office. There is another establishment too which I will not talk about because of the respect I owe my good mother who raised me properly. I am in good health and my bag was fairly heavy when I left Colorado. The mines have been emptied. I have become a carpenter because every day one house and sometimes two are being built here. The other houses are made of earth, like those in Mexico. Trees are being planted too. When I've finished building the city, if my belongings are not stolen, I shall go back to Colorado. Dear mother, I am ready to marry and there will be no lack of either affection or savings. I want to become a farmer. I have decided to stop walking. There is no end to America. Now I shall tell you what has happened.

It will give you one more reason to pray for your son. I was in a part of Santa Fe called French Town. I was in a bar. That's a place, dear mother, where people drink. By day, people work, and at night they drink. They drink because they're thirsty. A stranger told me he was from Canada and that his name was Duval. He told me he'd lost everything. Bandits had attacked his train, taken the travellers' weapons and their bags and emptied their pockets. Duval and I should not have drunk so much. We decided to take our revenge. Since Duval had been robbed on a train, we decided to attack another train so he could be reimbursed. Pray for me, dear mother, even though we didn't steal anything. Duval and I were sitting in the coach like ordinary travellers. We were studying the people. We were scrutinizing the bags they were transporting with them and, in particular, how they were armed. A gang of bandits were faster than we were. They swept into our coach, firing at the ceiling. Duval did not want to be robbed a second time even if his pockets were empty, while I didn't want to be robbed for the first time. We both jumped out a window. The train was going over a bridge so we landed in the river. We don't know how to swim. We sank to the bottom. Fortunately, it's not very deep so we got out, as wet as fish. We told each other, Duval and I, that our mothers must have said prayers for our protection. Thank you, dear mother. After that, we walked for a long time. The snakes were not our friends. I tell you all this, dear mother, so you won't be too worried about your *Canadien errant* who is travelling in foreign lands. I want to head back to Colorado. My health is still good, old mother, and I'll be able to take care of a piece of land and a wife. I would like to grow flowers. The future is leaning towards flowers. Your affectionate son, Joe Wood. That's my name in this country.

Could this Joe Wood be Dubois? The technique of the historian requires Robert Martin to consider every possibility. His document-hunter's instinct assures him this letter is important. His heart stirs. Why does Wood (Dubois?) want to grow flowers?

"Find me more letters from Joe Wood!" he orders his research assistant on the phone.

He goes out. A walk in the springtime air of Quebec City is an intoxicating delight. Even with her old stones, Quebec never seems truly ancient. He is free. He doesn't have to work tonight. Miss Camion is in Ottawa with her accountant. The too-pretty hairdresser must be getting ready for the great return.

The concierge tells him he's received another message. It's another document his assistant has faxed. The writing is clumsy:

Dear parents of Joe Wood in Canada, I don't know if you're still alive on this earth or if the good Lord's come and carried you off, but I'm obliged to tell you that your late son Joe took a bullet in the heart. I myself was forced to deliver the bullet to that spot. I assure you I'm no killer, I'm an honest man most of the time. If I were a murderer I would ask for your prayers and I'd give you my apologies. We were friends, your son and I. We met at the mission in Santa Fe. Today, we played cards. He lost. He accused me of cheating. I'm a gambler and a drunk, but I'm no cheater. Specially when I gamble with a friend. He got mad on account of he was losing. He fired at me but he missed. I said: "I thought we were friends." He said: "You cheat." So then I fired too. I ask for your prayers, for him and for me. I'm not a killer.

I've become a farmer who loves peace. Your son was buried
without the sacraments, on a knoll. He's got a fine view from
up there but he won't be able to cultivate his land. That's
what he bet when we were gambling, and he lost it. Forgive
me, wherever you are, I can't remember the name of the village Joe Wood came from. I've got a French-Canadian name,
but you'll understand why I won't sign it at the bottom of
this letter. When the missionary comes, if he's a Catholic I'll
ask him to sprinkle holy water on the knoll where my good
friend Joe Wood lies buried.

There's no date on the letter. He'll have to search, again and again.
The past is as impossible to grasp as the future. Why be surprised
then that the present fluctuates so much?

After leaving the Château Frontenac, Robert Martin strolls in the
direction of the Grande Allée, his head throbbing. The north country and its forests, the south and its fields spread over the city a
country odour that mingles with the scent of seaweed from the
great river. On his Île d'Orléans in the middle of the St. Lawrence
some kilometres away, Jean-René Goupil is reading his mother's
confession. The man must be crying as he cried at his birth. Quebec City is so peaceful. The historian walks with delight.

Miss Camion is a great ray of sunlight. She's a woman who has
happiness in her bones. "Thank you, Miss Camion, the time we
spent together was a happy time!" Why is he so close to tears?

"No one has ever truly written history," he soliloquizes.
"They've written the lives of those who left documents behind,
but the most elementary history hasn't been written. No one can
write the history of the dust stirred up by the footsteps of people
pursuing their dreams. The true history of America is that of the

water droplets at the tip of the voyageurs' paddles, of the autumn leaves crumpled by passing hunters and loggers, of the needle stuck into a garment by a woman's patient hands." This theory, which he'll proclaim in the introduction to his book, will be cited at conferences. And his university colleagues, those slaves to intellectual conformity, can go to hell!

He slows down as he passes the opulent-looking houses on the Grande Allée. The notables who built them at the turn of the century were conservative, soft and nostalgic for Europe. "They were also pompous," Robert Martin deduces as he lingers over the turrets and the corbels. Has Blanche Larivière's house been debased by the notables of today, who have turned themselves into innkeepers? He'll ask Jean-René Goupil where number 33 stood.

On the Plains of Abraham, lovers walk hand in hand towards the river. "They'll lie beneath the stars," he thinks. Why isn't he their age? Robert Martin is lonely tonight. He feels old enough to be the father of history. In this spot on 13 September 1759, a brief battle was fought. France lost. England won. The French Canadians had to submit to the English. The bullet that pierced the chest of General Montcalm shattered the dream of a French America. Remembering that, the historian feels a painful twinge of sorrow. What would Canada be like if that battle had been won? No important book has been written about that night when the destiny of a people and a continent were changed. That's the project to which he ought to devote himself instead of trying to track down some Farmer Dubois who refuses to let himself be resurrected.

So many projects would be fascinating. The life of Blanche Larivière, for instance. . . . How could her husband have thought he was the father of that son whose features are those of a pure aboriginal American? How could he not be aware that his son didn't have the pale complexion of those who, generation after generation, examine marriage contracts and wills? Notary Goupil, the father, must have believed that, a century or two ago, his ancestor hadn't spurned an Indian woman.

As for his farmer who was nowhere to be found, the historian's assistants have questioned many Dubois families. None of them has any recollection of him. Along the paths and roads of America, always anxious to arrive somewhere else, did Dubois forget where he came from? Fascinated by the future, he'd got rid of the past. His dreams were more exciting than his memories: that was the great principle on which America was built. Farmer Dubois didn't worship the past; that's why he did nothing to ensure he would be remembered.

Last year, Robert Martin fled to the United States because his heart was broken. Could it be that Farmer Dubois fled to the United States to forget the pain caused him by a woman? Could it be that his expedition was nothing but a vast love story? He was thought to be hunting for gold. Will it turn out that he was looking for a woman?

The stars are bright above the Château Frontenac. Some of those stars have long been dead, but their light is still beautiful. Farmer Dubois is like one of those stars. He is long since dead, but the flame from the wick of his lantern still shines in the past. Robert Martin has borrowed that idea from a novel that was famous in his adolescence. Oh, how he wished he didn't have to write that book and could read, read till he was drunk with words! The past is contained in the present as the present is in the past. The historian will jot down that phrase when he gets back to the Château Frontenac. He mustn't forget it. He will place it as an epigraph to his book. This walk has not been useless.

He also jots in his notebook:

Hundreds of thousands of French Canadian emigrated to the United States. Some became adventurers, gold diggers, miners, hunters, fur traders, explorers; others became slaves in factories, in the service of the accelerated mechanization of the time. Those who were honest, submissive Catholics ended up in the factories. Scoundrels and non-believers became free hunters of gold—and often found it!

The idea is appealing. A few old geezers will choke when they read it . . .

28 "Goddamn poetry!"
Jean-René Goupil is devouring the manuscript given him by the historian. He turns the pages as avidly as a cowboy slurps his soup. Suddenly this man who has a professional respect for words and paper flings to the floor the pages on which his mother's dancing pen drew florid characters.

"Poetry drove my mother crazy! On top of everything else, she named me for a missionary who got himself tortured by the Redskins! What a moron he must have been! Goddamn poetry! . . . And my poor father put up with it! My poor father who wasn't my father . . ."

He knows everything. He does not wipe the tears from his eyes. His father wasn't his father. The man who loved his mother doesn't know he has a son. Jean-René Goupil doesn't know his father.

"She should have knit instead of writing those verses. No one goes crazy from knitting."

So his father is supposed to be some Indian from Arizona. Should he believe his mother? His poor father, the notary, believed her, and he never got to know the truth. Why should he believe her? Because she's dead. Why do some people have to die before they can tell the truth? Jean-René Goupil has crossed Arizona several times on his motorcycle. Was his father one of the old Indians who watched him drive by with his girlfriend sitting behind him, her hair like a flame down her back?

This manuscript has taught him that he's barely been born. Isn't a man's childhood the time when he follows his father, to learn what he knows and what he doesn't know? With her silence, his mother robbed him of that segment of his history. That which his false father taught him is no better than a lie. A man can learn the truth only from his father, whom he resembles.

"Goddamn poetry!"

Until she died, his mother was submissive to a man she didn't love. She imposed him on her son. And her son, who doesn't know his real father, is condemned to be as unhappy as his mother. Always he will be an orphan, just as she was nothing but a widow.

"She killed my father!"

From the bedroom where she is resting because she wanted to leave him alone, Isabelle hears this cry. Then the sound of boots pounding the hardwood floor. Doors are slammed. Jean-René Goupil goes outside. And then a shot rings out.

"Good God!"

The young woman feels as if she's about to faint. Has some great disaster just struck the Île d'Orléans? The shot echoes and rumbles like a heavy cart along a wooden bridge. Another shot! The young woman rushes out, revived now. The tragedy she expected hasn't happened! Another shot! Then another explosion. And another. And another. In the night the young woman can make out her husband, who is firing at the stars.

"Goddamn poetry!"

His ammunition spent, Jean-René Goupil lets himself fall into the grass to cry. His young wife, his very last wife, Isabelle, goes up to console him with tender, motherly gestures. Her husband is as old as her own father. Fingers stroke forehead and temples. The hand settles onto the chest where a heart is trembling in all its pain. He is like a child who doesn't understand the mysteries of the world.

"Tell me why you're sad."

The wounded animal stiffens.

"I don't know who my father is. I don't even know who *I* am."

Shaken by his words, his sadness, she falters but she's also quick.

"Tell me how I can help you . . ."

"I know how a woman can hurt a man."

He stares at her as if he hated her. Then he gets up and rushes to his jeep, which lurches forward with a roar, throwing up pieces of gravel.

"Jean-René!" she calls.

He can't hear. Preoccupied by her man's dismay, wounded as much by his silence as by his words, she goes inside. The document he was reading is scattered across the bearskin in front of the fireplace. Page by page, she discovers the secrets of the mother of her man.

It's surprising, in the elegant lobby of the Château Frontenac, to hear somebody scream. The guests stop whispering. They turn their gazes in the direction of a tall man dressed like a cowboy who is running towards a skinny, bespectacled little man who is waiting for the elevator. The tall one shouts at the little one, who is sniffing a flower. Some of the ladies bite their fingers. The little one is going to be flattened. What appalling behaviour! These people conduct themselves in hotels just as they do in taverns.

"Did I ask you," the big one shouts at the little one, "to bring me your old papers?"

The cowboy's powerful hand grips the shoulders of the intellectual, who goes pale.

"Did I ask you to tell me that my father wasn't my father?"

The bespectacled little man is hurled to the ground.

"Did I ask you to come and tell me that my mother took a jaunt to Paris with an Indian?"

The cowboy has thrown himself at the little man and he's shaking him against the floor. His glasses have slipped off. Fortunately, the carpet is thick. The security guard, who has noticed the size of the attacker, runs up slowly. Robert Martin doesn't know how to fight. He doesn't want to fight.

"I thought you'd be interested . . ."

The other man is out of control. Frightened, forced to defend himself, Robert Martin manages to knee the cowboy. The angular bone crushes the cowboy's balls and he releases his victim. The scene has ended.

A photographer happened to be present. He recognized the local hero, the historian who wrote the famous book about Farmer Dubois. He captured several stages of the assault on film. Tomorrow, Robert Martin and Jean-René Goupil will be on the front page of the *Journal de Québec*. Now that peace has been restored, the security guard steps in and, in an authoritarian voice, orders the hostilities to cease.

"Did I need to know that my mother's poor husband was a cuckold every day of his life?"

"Your mother loved her husband; otherwise she'd have gone and joined your father in Arizona . . ."

"My mother preferred a house on the Grande Allée to a shack in the desert . . ."

The spectacle isn't interesting now. The bystanders scatter. The security guard makes sure no risk of violence remains. The cowboy and the historian are face to face. They're uncomfortable.

"Historians," says the notary reproachfully, "ought to let sleeping dogs lie."

"There's no past. Everything belongs to the present," Robert Martin assures him, replacing his glasses.

"Historians ought to let oblivion do its work. A person with too many memories lives in the past. It's the present we have to occupy."

"Even if you hadn't read *A Bottle in the Sea*, the facts would be the same: you're the son of an Indian whom your mother loved."

"For a man, one father is too many. But two..."

"Without your mother's manuscript you'd never have understood why she entrusted that painting of the handsome Indian chief to you."

"I'm remembering all those books she kept shoving at me! I didn't want to open them. She'd shut me away so I'd read them: *The Last of the Mohicans*, *The Deerslayer*, books with Indians on the covers. She filled one whole shelf in my room with her books about Indians.... Now I'm glad I know. I'm angry, but I'm glad. More glad than angry. I have a new father. A new life is beginning. We'll celebrate the event in the wigwam! Come on, champagne's on me! The only sad thing is, my parents aren't here to celebrate their little Indian's birth!"

"Then you're making peace with me?" the historian asks cautiously.

"There was a book my mother gave me—*Son of a Redskin*, something like that.... About a little Indian boy some kind white people adopted after his parents were killed in a skirmish. She told me that story a hundred times and I hated it. There was something in those books I didn't want to know. Tonight, I understand it."

The bottle of champagne is on the table. Is this the moment to inform the notary that there's an old Indian in Arizona who keeps repeating the name of Blanche Larivière? Robert Martin raises his glass and clinks it against that of the old man's unknown son. No, it's not yet time to tell him what he knows.

"To my father's health!"

"Welcome to your second life! What a privilege! Most humans have only one."

"I liked the one I had. I would have liked it to never end. Actually, I've never accepted the fact that life has an end. Humans ought to be eternal.... We should all have a thousand fathers and a thousand mothers."

With the third glass, they've become friends. Robert Martin confides:

"I too will have a second life.... My wife left me last year. Now she wants me. I'm going back. I'm starting over. I'm as nervous as if she were a perfect stranger."

"Women are always perfect strangers. If every woman is equivalent to one life, then, my dear professor, I'm eternal!"

With the fifth glass, Robert Martin remembers what he still has to do. First of all, leave Miss Camion and go back to his wife. Second, speed up the research for his book about Dubois. The project has become as heavy as an overloaded wagon in the ruts of the Oregon Trail. Abruptly, he announces:

"I'm going to sleep. It's late. Very early tomorrow I return to Montreal. I'll be back. I've got more of your mother's manuscripts for you to read."

"More manuscripts? Why didn't you bring them all today?"

"Where papers are concerned, historians are just as cautious as notaries. Goodbye."

"I'm convinced I haven't had enough to drink," concludes the Indian's son.

Robert Martin has gone up to his room. Drunk, he's already asleep. Jean-René Goupil drives his jeep into the night that resembles a great peaceful river. He feels like a newborn who is opening his eyes on the planet.

29 Blanche Larivière accumulated photographs during her trips to Paris. Then she pasted them into thick black albums and spent long moments dreaming over them, absent, as if she hadn't come back to Quebec. "What's become of those albums?" wonders Jean-René Goupil. "Did she give them to the Archives, too?" Did the second wife of his notary father make them disappear to wipe out every trace of the poetess from her husband's life? As a child he'd been jealous of those photographs. When his mother looked at them she'd set off on a journey again. He was as alone as when she boarded a plane with his father, his false father. In the photos, she would be standing in front of an old stone wall, a castle from centuries past, a Romanesque church or the Eiffel Tower. Most of the time she was alone. Occasionally she was holding her husband's arm. They took this trip religiously every two years. Jean-René would stay with his grandmother then, on the Île d'Orléans. In the photos, the two travellers were always smiling. Jean-René remembers: it used to make him sad; he assumed his parents had forgotten him.

The notary was unaware that before him an Indian warrior had walked with his mother over paving stones worn down by generations of footsteps, past buildings blackened by the soot of time. Did his mother hear the Indian's voice, then, in her memory?

Now he knows: the poetess left signs everywhere. He has to get those photos back. When she was looking at her albums, his mother was contemplative, as if she were praying. While the notary, drowsy from wine, dozed over the news of the world, was she travelling into the time she'd spent with the man who had given her this child who was so jealous of her dreams? Could her photographs have been like the breadcrumbs dropped by Hansel and Gretel when they were wandering in the forest?

What name should he inscribe now on his office door? Longfeather Larivière? Hawkeye Longsong? Sharp Arrow Goupil? He prefers Little Tornado Man, Notary. . . . Is his real father still alive?

How mysterious are the ties that bind human beings! His mother in the northern wind and snow; his father in an Arizona desert; time has passed between them like the river between its shores. Jean-René Goupil has never been able to love a woman the way his mother loved her Indian. Is it because they were apart that her love was so enduring?

It's his notary father he should be thinking about. The poor man must have often sensed his wife burning with love. Did he suspect that she wasn't burning for him? He warmed his soul with wine. He must have realized that his son looked less like him than like the Indian chief in the painting over the fireplace. Did his notary father, that decent man, never recognize the shadow of an Indian between them as they strolled the streets of Paris?

A delicate poetess, his mother hadn't wanted to hurt anyone. She wrote out her confession and left it to chance. . . . She hoped that chance would be slow. Perhaps she didn't want the truth to touch her son. Jean-René Goupil is confused, agitated, overwhelmed, but he's not suffering. Is the old Indian in his Arizona desert suffering—if he's still alive—because he doesn't know that up north with the Whites he has a son he made with a beautiful white woman one night in Paris, to celebrate the peace?

The Île d'Orléans has sunk into the sea of night and the two beams from his jeep are painting the road like a dream. The jeep is carrying away Jean-René Goupil, and he is drifting along with it. Today, he died. Today, he was born. Today, he has become his own half-brother. He has become a stranger to himself. He is no longer the man he was yesterday. His thoughts are tangled, like his laughter and his tears.

"When I tell my friends in our fancy golf club I'm an Indian!"

He bursts out laughing, the way the first man on Earth must have laughed when he discovered it's not necessary to cry all the time. His passion for setting traps for hares, squirrels and porcupines; his patience with nets for catching birds; his knack for fishing, once he was finally free of school and could cast his hook behind the damp alders in July and August; did he inherit all that from his Indian father? When his son came home with his catch, muddy, covered with scratches and soaking wet, his notary father often exclaimed:

"Look at our little Indian."

His mother would say nothing. He was right. How sad the love they shared must have been. . . . Just before she died, she'd whispered, with her bony little yellow hand in her husband's: "I'm not sad because I'm dying; I'm crying because I'm leaving you." Jean-René Goupil remembers her words very well. She talked like that because she was a poetess, but surely poetesses who aren't in love don't use such touching language. If she hadn't loved his notary father, would she have tolerated every morning, seven days a week, straightening his bow tie that was always crooked? She loved that little man who believed himself to be a father just as she never stopped loving the man who was no longer there. How painful it must be to love only a memory!

Of course she consoled herself with her poetry, which was no doubt another way of loving. Poetry must have replaced the "absent flesh," as Blanche Larivière put it in one of her poems. The literature teacher had read those hateful lines in class. Jean-René Goupil maintained then that his mother's poem wasn't really poetry because, he argued, his mother wasn't crazy and you have to be crazy to write poetry. The teacher had sent him to the prefect in charge of discipline to repeat his poetic principles.

"Papa!"

This cry in his own voice startles him. His notary father is buried in the soil of the Île d'Orléans. Is his Indian father still alive? So far from the Île d'Orléans, like Jean-René's deceased father he can't hear the son who is calling to him.

Does he look like his father? When his mother died, Jean-René Goupil was about the same age the young Indian had been when the heart of Blanche Larivière beat for him. When her gaze fell on her son in her hospital room, did she see the man she had loved that night when peace came back to Paris like an extraordinary springtime?

The jeep stops in front of his house. He doesn't want to go inside because there are tears in his eyes. His thoughts are agitated, feverishly confused. He walks along the path to the old pine tree. The stones are wet with dew. He leans against the trunk. The river seems to be a small portion of the daytime lingering in the night. So many times he's come to this place to think things over when he was unhappy. So many times he's taken refuge under the branches of this old pine tree when his fate seemed difficult to him.

So he's the son of an Indian from the desert. Is that why he didn't want to take the bourgeois road that his notary father, who had followed in the footsteps of his own father and his father too, had pointed out to him? Is that why little Jean-René used to go to school like someone being punished? He detested books as much as the medicines his mother made him swallow. When he bent over a page the words would fly away like frightened insects. He liked only what didn't come into the school. His notary father was deeply disappointed. His son was not responding to the call of the hereditary vocation. His mother didn't panic. Their child, she explained to her husband, had a great deal of curiosity. If he learned to read from the great book of nature, he would certainly learn to understand books by humans. His mother knew where her son had come from. Tonight he recognizes her patient goodness.

When he reached the age for entering university, he chose the faculty of law. As soon as his family was reassured and he himself was dying of boredom, he jumped on his motorcycle and disappeared along the roads of America. Some years later, he was captured again by the mysterious family trait. He went back to university. Like all the males in his adoptive family, he became a notary.

He'd always thought he knew what he was running away from. He had rejected a future that was waiting for him like a piece of clothing that was too tight. Tonight, he understands: he was looking for the one person who could teach him another way of being—his father, the unknown Indian. Leaning against the pine tree, he feels against his back a force that is rising in the night. In the breeze, the branches are swollen like a sail.

It had always bothered him that his notary father was such a short man. At the seminary, when the parents were invited, it pained him to be seen next to a father who'd stopped growing too soon. He'd always known he was a giant's son.

When he rode his motorcycle, his soul suspected he was descended from a race that doesn't tolerate borders. They tried to educate him the way notaries' sons are educated: he, the son of an Arizona Indian. They wanted to constrain him the way the sons of bourgeois white people are constrained.

Tonight, everything is clear. And everything becomes a mystery. This stranger whom he doesn't know, with his back against the pine tree, his eyes glued to the river, is him: the man without a name.

His feet are on a stone that sat at the bottom of the water when the sea covered the Île d'Orléans millions of years ago. Pressed against his back is the venerable patience of the pine tree. The eternity of stone vibrates under the soles of his urban cowboy boots. His body is huddled around his agitated heart beneath this night laden with dreams. He's not altogether here, on this point of Earth. Another part of him is calling far away in the south.

He remembers a furious rage against his teachers. After days and days of travelling on his motorcycle, he ended up outside an ancient Indian city built in the shelter of a sandstone cliff. It was a city of stone with towers, an elegant, planned city. No one had taught him that the Indians, who shrieked like starving dogs in American movies, possessed the skill to build cities. The stones that still sat on top of one another, the collapsed walls and deserted rooms watched over a terrible silence. His teachers knew nothing of these vanished American cities. Yet they knew everything about the ancient cities of Rome and Athens. Standing in the Indian city, Jean-René Goupil remembered again the ornamental "triglyphs, metopes and griffins" of Greek architecture. He remembered, he still remembers, the "golden mean" to which the construction of a Greek temple was obedient. He remembered, he still remembers, that the corner pillars of Greek temples were seven centimetres off plumb, otherwise they'd have seemed to lean outwards. He remembered, he still remembers, that the corner pillars of Greek temples were sixty-four millimetres thicker than the others so that when they were eaten away by the light they wouldn't look more spindly than the others.

All that useless baggage with which his educators crammed his memory! Facing the destroyed and deserted Indian city, he cursed the ignorance his masters had passed on to him. Jean-René Goupil had been educated as if he were White and Whites were taught that Indians slept under the trees.

Under this pine tree that witnessed his childhood sorrows, his adolescent anxieties, his worries, his rages, his dreams, he swears that he is glad to be an Indian. His soul rises up like Earth's crust when a volcano bursts. A new breath sweeps over him: it is the history of America, the history of Whites and Indians alike, that wells up in him.

In Europe some fifty years ago, at the end of the Second World War, the history of Whites and the history of Indians were united in the body of a pretty white woman from the city of Quebec. That night, the history of the Whites and the history of the Indians met in her body. However, Jean-René—Jean-René Without a Name, because he doesn't want to be called Goupil any more—won't be silent as his mother was. He cries out as if he wanted his voice to be heard in heaven.

"I'm an Indian!"

There is no echo. Only one small animal has stirred in the underbrush. The blue silence pierced with stars hasn't been disturbed. The water in the river murmurs as it runs to the sea. His young wife runs up to him.

"Jean-René! . . . Jean-René! . . . Are you all right?"

He is silent.

"Jean-René, I've read your mother's manuscript. It's incredible . . . Jean-René, you mustn't cry . . ."

"I want to make love to you. Now. Right here, beside the river. Under the sky."

"Oh, Little Tornado Man, with all those stones . . ."

"Let's do something wild! I want to share what I'm feeling with you."

"Let's go inside."

"Indians make love under the stars . . ."

"Let's go inside. I promise you . . ."

On the bearskin, without knowing it, riotously, they repeat the same ceremony, oh so human, that Blanche Larivière and René Goupil the notary feverishly performed half a century earlier, in this same place. Then, calm and covered in sweat, they slowly return from their journey to the land of love.

"My false father had no idea my mother was thinking about an Indian from Arizona when she did this . . ."

"Don't be so cynical, Little Tornado Man. Cynics are always wrong. It was important to your mother to give you a family. Do you think that back then she could have packed up her little Paris dresses, taken you in her arms to nurse you at her breast and gone off to look for the Indian who'd turned her legs to jelly? You shouldn't reproach your mother for not loving her husband. It was you she loved."

Jean-René Goupil stops trying to hold back his tears. They are the tears of a child.

30 Robert Martin is driving down the highway. The morning is new upon this flat green expanse that separates Quebec City from Montreal. A full day awaits him. Today he will go back to his wife, to his home. He'll be reunited with his children, his house, his books, his bed, his chalet, his sailboat. Today, he will see her before him. She will open the door to him. Invite him into his house. Hold out her arms to him. His too-pretty hairdresser will have a smile on her face as beautiful as the sun after a storm.

He drives through patches of fog. The night is fraying as it breaks away from the day. Here and there are trees set ablaze by the rising sun. Now the historian can think about what's on his mind. His book on Farmer Dubois has become a trap and he's a captive. The people in Miss Camion's special projects division are demanding a synopsis so they can tackle what they call spinoffs. He received a substantial advance. He's not making much progress. Is it his fault if the farmer didn't leave a diary as Blanche Larivière did?

He will be back with his wife and his children. As though after a long journey. They have lived together all these years. He will go back in spite of the grief, the humiliations, the accusations. He'll go back because there is perhaps no other way to heal his wounds. Why is he nervous at the thought of going home? He's afraid. As he was afraid the first time he called a girl from school to ask her to go to the movies. Riding his bicycle to a phone booth where his brothers and sisters wouldn't hear him, his hands trembling on the handlebars. When she answered, his throat tightened around his words. . . . Now, on his way back from Quebec City to Montreal, in spite of the years that have scratched his face and his soul, he's still the same boy who was afraid of being told no.

The day is young. It has not yet fully regained its hold over humans. The historian's thoughts are free to drift, like the mist. He thinks about Blanche Larivière's moving confession. Archives aren't a graveyard. Not only do documents tell what has been, they also announce what will be. The past is the beating heart of the present. Woe to individuals, woe to peoples who have no history. Wretched slaves, they are condemned to bear on their shoulders the present of other people. The road is long. He's a little delirious. . . . Couldn't a study be done on the delirium of the adventurers in America? For months they travelled by canoe along unknown and menacing rivers. For months, they travelled through landscapes that unfolded like eternity. Because of their solitude, because of their anxiety, because of the vastness, these people must have become drunk on dreams. Might death not loom up from behind a rock or a tree? Those people must have been driven mad by thirst, by hunger, by dwindling time, by lengthening distance. We will understand nothing about the history of America unless we realize that it was established by people who were in the grip of vertigo. The vertigo of immigrants come from far away who disembarked from their boats, foreheads burning with misery and hope; the vertigo of those who have crossed forests where even the birds lose their way; the vertigo of miners who dug in the black rock by the flickering light of the golden flame of their desire. What vertigo led Dubois to the mountains of Colorado? Now there's the story that ought to be told: the vertigo of Farmer Dubois!

Crossing the bridge to Montreal was not too difficult. First he stops at the National Library. The door is locked. "It's a good thing America already exists; you don't build a continent with lazy slugs like that!" Robert Martin regrets his reaction. Now he's thinking like a captain of industry. Miss Camion would have made the same remark . . .

He should call her before he goes to his apartment to pick up his books, papers and clothes. A still-sleepy voice answers:

"It's you, my little love! . . . Ah, I'd love you to come and tell me everything, everything. . . . I . . . I'm in a meeting with my accountant. California's causing us a lot of problems. As soon as he's gone I'll be with you. . . . Call me back, my little love."

"I hope I didn't wake up your accountant."

He hangs up. He didn't really want to say those words he'd only muttered. Why is he suddenly so sad? Isn't he going back to his wife, going home to be reunited with his children? His normal life has been restored to him.

His wife had left a modest history professor looked down on by his dean. Now when the too-pretty hairdresser opens the door to him, she will see the return of "the only historian who has won the people's heart," as *L'Écho des montagnes* has written, "a historian who has received bigger royalties, for a book not yet written, than other historians get for the whole of their published work." He ought to be singing for joy this morning.

With all the trouble raining down on him because of this Dubois, how can he fail to be worried? What's going on in the office? He makes a phone call.

"We've got another piece of the puzzle," a research assistant announces. "Farmer Dubois may have been a priest. We've located an Abbé Joseph Dubois.... Let me find my paper.... Here.... It's a brief notice in a Boston newspaper. Father Dubois taught Latin in a Boston school. On June first, 1863, the paper tells us Dubois was dismissed from the school before the summer holidays because of heresy."

"Boston you said? But our farmer lived in Colorado!"

"We've already identified traces of Dubois in the Yukon, in 1869. The heretic could no longer teach in Catholic schools. He had to disappear, keep a low profile. The Yukon gold fever is exactly what he needed."

"I'm writing history, not fiction ..."

"Our correspondent sent us a photocopy of a pamphlet written by Father Joseph Dubois ..."

"A pamphlet? Don't we already have something by Joseph Dubois: a pamphlet on whale hunting? Compare the dates ... Are all these pamphlets going to lead us to the complete works of

Dubois, an unknown author?... If you can establish a link between these two leaflets, I've got my man and my book is done!"

"The title of the pamphlet is *The Miracle of Levitation Made Accessible to the Pious Christian*."

"A mind preoccupied with levitation doesn't go to Colorado to raise cattle."

"Listen.... Have you got a minute?" asks the research assistant, who goes on without waiting for his reply. "Dubois drew up a list of the prophets who soared like birds: Enoch, the father of Methusaleh, who flew to heaven; Elijah, who broke away from Earth in a chariot of fire; Habakkuk, whom an angel pulled by the hair from Judea to Babylon, so he could bring food to Daniel in the lions' den..."

"Did you say Habakkuk? I've never heard of him. And we're a long way from Colorado."

The research assistant isn't listening.

"... and above all Jesus Christ at Bethany, who rose into heaven while his friends looked on. Dubois also lists a group of holy individuals who flew like helicopters when they prayed: Saint Anthony the Great, Saint Ladislas, Saint Bernard of Clairvaux, Saint Dominic the preaching brother, Saint Stanislas, Saint John of the Cross, Saint Joseph of Copertino, Saint Stephen, King of Hungary, who rose into the air with his tent while he was praying with his army; Saint Dunstan, Bishop of Canterbury, who, when he was levitating, struck his head against the vault of his cathedral; and Saint Colette of Corbie, who rose so high into the sky, people lost sight of her: '*oculi evanescens*,' the pamphlet points out. And there're many more..."

"That's enough."

"Listen to Abbé Joseph Dubois's conclusion:

At all times, human beings have wished to escape Earth's attraction. They have wanted to fly when awake as well as in their dreams. The human soul is as light as God created it. In taking flight, the soul has the power to take along the body in which it temporarily resides. Human beings have always wanted to fly, they have always flown and they will certainly fly in the future.

"Abbé Dubois was a prophet.... Listen to this. A little later he writes that in the accounts of their journeys, certain missionaries talk about a humble cactus, the peyotl, which contained a substance the Indians 'absorbed, and it made them take flight from the realm of the Earth.'"

"We're light-years away from our Farmer Dubois who bought fifty-nine head of cattle in Colorado."

"Listen to this.... One night, Abbé Joseph Dubois is wakened by a disturbing noise. Quickly, he lights his candle. What does he see in his bedroom? An unknown man, baffled, scrawny, dirty, who doesn't know where he is. Abbé Dubois realizes the man is harmless. He says to him: 'Where do you come from? Tell me where you've come from.' The intruder explains that he's been travelling for weeks in the mountains of a land called Colorado. He fed himself on what he could kill or gather. Here's the last thing he remembers. He was leaning on his bag to rest for a while. Beside his bag he noticed a beautiful big flower with yellow petals streaked with red lines. He was hungry. He ate the flower. And all at once he finds himself somewhere else, in a bedroom with someone he doesn't even know. And he hasn't got his bag. In his pamphlet, Abbé Dubois goes on:

America is an endless continent; her inhabitants want to reach all her borders, cross her valleys, climb her mountains, travel through her deserts, her forests. The dazed stranger in my room had discovered by chance the flower that lets people fly. The person who offers America the flower of flight will get rich.

"The magic flower grew in Colorado," the historian concludes. "Out of all the possible places in America, Farmer Dubois settled in Colorado. There's a connection. Unfortunately, the episode of the flying travellers is totally incredible. But let's not close any doors . . . Everything is possible, even the incredible."

"We've caught our Dubois!" declares the research assistant. "The farmer went to Colorado in search of the flower that lets people fly. I'm sure of it."

"Compare the style and the vocabulary in this pamphlet with those in the first one. And compare them with the letter from Joe Wood to his parents, remember?"

"Listen to what Dubois says:

I can certify that the traveller's fabulous tale is authentic. Basing my judgment on details in the sincere, total and complete confession he made to me, here are the characteristics of that precious flower . . .

"Unfortunately, the page is torn here."

"Find another copy of the pamphlet, for Christ's sake! Why do I have to tell you?"

"An interested reader must have torn out the page instead of copying it. To me," the research assistant assured him, "it's perfectly clear. After hunting whales, young Dubois becomes a journalist, he gets some education, becomes a priest and a Latin teacher, leaves the priesthood, goes to the Yukon in search of gold to give himself a financial base, then he sets off for Colorado determined to discover the flower that lets people fly, to cultivate it and market it so all America can soar."

"Let me tell you once again," says Robert Martin impatiently, "I'm writing history, not a novel."

"America is a novel!"

"I've sacked assistants for having simplistic ideas like that."

Robert Martin is bored with seeing his research assistants sink into dreams one after another when the history of America is being told.

"You shouldn't imagine or invent what Farmer Dubois might have been. We have to find his trail."

"His trail.... Every time we think we've got a glimpse of Dubois in one place, he turns up somewhere else. His trail.... According to notes we've received from the library in Montpelier, Vermont, one J. Dubois fought in the Civil War."

"Fifty thousand brave French Canadians took part in that war. Dubois may have been one of them. That's another forgotten chapter in our history. Tell me about that Dubois."

"J. Dubois worked for a textile mill in Winooski, Vermont. He volunteered as an artilleryman in the Vermont Light Regiment, which was part of the Army of the Potomac. It seems he took part in the Battle of Wilderness, in northern Virginia, on May 4, 1864."

"I don't want any more hypotheses or suppositions. I want facts: real, proven, true facts."

"Wilderness: that was a forest of oak and pine trees tangled in impenetrable brushwood. The soldiers were ensnared there like mosquitoes in a spider web. Entire brigades got lost in it. They didn't know in which direction to fire. It was impossible to get even a glimpse of the enemy flags. When a shell landed, you couldn't tell where it came from . . . There are good reasons to believe that Dubois took part in that battle."

"Don't just look, find! History punctuated with maybes looks like the patched-up tapestry of a novel. We're writing history, god-dammit!"

"Our discipline is a science. Life isn't scientific. Sheer chance led us to find the following letter:

Since my last letter some months ago, we have arrived in Wilderness. There were enemies everywhere and they were furious. I hid my nose and everything else behind an oak tree. Suddenly bullets were spitting on the bark. My heart was pounding like a devil in holy water. We were surrounded by enemy soldiers hidden in the brush and smoke. My throat was tight, my mouth was dry. I tripped over a soldier who had fallen on the other side of the big oak. There was a hole in his forehead just over his left eye. His brain was leaking out of the wound. I closed his right eye. His skin was still warm. I don't know his name. Besides that, it was raining.

"The letter is signed Soldier J. Dub. . . . The rest of the name is washed out in a spot of grease. It's probably Dubois."

"I told you, I don't want to hear any more probablys or maybes."

"You see, we aren't wasting our time."

"Can I write even one page of the history of Farmer Dubois with the questionable information you're giving me? Get me some facts!"

The conversation ended there. "Educated by television, the young generation lacks rigor," thinks Robert Martin. "Fortunately though, it's full of beans."

The National Library has finally opened. People are assembling Blanche Larivière's documents and making photocopies for the notary on Île d'Orléans. While he waits, Robert Martin leafs through Volume 30 of the *Cahiers des dix*, which contains letters from a French Canadian on the Oregon Trail. Soon everything will be ready.

"Hello, Mr. Goupil? I'm sending on your mother's documents, as promised. What's your office address?"

"I'm staying on the island today. I'm not going out. Professor Martin, may I think of you as my brother?"

His voice breaks. In spite of all the landscapes he's explored, in spite of all the women, in spite of all the days he has devoured, the notary, the cowboy, is a child in a man's body.

"I've never had a brother."

The historian knows what it feels like to be a man who is crying. During his flight to the United States, he cried while he drove along the roads.

"Yes, of course I'll be your brother. . . . Now listen carefully, brother, to what I'm going to say. This is not a dream. In Arizona, there's an old man who can pronounce very clearly the name of Blanche Larivière."

"You don't have to invent things to make me happy."

"I repeat. Listen carefully, brother. In Arizona I met an old Indian who remembers your mother's name."

"Brother, you've really decided to mess up my life."

"I haven't decided anything."

"Are you a sorcerer? A schemer? Some kind of swindler? A braggart?"

"You're insulting me."

"It's no insult to insult your brother."

"As soon as you're ready we leave for Arizona!"

As he hangs up, Robert Martin wishes he could take back the words he's just said. Can he go to Arizona? What will his wife say? "You're no sooner home than already you want to leave me." He hates this feeling of not being free. Should he speak to his lawyer before he goes home? No. The situation is clear. His wife who rejected him now wants him back. He goes into the bathroom, where men often have profound thoughts. Standing at the mirror, he straightens his tie, smooths the few hairs on his head. He will step inside his house without knocking, as if he were just coming home after a day's work.

In the car, his heart is beating too hard. What will he say? Should he choose his words in advance? After pushing open the door he'll let his heart say what it will, automatically, the way we struggle when we fall into the water. He's forgotten to buy flowers. There must be flowers. "Say it with flowers." Roses. The flowers of love. Flowers with thorns. . . . A side trip to look for a florist.

When he lays the flowers on the back seat he remembers that the too-pretty hairdresser likes chocolate. When he sets the box of chocolates next to the flowers, he remembers he's forgotten the champagne. This is a big day. It's a new beginning. A new season. It's as if he were marrying her! That's what Robert Martin will say when the time comes to say something.

What traffic! A city-wide bottleneck. Stuck in their cars without moving, city-dwellers will find their legs beginning to atrophy. In a few centuries—as the population increases, traffic will multiply—traffic jams will last longer and city-dwellers will be powerless. Maybe they'll grow wings? Robert Martin should buy gifts for his children. For his wife, too. She used to be happy when he surprised her with a scarf or perfume. . . . Why not a blouse? Another side trip . . .

That soldier in Wilderness, shot down behind an oak tree, with a bullet-hole in his forehead.... The story of that nameless soldier: now *that* is genuine history. It's genuine because it cannot be told. What can be told is narrative, not history. Prime ministers and generals who leave records behind hope their history will be written down. That's not history. The only history, genuine history, is that of the voiceless characters who have left no trace. The story of the Unknown Soldier: *that* is a country's genuine history. In his way, Dubois is an unknown soldier. Ah! there's some powerful reasoning for his book. It will shake up the snoozing community of historians. His dean will fall out of his upholstered chair.

Like a well-trained dog, his car has come back to his house. Robert Martin feels shy. His heart is beating too fast. He's hot. He's shivering. His legs hesitate. He gathers up flowers, chocolates, champagne, gifts. He walks to the door. The lawn needs watering. The paint around the windows is peeling. He tries not to think. He feels as if he's come back from a long journey. Nothing has changed. The bricks need pointing. That's expensive. He is back home. He loves his house. He loves his too-pretty hairdresser. Better not try to understand what happened. It shouldn't have happened. He should have come back sooner. He shouldn't have waited for her to ask him.

The door opens. She steps outside. Takes two steps. Looks at him. He's brought flowers, chocolates, champagne, presents. She has changed subtly. Her face seems rounder. There are circles under her eyes. Her hair is different. He offers her the flowers. His words are stuck in his throat. He says stupidly:

"They smell good."

"The only thing I can smell is another woman's perfume."

"I've come back," he pleads.

"You can come back when her perfume's evaporated."

His too-pretty hairdresser steps briskly back inside the house. She slams the door. Robert Martin hears the key turn in the lock. The curtain stops stirring.

"That wasn't the right way to come back," he concludes.

His arms are full of presents. Should he take them with him? He feels ridiculous. Isn't she his wife? Isn't this his house? Didn't she let him know herself that she wanted him back? With all his presents he looks like a peddler. The door has been slammed in his face. He deserves more respect. He drops what he's holding onto the grass and turns his back.

He gets into his car. There's work waiting for him in his office. He has to go through the new documents on Farmer Dubois. Fortunately, there is the past.

31 In Arizona, it's the end of June. Behind a cactus, a swarm of bees is engaged in an all-out battle. Charlie Longsong has often observed this war among the bees. They fight until only one male survives. The winner can then couple with the female who is waiting for him among the lifeless males. Little Tornado Man fought a war too, but he can't recall why the men were destroying one another.

Far away, high in the sky, from its source in a black cloud, a dark river is seething. Though it is still very far away, the rain will come. That will be good. The earth is thirsty. Charlie Longsong goes to prepare his barrel to receive the water from the sky. When the rain comes he will allow it to wash him. He goes back to his *hogan*. He'll sit on his doorstep and wait for it to come.

As the rain draws nearer, the earth grows dark. Yet over there, on either side of the grey river, the blue sky lights up the desert. This downpour will waken the plants and fill the *arroyos*. Something is going to happen. The clouds are laden with signs. He has a foreboding that this time is not like the other times. The air is scented. He imitates the animals who raise their nostrils to the wind to identify a foreign presence on their territory. Today, the passing time has an unaccustomed fragrance. The air is cooler. The rainfall will be abundant. It will provide a generous store of water. He hopes his roof will hold out. Sometimes the rain is heavy.

Soon the rain before him is no longer a river but a wall of anger, a wall that's nearly black, that hides the desert and the mountains from him. It isn't rain, it is hail that is now skipping across the gravel. The hailstones are the size of hens' eggs. Will his roof cave in? It's like a rain of pebbles. Hailstones clink and clatter. The column of hail rumbles as it advances. Charlie Longsong goes inside his shelter and rolls himself in a blanket, wrapping it first around his head. The hailstones hammer at it but his roof does not give in. They gleam on the ground as they cover it. The sky empties. Charlie Longsong has never seen hail so powerful, so relentless. Then the storm subsides. The dark wall is rubbed out like smoke driven by the wind. The dark clouds drown in the return of the intense light. Charlie Longsong drops his blanket. It is June but his desert is as white as if winter were at his feet. A man hasn't wasted his day if he's been able to admire such a hailstorm. That man has seen what the gods are capable of doing in just a few moments. The daylight that flared up on Earth has not been wasted, because the man who has witnessed a force so powerful feels the need to be silent for the rest of the day. The hail has come to warn him that great events are about to happen. Everything that happens does so for a reason.

Since morning, Charlie Longsong has been thinking of his story about the snakes. Why did that story seep into his memory today? The snakes carry messages from the Indians to the gods. Would the snakes bring messages from the gods to the Indians as well? He hasn't yet told the young people of the mesa the story about the *bohana* Dooboy. He told it to Blanche Larivière, he remembers as if it were yesterday. She laughed a lot, especially when he danced on the bed to imitate Dooboy. The young people of the mesa will enjoy it when he dances as he tells his story. It's the funniest story he knows. It was given to him by his father. His father's father told it. His father's father saw Dooboy dancing for the snakes with his own eyes.

Back then, the *bohanas* had killed so many snakes there were hardly any left in Arizona. When they spied a snake, they thought they were supposed to break its head. They didn't like snakes any more than they liked Indians.

One day, Dooboy turned up on the mesa. Like the missionaries, he was unarmed. His mule was carrying a device for taking photographs. All he wanted was permission to plant his device in front of the Indians, in front of their houses, their women, their children. Then he made an explosion above his head and he set off again with his box filled with images. The Indians saw a lot of photographers who begged the men to put on their ceremonial trinkets even if it wasn't a ceremonial day, or their war costumes even if they were at peace. They encouraged the chiefs to don their most precious attire. They threw candies to the children. The photographers were less dangerous than the missionaries or the surveyors. They only wanted to take their pictures. Initially, the Indians, who were very cautious, didn't want their image to be stolen. In time, though, they had tamed the photographer's device. Soon they took a certain pride in posing.

A number of them wondered if these unarmed men who left

without any booty were really men, or if they were of the same sex as the Catholic missionaries. None of them was as famous on the mesa as Dooboy.

Back then, the chief was worried. He was afraid of running out of snakes. If the snake dance didn't take place, the snakes wouldn't know which were the Indians' prayers. In their land of darkness, they wouldn't be able to pass on the Indians' requests to the gods.

To ward off such a disaster to the tribe, the chief began first thing in autumn to collect snakes for the following summer. When he was out hunting or walking, if he met a snake he'd grab it and drop it into his bag. Then the chief would empty his bag in an uninhabited cabin just outside the village. The snakes would be kept there until the ceremonial day. That was foresight. Soon the November winds would blow.

The reptiles went into their dens under the cabin floor, to doze. Early in December, a fine rain after sunset turned into snow that resembled white powder. At dawn the sun appeared, but the snow withstood it. The old people at their windows understood that the winter would be cold.

That winter, the earth became as hard as ice. The wind buffeted the poor Indians. A fine coating of white dust swirled and covered the ground. That was the day the photographer Dooboy appeared out of the blue. He'd come from very far up north. They had never heard anyone talk the way he did. Because of the cold wind that blew right through his tent, his blankets and his clothes, he hadn't slept for three days. He asked if he could take shelter in the uninhabited cabin just outside the village. There, he would have walls against the cold and a roof against the snow. No Indian would refuse shelter to a *bohana*. But they didn't know the chief had already sheltered some guests in the cabin. The sun rolled to the other side of the country, leaving just a trace of light behind.

As soon as he entered the deserted cabin, Dooboy noticed the hood of a fireplace. This lodging would be as comfortable as a hotel. All he had to do was find a few sticks of wood. With a fire, it would be as warm as a day in June.

Soon he was sweating. He took off his shirt. Bare-chested, he cooked a hare over the crackling fire. They could hear Dooboy singing with pleasure in a language they didn't know. In spite of everything, the day was good. He had collected some fine images, he would sleep under a roof, it was warm and the meat was juicy. He had drunk a few sips of bourbon. Pleasant memories were stirring.

Suddenly he thought he heard something prowling around the cabin. A drawn-out slithering against the wall. Probably some nosey person wanting to observe him. No. He listened some more. It sounded like a ghost with chattering teeth.

"There! There!" he cried out to himself, pointing towards a dark corner.

He lost his voice. Slipping out of the shadows, a rattlesnake was approaching the table to join the feast. Dooboy couldn't race to the door without walking over the snake, which was barring the way with the whole length of its body. Dooboy jumped to grab hold of a beam that ran across the cabin. From another dark corner, another snake appeared. Then another. And another. Finally, the floor was covered with sleep-numbed reptiles that were slowly approaching to relieve their hunger.

With the heat from the photographer's fire, the chief's guests thought it was already April. They were emerging from their den.

Terror-stricken, Dooboy shouted at the top of his lungs like a child who's lost his mother. His voice went all the way to the inhabitants of the village. They didn't understand his cries for help. He was using words in a language nobody knew. They told themselves he must be living it up. Some, more curious than the others, went to the cabin, which was being shaken by poor Dooboy's moans. Cautiously, they approached the window. What they saw there was hilarious! Choking with laughter, they called the others. They took turns observing what was going on inside the cabin.

No doubt because he'd drunk too much, the half-naked Dooboy was doing some peculiar dance, clutching a beam in the ceiling. *Bohanas* behave very strangely, but this one was the strangest yet. Doubled over with laughter, the bystanders went home, leaving Dooboy dancing and singing in the manner of his tribe, or so they thought.

Suspended from his beam for hours now, Dooboy was paralysed, nearly dead. Eventually the snakes pretended not to notice he was there. Perhaps they were simply waiting for him to fall like fruit from a tree? The fire died down, became embers, then ash. Slowly, the icy night wind seeped into the cabin. Soon it was as cold there as it was outside. After this too-brief summer, the snakes went reluctantly back to their hole. Daylight had long since returned when Dooboy ran out of the cabin, half-naked in the piercing cold. He hadn't even picked up his shirt. He left behind an old canvas bag in which they found a book like the missionaries', some paper covered with writing no one could read and some photos of the great chief Geronimo.

Thinking back to this funny story, Charlie Longsong smiles. When his father told it, he often had to stop in the middle because the people were laughing so hard at this *bohana* who danced with the snakes. Why has he told it to himself today? He's forgotten why he started it. Across the sea, Blanche Larivière had found the story of Dooboy and the snakes hilarious. Afterwards, she hesitated before getting out of bed. She dared not set her foot on the floor of her small room. She was afraid of the snakes that might have emerged from the shadows.

"You're very brave, Little Tornado Man!"

For some time now, Charlie Longsong has sensed that great events are coming. Around him, something is brewing. Now that he's an old man, he should be wise enough to expect nothing more than the morning when his eyes will no longer open on the desert. But he is feverish, hopeful, he's on the lookout the way Little Tornado Man used to be when, as a small child, he waited for his father's return after that brawl and fired that shot.

Somewhere in the clouds, his father knows that his son, the old man, is pining. Isn't it time for him to come back on his black mare and visit him? If Charlie Longsong's time is nearly over, shouldn't his father take him with him into the clouds to join the ancestors? Because he has no son, Little Tornado Man is still a child himself. That's why he is allowed to call to his father.

And what if time has prepared for the arrival in the desert of Blanche Larivière, who has come down from the north because, before she dies, she wants to see again the soldier with an amputated arm who made her dance near a fountain in that immense city on the other side of the ocean? And what if Blanche Larivière, who invited him into her little room with a window open onto the sky above rue Gît-le-coeur, wanted to see Little Tornado Man again before she too closes her eyes? And what if she's come to tell him she's thought about him always?

32 Seated side by side in the airplane are two men with tears in their eyes. They've drunk a lot and they've talked a lot. Robert Martin talked about his divorce and his flight to the United States, when he hoped that somewhere the road would stop at the edge of a cliff where he would fall forever. He described his vertigo as he plunged into an endless America, he who had

travelled mainly in books. He described his emotion when he read the name of Dubois, his careful signature, on the first page of a ledger that was a simple schoolchild's scribbler, in the museum of a ghost town. The historian who had lost his love, his children, his house, was finding a French Canadian like himself, lost, like him, in the densely covered mountains of Colorado. Was Dubois also running away from grief? For perhaps the tenth time, he tells his new brother how, sinking into America as into oblivion, he met an old Indian who spoke to him, in an unforgettable manner, the name, unknown to the historian, of Blanche Larivière.

Since that journey, the past has taken over his life. He's started a research project on Farmer Dubois. He has not yet been able to pick up traces that are unmistakably his. And now the poetess whose name he heard for the first time in Arizona has revealed to him her most intimate secrets. Thanks to the rediscovered documents, the son of Blanche Larivière is going to meet his real father. All that past is going to become the present. All that past is going to be transformed into the future. No, the past does not exist.

"One day my little girl, whom I haven't seen since last summer, said to me: 'The past is when there used to be fairies.'"

With a sound like sliding on snow, the airplane descends into the foamy clouds. Jean-René Goupil's nose is pressed to his window. When he was playing a modern-day knight on his motorcycle, he explored this region. He idled around these megaliths carved by the tools of the centuries. Afterwards, he mocked his sculptor friends, calling them dilettante insects. To his painter friends, he said: "No artist can combine colours as the light on a canyon wall can do." Often, he stopped to lean over a cliff and drink in a little of eternity. He remembers a delightful night of love next to his motorcycle, protected by a rocky spur that resembled an old monk at prayer. Ah! to fall asleep in a night so beautiful that the sandstone turns into a delicate shadow ...

From his window, Jean-René Goupil interrogates the earth that seems to be rising up to meet him. He's like a child just expelled from his mother's womb. Down below, on this grey earth, in his desert, is his unknown father still alive? Will he arrive too late? Does he look like that man? What will he say to him? Will his father want to welcome him? How many brothers and sisters will he have? He regrets having hated his mother's poetry, having been ashamed of the sorrows she laid out in verse in the Quebec City newspapers. At the Petit Séminaire his stomach used to knot when the literature teacher handed out one of her poems, always surrounded by those goddamn drawings of flowers. He envied his classmates with normal mothers who didn't write poetry and didn't read it.

The day when he hopped on his motorcycle to hurl himself into adventure, he thought he was escaping from his family, freeing himself from the father who was a mere notary, too short, too timid, too weak, too fearful—and boring, too, with his predictable habits and rituals. Without knowing it, he was searching for his real father. Without knowing it, he was obeying a force of attraction that has brought him today to a small airport in Arizona. From here, he will set out in search of the Indian who apparently knows his mother's name. Jean-René Goupil is a little jealous of Robert Martin. This funny little man who looks like a book shouldn't have read Blanche Larivière's words before he did.

The historian hopes he won't be moved. He doesn't want to be sad. His too-pretty hairdresser has rejected him again. He wishes he had a heart of stone. He hates feeling distraught. In order to think of nothing, he mechanically turns the pages of *Time* magazine. A headline blinds him like the bright glare of the sun. He rereads it: "Du Bois, the Moses of the Blacks." He reads again. Du Bois, William Edward Burghardt, was born in 1868. Du Bois, this Moses, was black. The photographer has evidence to prove it. The article points out that Du Bois, this Moses, had Dutch, African and French blood. Farmer Dubois could have had a black son. The Moses of the Blacks is a prominent figure. The historian should be better informed about his subject, but he knows that his ignorance of American history is as vast as the continent. Du Bois, who obtained a doctorate from Harvard in 1895, he reads, fired the conscience of the black intellectuals of his day. He gave back to his brothers their history, of which they'd been dispossessed. By doing so he restored their pride. The black son of a white farmer couldn't have restored their lost history to the Blacks ... He must check the dates and the facts. Is it possible that Farmer Dubois was the father of the Moses of the Blacks? What if it's true! No, impossible. ... If it were true though, what an amazing chapter it would make! What a fine American paradox! The black son of a white farmer, the black son of a French Canadian, becomes the guide of the Blacks on their march towards freedom! Farmer Dubois, father of that modern Moses? He must check the facts.

Tears are running down the cheeks of Jean-René Goupil's broad face. He tries to hide them by pressing his nose against the window. This grey land seems uninhabited. Only one lost car is following the black road. Because of his mother's confession he is looking for his father, but can he believe this story about an old Indian who remembers his mother's name? The historian's encounter with the man is absolutely unbelievable. So much coincidence defies logic. He may have misunderstood. The old Indian was speaking in his own language and Robert Martin thought he heard the name of Blanche Larivière. His own wife had just left him; when a person is suffering from the pains that love can cause, he doesn't always listen very carefully. Anyway, remembering the name of Blanche Larivière is no proof of paternity. The old Indian must be dead. They're coming too late. The notary insisted on believing he could shake his father's hand, but that's impossible.

Events don't fall into place according to our wishes.... At the same time, he fears the moment when he will see his father, when he'll walk up to him, hold out his hand, the moment when he'll hear him speak. Robert Martin and he are heading towards a mirage in the desert.

The notary wishes he could remember the poem his literature teacher had handed out. The whole class had laughed because his mother was saying words of love to an Indian. The airplane's shadow creeps across the desert. How he wishes he could recite some lines of his mother's . . .

Even in the details of everyday life, Robert Martin behaves like a historian. During his trip last year, haphazardly following the American roads, he'd used a green felt pen to trace his route on the map. From the airport, then, it's easy to drive towards that spot in the desert where it all started, to the trading post where he first saw the one-armed Indian.

"Do you know your father has just one arm?"

"My father is a war hero!"

Jean-René Goupil doesn't believe in this story that soon will end, like all the stories we make up because we refuse reality. But why is he also bothered by a constant pain in his right arm? Why did he have the accident that broke his right arm?

"It's a sign," his mother the poetess would have said.

The historian's travel notes won't be useless. They've determined where some precise landmarks are. Eager now, they have no curiosity about Walnut Canyon. They're impatient to reach a secondary road, marked in green on the map, that runs along the Painted Desert. Will Jean-René Goupil's father loom up from behind some cactus? Robert Martin jotted a few paragraphs about that desert last year. It's of no interest. He was too filled with grief; he saw nothing. The world was nothing but a great wound of love. Those pages in his notebook may be useful for sketching out the landscapes in his biography of Farmer Dubois. No hypothesis should be rejected until it's verified. It's not unreasonable that Farmer Dubois could be the father of the Moses of the Blacks.

"Is a man allowed to piss in the open here?" asks Jean-René Goupil, opening the door as if the car had already stopped.

Robert Martin parks on the shoulder. His travelling companion walks away into the dusty shrubs. Why did his too-pretty hairdresser ask him to come back if she doesn't want anything to do with him? Was it to make him suffer a little more? It worked. He hasn't stopped loving her. If she asks him to come back again he'll simply refuse. But he can't deny that afterwards he'll buy chocolates and champagne for her. Miss Camion doesn't know what happened yet. That woman. . . . There's more life in her than in an entire century! Dear God but he was happy with that woman! A real woman, who knows how to make a man grow taller . . .

Jean-René Goupil comes back, shamefaced:

"I must be a little nervous. My bladder was bursting but I couldn't piss on my father's cactus."

The car starts up again.

"Brother, do you know how to write?"

"I'm not even officially an Indian yet and already you're prejudiced against me."

"I'm prejudiced against notaries. Take my notebook from my jacket pocket in the back and write down clearly what I'm about to dictate. *Was Dubois the Moses of the Blacks? Should my hypothesis turn out to be correct, the march towards the liberation of the slaves began with the wandering of a modest white farmer, a French Canadian, exiled in America.* Exclamation point!"

"What's my father like?" Jean-René Goupil interrupts, jostling the historian from his musing.

"What?"

Amazed to find himself nearly motionless in the middle of the road, he starts up vigorously again.

"What's my father like?" repeats the cowboy from the Île d'Orléans, who is shivering in the air conditioning.

Outside, the breeze passes like an iron over a shirt. Robert Martin recites lines that Jean-René Goupil struggled not to learn at the Petit Séminaire.

> *O my young Indian brother*
> *You have left your desert*
> *For the great ritual of fire*
> *And you took my heart*
> *On rue Gît-le-coeur*
> *And you gave me yours*
> *O my young Indian brother . . .*

"Even when you're the one reciting it, my brother, it's touching."

The mountains that block the horizon are clad in light. Mauve, maroon, red are superimposed without running together or obliterating each other. These mountains crumbled by time have made up the desert. It is gravel studded with burnt grass. Yellowish vines cling and creep. Here and there, bushes of silvery thyme. No human habitation. In the distance, spinning like a top, one of those dust eddies that roll in the wind: "dust devils," the pioneers called them.

"In this country," the notary observes, "it's a long drive to buy a cold beer."

"We haven't come here for beer . . ."

"Is my father a noble, handsome old man?"

"You mean is he as handsome as the painting over your fire-place?"

"I'm trying to imagine how all this is going to upset my habits. . . . It's inevitable that, with a new father, everything's going to be different. So what will I be like? It's taken me nearly fifty years to adapt to my first identity. I can't jump into my second one as if it were a new pair of pants. Ever since I boarded the plane, all I can think of is: What kind of man is my father? I was nothing like my notary father. . . . He was the best father I could have had: he always found a way to prove me right. . . . If I'm like my Indian father, do I really want to be like him? Stop here, I have to take a leak."

Robert Martin would rather be somewhere else, tracking down the mystery of Farmer Dubois. On the other hand, he couldn't refuse to take his new friend to his unknown father. A jarring uncertainty has his stomach in knots. There's no guarantee that the old Indian is Jean-René Goupil's father. Memory often plays nasty tricks. With malevolent freedom it selects what it wants to hold onto. Memory bears a marvellous resemblance to dreams. Would he be prepared to swear on the Bible that the old Indian really said the name of Blanche Larivière? Memories are often the fruits that the present desires. Robert Martin knows enough history to be certain of that; that's why each generation reinvents history. In spite of itself, history lies. Writing history means lying a little. The closer he comes to real places, the more the historian is perturbed by doubt.

Why was he incapable of phoning Miss Camion after the too-pretty hairdresser rejected him? He wanted to talk to her. He needed to confide in someone. He was thirsty for her sensual voice filled with lights and birds. He wanted to feel the force of that woman who is charging towards the future like a truck in her flowered dress. He couldn't. He was intimidated. As if she were a stranger. . . . It was impossible for him to confide his pain. Miss Camion, he told himself, was busy elsewhere. He was afraid that she too would reject him.

The cowboy from the Quebec Chamber of Notaries comes back to the car.

"I flooded the desert. Flowers will spring up there. Good God! I'm about to see my father for the first time . . . and I'm already a grandfather myself. . . . I'm a lot more nervous than I was the first time I took off my clothes after I'd undressed a girl. I was terrified. I was sure she was going to say no. Do you think my father will say no?"

"We have to find him first. Now we have to pay attention. . . . Me too—I've always been afraid of being told no by a woman . . ."

"Hundreds of women have said no to me. It always hurts. . . . You remember the ones who say no . . ."

"Here, make yourself useful. Take this map. Navigate. If we make a mistake here you'll never see your father. We must be getting close . . ."

Ahead of them, in the west, the sun is transforming the mauve mountain into a fabulous temple.

"There aren't any landmarks in the desert," mutters Robert Martin. "Everything looks like everything else but nothing's the same."

He is impatient. Anxious to arrive. Anxious for it to be over.

He wants to get back to Farmer Dubois. Why did he throw himself into this adventure of finding his new friend's father? He still needed to run away from his own grief, the way he took to the American highways to run away from it last year. Run away. Run away. He hates knowing that he's constantly running away. This knowledge irritates him, gets under his skin. Jean-René Goupil observes his bad mood.

"Since you ask, I'm going to help you orient yourself," he offers. "After all, I'm more or less from here. . . . At the Petit Séminaire in Quebec, when my dear classmates wanted to insult me they'd call me a 'goddamn savage' . . . I'd defend myself. . . . I'd fight like a goddamn savage."

They drive along from curve to hesitation, turning around, arguing, bending over the map.

"Why should I have marked my route more carefully? I had no intention of coming back to this lost planet that looks like the Moon. There's nothing here. You can see for yourself there's nothing . . ."

"I beg your pardon! My father's here. My roots are here. That's not nothing."

After crossroads where they have no choice but to let chance decide which direction they will take, they follow some gravel roads lined with sage and cactus. After making some hesitant turns, ten times they have to retrace their steps, try another direction, another unmarked road.

"This landscape is as boring as a month of rain," the historian decides.

"It's my country, brother. Show some respect!"

A winding trail of dust creeps through the dry bushes. The thin shadow of a coyote appears beside a cactus, sniffing the wind. The windshield wipers have smeared the glass. The sun, behind the mountains now, is sending out blinding arrows. Robert Martin sighs.

"It looked like this. With the antique shop next to it. . . . It's the trading post. Yes. This is it. I remember some cactus as tall as a spruce tree. It was just there. We've arrived. Last stop!"

"Do you think there's a can? I've never been so nervous in my life."

Robert Martin bursts into a laugh that could choke him. Surprised at first, Jean-René Goupil joins him and laughs uncontrollably till they both have tears in their eyes. Nothing funny has been said, but they laugh because no words can express what they're feeling. And if words could do that, the two friends wouldn't dare say them because of their male prudishness; it's easier to make faces like little kids than to tremble like men in the face of the unknown. The laughter dies down. The two men wipe their eyes. And then it starts up again. Like a pair of drunken tourists, they walk into the trading post.

At first, Robert Martin thinks he recognizes the cashier. No, it's not the same one. The one last summer teased the regular customers. She had long hair. And the shelves aren't arranged in the same way. He doesn't remember seeing those rifles chained to the wall last year. And those tables weren't there. The historian is confused. His memory is hazy. And if he can't even remember last year, how does he expect to reconstruct Dubois's trajectory over the last century?

"I've made a mistake," he concedes. "This is the wrong place. Let's keep looking."

The customers sitting over their Cokes aren't talking. They all look nearly a hundred years old. They're staring at Jean-René Goupil as if no one has been here for a long time.

"Would you mind telling me why these old geezers are gawking at me like that? Have they never seen an Indian before?"

They are peering at him with insistent curiosity. They've screwed up their eyes as people do when they slowly recognize a

person who's returning from a distant past. Jean-René Goupil
sticks out his chest so he'll look more impressive. The old men
are whispering. They're talking about him. They must be.

"Miss, would you mind telling me where we are?"

The cashier assesses them with her gaze.

"That depends... Where do you want to go?"

"We're looking for an old man with one arm."

"Charlie Longsong?"

"He claims your store belongs to him..."

"That's Charlie Longsong. He's been minding his manners for a
while now. He must feel death coming."

"Miss, why are those old men looking at me?" asks Jean-René
Goupil.

"Men," shouts the cashier so that even the deaf ones can hear
her, "why are you staring at this gentleman?"

"Because he looks like somebody we used to know way back
when..."

"'Looks like' doesn't mean anything," concludes the cashier.

"Can we see this Mr. Longsong?"

"It's over that way.... Three hundred feet from here you take
the gravel road on your right, then keep your eyes peeled on the
left and you'll see three big cactuses standing close together. Now
pay attention; if it's not too dark you should see the tracks of a
truck. Follow them slowly and say your prayers. If Charlie Longsong misses his shot because he's too drunk, you'll be able to see
his shack. Want me to warn the undertaker, just in case...?"

With meticulous attention, they follow the cashier's directions: they
travel a hundred metres, they turn right, they spy three cactuses.

"It's this way, brother..."

Robert Martin is impatient.

"How do you know? These goddamn cactuses are everywhere!"

He regrets his outburst but doesn't apologize.

"I feel the way I felt in my mother's womb when she'd been carrying me for nine months and three days. . . . See those truck tracks? Follow them. . . . Watch out for the cactus. Careful! You're going to hit the opopanax."

"Opopanax? What's that?"

"I see you didn't have a poetess for a mother, ignoramus!"

"The tracks are disappearing into the brush."

"Keep going, we'll find them."

"I hate this. We're driving blind. We have no idea what's ahead of us. . . . This isn't the Grande Allée in Quebec City . . ."

The opaque night hugs the car despite the beams of light. Whipped by the glare of the headlights, a crowd of cactuses files past like strange pilgrims. The car is shaken, it twists in the potholes and dried-up ravines. Stones scrape the gas tank. Sometimes a wheel gets stuck in the gravel, spins, then grips again. They move forward. They'll never arrive anywhere.

"How hard it is to have a father!" the notary philosophizes.

"He's your father. . . . I've never asked you to help me find mine . . ."

"I'll do the same for you, brother, once you get your hands on your mother's diary."

"Prove to me you're a real Indian; tell me which of the constellations is the Big Dipper or the Little Dipper."

"I don't feel like passing on my knowledge to a white man . . ."

Bushes with claws scratch the sides of the car. Small animals with sparkling eyes scatter when the light brushes them. The historian is tired. Despite the air conditioning the back of his shirt is soaking wet. He hates to drive. And look at him now, out to conquer the desert. What an idiotic escapade! His car is exhausted too. It won't hold out. It's going to collapse somewhere like a mule that doesn't want to go any farther. The memory of his impressions in the desert should be useful when he writes Farmer Dubois's story.

This night is like a dense forest. Robert Martin is troubled by a benign giddiness. He knows this sensation. He remembers the first time he felt it. He had climbed onto the roof of his house, when he was still allowed to live in his house, to rescue his son's kite. How he wishes he could hold his children in his arms! He and Jean-René will spend the night in this desert. If they set foot outside they're liable to step on a snake's tail. He is a civilized man: he's driving a car; he has a Ph.D. Yet terror is stirring inside him. It nearly makes him tremble. Robert Martin decides he has to stop.

"Keep going," insists the cowboy. "We're nearly home."

"You've waited fifty years to meet your father. If we wait till it's light before we continue on our way, it won't make a lot of difference."

"You talk like that, my brother, because you knew your real father."

"Let's go to your father's place then!"

Tonight he must set down his emotions in his notebook before he goes to sleep. That will give his book on Farmer Dubois the authenticity of real-life experience that history so often lacks. Jogging along like a recalcitrant camel, the car spits, moans, rebels. Slumped in his seat, Jean-René Goupil can finally recite without a mistake:

> *And you took my heart*
> *On rue Gît-le-coeur*
> *And you gave me yours*
> *O my young Indian brother*

We made peace
In the month of August
on rue Gît-le-coeur
In Paris.

"Put on the brakes! The brakes!" he cries. "The brakes! You're going to run over a man!"

Robert Martin can only see the light of his headlights.

"There's a man!"

Robert Martin sees no one.

"It may be my father . . ."

"Call to him. Call: 'Papa!'. . . Then we'll see. . . . Where is he?"

"Look to your right, just outside the light. He's armed. Can you see the glints from his rifle?"

"Should I back up?" suggests the historian. "We're not armed."

"I'm going to ask him his name. We'll see if he's my father. . . . Shit! I forget his name. What's my father's name?"

"Shit! You made me forget it. You're so nervous you're getting on my nerves! Can you see how many arms he has?"

"Papa!" ventures Jean-René Goupil out the window.

The silence wafting on the breeze shakes the dry bushes, stirring the warmth that's sleeping in the ground.

"Let's get out," suggests Jean-René Goupil. "I'm going to talk to him."

"I can't see anybody."

The cowboy from the Île d'Orléans pushes open the door. The hinges creak oddly in the unfathomable quiet. His body unfolds with cautious slowness as if he were stepping into cold water.

"Hi! I can't see you. I'm looking for my father, who lives around here."

A shot rings out. Jean-René Goupil saw the fire spat out by the rifle. He thinks he's dead, but he dares not roll to the ground for fear of snakes. Realizing that he's still alive, he comes back to the car. Another detonation whips the desert.

"We should've got the hell out of here ages ago," says Robert Martin regretfully.

"If we move, we're liable to get a shattered windshield."

"And I still haven't seen a soul."

"But it's not cactuses that are exploding! Stop the car. Switch off the headlights. We're better off not moving. That'll reassure him."

"And I say the smart thing to do is get the hell out of here."

The car is barely moving. The left front headlight shatters with a metallic sound.

"Looks like your father's not exactly thrilled to see you."

"Turn off the other one before he blows it to smithereens..."

The historian is suffocating in the heat. The notary is cramped inside this second-rate car.

"We should have rented a tank."

"If you're so sure the invisible man is your father, call out your mother's name to reassure him."

It's the only reasonable thing to do. Jean-René Goupil rolls down his window and enunciates very clearly:

"Blan-che La-ri-viè-re!"

The mountains that have disappeared into the night send back into the desert the name of the poetess who loved an Indian from Arizona.

"Blan-che La-ri-viè-re!"

The two travellers wait for a reply, for another rifle shot. It doesn't come. They wait some more. It must come. The rifle remains silent. The silence drags on; the time becomes heavy.

"Roll up your window or the mosquitoes will eat us alive."

"Without air conditioning we'll die."

"He's got a nasty disposition, your old man!"

"We're going to be steamed like Chinese beans."

"If you're really that sharpshooter's son, he'd feel it in his genes. He'd want to hold you in his arms."

"In his arm. . . . If I get out to piss now I'll be risking my life."

"We should've stayed on the Île d'Orléans."

33 This morning, the sun caught fire abruptly above the desert just as the light in the dormitory at the Petit Séminaire, switched on by the monitor's perverse hand, would slap the sleepers' faces. In the car, already blazing hot, the two passengers wake up grimacing, one on the front seat, the other in the back. Their bewildered gazes scrutinize the desert: buttes, sagebrush, tufts of creosote bush, a disorderly battalion of sequoias and a shack covered with rusty tin, a pitiful shelter built from a bunch of rubbish. Seated in the shadow of the doorway is a sleeping man. A weapon lies across his knees.

"Which of us gets out first?" asks the notary.

"You're wearing cowboy boots; you're braver," decides Robert Martin.

"In which ancient Greek myth is the son killed by his own father?"

"I don't know. Isn't it Chronos, the god of time, who devours his children?"

"Put on some music like they play in the movies when the cowboy walks up to the armed man."

The radio sends out a sombre lament by Johnny Cash, who relates the sad story of a young man whose mother begged him not to take a knife when he left for town. He didn't obey her. The whole desert listens to the bleak tragedy. The young man will die in the end. Jean-René Goupil stays in the car.

"I had a strange dream," says the historian. "Last night I felt a presence near the car. I looked out. A horse was approaching the car. I was wide awake. His hooves were silent. Then the horse and his rider trotted away, going towards the Moon. It was a dream, but I can remember it as if I'd seen it with my own two eyes."

Jean-René Goupil interrupts the ballad of a cowboy who's looking for a cowgirl who looks like an old photo of his mother.

"Did I talk in my sleep?" he asks. "That's my dream you just described. It's incredible! Did I tell you what I dreamed?"

"No. Not your dream or anything else."

"This is impossible! You and I dreamed the same dream! I swear I heard a horse galloping towards us. His hooves didn't make a sound when they struck the ground, but I could hear the silence of the hooves as if it were a sound. The horse moved like a shadow. I heard him approach the car. I didn't dare move. He walked around the car and then I went back to sleep. After that I dreamed I was on the horse's back. A black horse. It's impossible. We had the same dream! I was on the horse's back. I can remember the smell: like damp leather. The horse was going towards the Moon. . . . We had the same dream. It can't be. One of us must have talked while he was dreaming . . ."

"We have to get out of here."

"If I don't get out to piss, I'm going to burst."

"I'll burst before you do."

Cautiously, each of them opens his door. They do their best to avoid any creaking. They don't want to waken the man who's asleep on his doorstep. The dust makes the hinges creak. He can't really be asleep: they've both seen westerns. They can sense his gaze, like the sharp tip of an arrow. Each on his own side sets his foot on the ground. No movement in the shack. They unfold their bodies, stiff after a restless night. Numb and limping, each selects a sequoia and runs to take shelter. The murmur of streams of urine like a flood. A blissful sensation fills their bodies and their souls.

A shot explodes. A bullet whistles above their heads. They crash to the ground.

"I haven't finished . . ."

The Indian approaches, his rifle pointed at them. He's a tall man shortened by age. He holds his rifle in his one hand. He walks with the confidence of a man who wants to remain master in his own house. He takes up a position by the car and waits for them.

"Why did you bring me here?" asks Jean-René Goupil reproachfully.

"Put your hands up. We have to show him we aren't as dangerous as we look."

"I'm hungry. It's time for breakfast. Ask my father if he'll fix us some French toast with maple syrup."

"Ask him yourself; he's your father."

The old man doesn't look as if he wants to lower his weapon.

"Do you think the old bugger wants to kill us?" worries Jean-René Goupil after a brief analysis of the situation.

The old man slings the barrel of his rifle over his shoulder and takes three steps towards them.

"I knew you'd come. You have to be wary of men in the night. I wanted to see you by daylight."

"It's my father!" exclaims the notary triumphantly.

"Way back then, I was no higher than a cornstalk that's still got some growing to do. One night strangers came. They wanted my father's land. They were looking in the ground for something that sold for a lot of money. My father wanted to keep his land. They said my father didn't have the right to keep his land. My father fought them. While me, I'd just left my mother's breast. I picked up a gun in both hands. Back then, it was before I went to war, I still had two hands. To defend my father, I fired a shot. It was dark. My father fell. The strangers ran away. Me, I was very small. I'd killed my father. Last night while I was keeping an eye on you, I fell asleep. I'm an old man and an old man sleeps a lot. My father came and visited my dream. He came on his fine black mare. My father spoke to me. He told me, 'You were a brave Little Tornado Man. You fought like a brave little Indian. You defended me well. The *bohanas* would have killed me but you fired first, Little Tornado Man. You were so small! You could hardly grab hold of my mare's tail.'

"My father bent over to take me in his arms. He sat me on his black mare and he said to me, 'Come with me, Little Tornado Man, I'm going to ride you around my land. You've done a good job of protecting it. Nobody's come and dug big holes in it. Hold on to me tight, Little Tornado Man, because I've come to tell you you've got a son. I'm going to show him to you. You and me, we're going to get our first look at him. Hold on tight, Little Tornado Man, because we're going to bring your son along with us.'"

"I'm the son of Blanche Larivière."

"Rue Gît-le-coeur," the old Indian recites, gazing far away, as far as the other side of the ocean, as far as the past of his youth.

His pronunciation of the French words is nearly perfect.

"What a story!" thinks Robert Martin. Instead of knocking himself out piecing together Farmer Dubois's odyssey, he'd be better off writing the biography of the poetess Blanche Larivière and her lover, Little Tornado Man from Arizona. After his own bitter divorce, how sweet it would be to tell a love story! It would let him insert a woman's presence into the history of America. The history of America populated only by men is just half the story. The unfinished story. America wasn't made without women. In the course of his research on Farmer Dubois, he hasn't often heard the rustling of a petticoat. Men like Dubois were blessed with a passionate nature. Their blood was hot and strong. In the forest, in the mines or on the plains, their animal instincts roared. Those men went for months without seeing a woman. Could Dubois have been homosexual? . . . No hypothesis should be rejected. Yet if he had been, how to explain the episode in the Yukon, when Dubois won the heart of the singer Emma Latour?

"Son, tell me where you come from."

The notary would like to say: "As of today, I'll have a story to tell." But he says nothing. With his white man's education, he's afraid of being ridiculous. To avoid talking, he takes a few steps. Charlie Longsong goes over and walks with him. In silence. With his father, he takes his first steps in the desert. Like a genuine Indian's son. But he's an adult. . . . He has the paunch of an adult and he's dressed up like a cowboy with his pointed boots.

"This old man is probably my father," the notary reasons, "because I've got the feeling we have nothing to say to one another. I had the same feeling about my poor ex-father the notary." Why didn't he simply stay on his Île d'Orléans? He could have been hanging out on his boat instead of exhausting himself in this desert. From the river he could watch the world burying itself under its troubles.

The Indian heads for his *hogan*. Jean-René Goupil understands that he's been invited to follow him. Why is his blood shivering in his veins? Why is there a lump in his throat? Why does he feel this awkwardness at the shadow of the open door? It's just a shack where poverty has built its nest. He's seen thousands like it all over the world. Is he frightened to go inside this one because it's his father's house? Dressed up like a cowboy of the vast open spaces, the notary hesitates to set his boot down on the dirt floor. "When you get close to poverty, you take on its smell," he has learned. The bird who has flown so far away is apprehensive about this nest that his father has never left. Is that why his legs feel lifeless? The son of the Indian from Arizona is choking from this profound, atavistic, uncontrollable anxiety that we feel in the face of the unknown.

If memory weren't a machine for producing oblivion, Jean-René Goupil would remember that once before he had shivered with this same fright. It was on the day when his mother was striving to bring him into the world; he was hanging on, for he preferred the warm familiar night to the unknown light that reigned over the St. Lawrence River.

The notary follows his father, that amputated, bent, furrowed giant. The old man exhales a stench of boiled meat or wet fur. Blanche Larivière, the distinguished lady who wrote her poems in ink on blue paper, wouldn't have tolerated his odour.

"Son, tell me."

Jean-René Goupil has been brought up as a white man in a small, white men's city. As an adolescent, he rebelled; his revolt was that of a little white boy taking a short break before returning peacefully to his classes. Yet he's never been a little white boy. He is the son of this Indian who is walking ahead of him, making the gravel roll beneath his feet. A shack made from tree trunks, plywood, cardboard and tin: that's where all those years have brought him. It's from here that he will fly away towards his new horizons. The notary knows that a man does not escape his father. He wishes he could read the old Indian's thoughts.

Jean-René Goupil has travelled in Latin America. He has read the history of its peoples. The Indians were warned that the white man would bring misery and disaster. He recalls that a great Mayan book, a sort of Bible, prophesied that the gods would return in the form of bearded white men and that their return would be terrible, because those white men, armed with lightning, would have the power to castrate the sun and to impose darkness on their empire. Is the old Indian in the midst of his silence trembling before his white son? Has Blanche Larivière spread darkness over Little Tornado Man's desert?

Charlie Longsong hangs his rifle over the two nails on the wall and makes his way to a corner of the shack, where he clangs together a saucepan and a frying pan.

34 Jean-René Goupil and Robert Martin have wolfed down the corncakes fixed for them by their host. The old Indian doesn't speak to them. He serves them tea. The teapot is black with soot but the tea is good. It's wild tea gathered in the desert. They drink from tin cans. His old hand doesn't tremble when he pours the tea. How to break the silence?

Charlie Longsong is sitting with them on the gravel, on the side where the shack provides shade. Slowly, he begins to talk:

"When the *bohanas* came to take my father's land, I was a child. A gun was so heavy. They attacked my father. I was brave. I fired. Can a sensible man ask a child to know how to fire a gun like a man? I should have been with my mother and the other children. But I was in the middle of a men's battle. It was night. The knives were shiny. The pickup trucks were roaring. And the horses were neighing. I wanted to help my father. I fired. And I hit my father. That's what I wanted to tell my son. My father cried out. I shouldn't have been there. The night was as black as the inside of a rock. My father wasn't afraid of death or threats or insults or gunshots. My father said to me: 'Little Tornado Man, you are young and I will never leave you alone on Earth.' After that, everyone fell silent. The *bohanas* fled in their pickups without putting on their lights. The horses were crazy. They escaped. I stayed by myself. It was so dark, I couldn't see my toes. Like any child my age, I called my father. I yelled. I yelled my father's name so loud I had blood in my mouth. I passed out. When I opened my eyes the light on the desert was so bright, I had to close them again. Thirst was gnawing at my stomach. I stood up. I looked around. There was my rifle. Intertwined tire tracks. Hoof-prints. There was a brown spot on the sand where flies were drinking. It was the blood that had poured from my father's heart. Hundreds of times I called him again: 'Papa!' Heaven helped me because the echo repeated: 'Papa!' From the other side of the clouds and from deeper down than the plants' roots, the gods had decided that on that very night, Little Tornado Man was going to become a man earlier than all the other children. A man who hasn't received a childhood cannot give one. With my father gone, I was alone the way a man is alone. He never abandoned me, even though I'd broken his heart. All his words poured out along with his blood into the desert soil. That was how he often talked to me. And it's the story I wanted to tell my son. . . . Son, tell me your story."

"I don't have a story . . ."

In this man's presence, Jean-René Goupil is ill at ease, intimidated. His father is too tall, too heavy, strange. A mild giddiness has clouded his thoughts. He sees himself in that fog, eyes misty with grief, following the coffin of his notary father to the graveyard: the coffin of the man he'd thought at the time was his father. Facing this old giant baked by the light of time, he has nothing to say and he lacks the words to say it.

"My mother, Blanche Larivière," he begins, "died about thirty years ago . . ."

Little Tornado Man bows his head to meditate over a pious memory. When he raises it, his small creased eyes meet his son's.

"There was the war. And then when the fighting was over, there was music and dancing. When the dancing was finished we went back where we'd come from, some to the south, others to the north. . . . Some remembered, others have forgotten . . ."

"This is the time to insert the most important question," thinks Jean-René Goupil. To formulate it, he has written it out on paper. He's worked at it, corrected it, started it again, polished it over and over, no doubt the way his mother did when she was writing her poems. He has turned it over in his head so many times.

"Do you remember the moment when you and my mother made me, in that room on the rue Gît-le-coeur in Paris?"

The old Indian looks past him as if he could pierce the horizon and see rue Gît-le-coeur.

"A man my age has done a lot of remembering and a lot of forgetting. Time passes like the wind and it chooses what it will carry along with it. . . . When a man looks for his father, he's looking for the man he resembles. The man who doesn't resemble his father is an orphan."

Jean-René Goupil doesn't push it. An old man has the right to be silent.

"I'm going to take you to rue Gît-le-coeur in Paris."

"I'd like to see the cliff I climbed in the war when I still had the two arms a mother gives her children. But an old man mustn't retrace the footsteps of his youth. An old man should go where he has to go."

"I'm going to take you to 33 Grande Allée in Quebec City, to Blanche Larivière's house."

"Wait."

Charlie Longsong disappears into his *hogan*. Jean-René Goupil stands up too. The sun is heavy. His travelling companion has stepped aside to leave him alone with his father. The cowboy hopes he's not lost—he who is used to following sidewalks. The light that the gravel reflects on his face is unbearable. His body, as much as his soul, is as sensitive as if it's been beaten up. He is thirsty. Why didn't his mother do like other women and keep her little love secrets to herself instead of turning her shivers into immortal poems? It was totally pointless. Today, nothing is immortal.

Charlie Longsong comes back with a handful of smeared paper, which he holds out to Jean-René Goupil.

"Son, here are some letters for Blanche Larivière."

The envelopes are marked "UNKNOWN. Return to sender."

3 5 In the plane bringing them back to Canada, the two companions don't feel like talking. Each of them is suffering a little. Robert Martin has wasted an entire year trying to reconstruct the elusive itinerary of one Farmer Dubois. He absolutely has to talk to Miss Camion.... Ah! to sleep with Miss Camion.... It's as if a warm ocean were rolling you in its waves all the way to the open sea, then bringing you back to shore. It's like exploring the landscapes of the Rocky Mountains. It's like driving down a highway at top speed.... Miss Camion can't be satisfied with an accountant. She's hungry for wide open spaces. That was why she liked the Farmer Dubois project so much. Surely she'll love even more the romantic and deeply moving fresco of the meeting between Blanche Larivière and Little Tornado Man, of their long-lasting love and their eternal separation. As soon as he arrives at the airport he'll call Miss Camion, tell her he won't be going back to his too-pretty hairdresser. Maybe he'll sleep with Miss Camion tonight.

Jean-René Goupil feels sad, as if he were returning from a funeral. With his two fathers he's more orphaned now than he has ever been. He knows what he'll do on his return to the Île d'Orléans. He'll walk to the big pine tree behind the house, right next to the river. He will sit down as he's done so many times, as his mother and his poor notary father did before him. Before the river that runs to the sea he'll read the letters from Charlie Longsong that his mother dared not receive. They will explain the mystery of who he is.

When he pulls up in front of his house, Jean-René Goupil doesn't go inside to kiss his young wife, he sinks into the shade of the leafy trees that play at pushing back the sun above the path. He sits against the pine tree, shivering, with these letters that will unveil the final secrets. As he's about to tear open the first envelope, his hand hesitates. It's his own life he should plunge into, not his mother's or the old Arizona Indian's. Jean-René Goupil should set out on his adventure as an Indian intensely on this planet—and elsewhere if possible!

"The wind's coming up, I must try to live." That thought has come to him from far away, from a poetry course. It was stifling, that class at the Petit Séminaire. Outside the window, beyond the St. Lawrence River, the world was opening, great and inviting.

One by one he drops into the rushing water the letters that will be carried away and sink to the bottom of the sea, where, it is said, everything began.

FINAL EPISODE

Isabelle, his young wife, said to him:

"You can't leave your father all alone in the desert like an old cactus."

And so what had to happen, happened. Jean-René Goupil is incapable of explaining why he left his father behind in his miserable shack in Arizona.

Charlie Longsong no longer thinks of anything but this unknown son who turned up one night and then immediately went back to the cold and the north as if he were afraid.

Jean-René Goupil is trying to imagine the arid solitude his father has known. He'll feel guilty to the end of his days unless he can make beautiful the final years of this man to whom his mother had given a great happiness. Because he is the son of Blanche Larivière, it's his duty to lavish on him a second happiness.

Charlie Longsong is the father of a son. He muses about all the things his own father taught Little Tornado Man. He adds up everything he hasn't taught his son. He will close his eyes for the great sleep without his son having heard his own story. What will this son tell his own children?

Jean-René Goupil needs to hear from his father's mouth how he arrived on Earth and what it was like before his arrival. He wants his father to guide his first steps in this new chapter: only an Indian can tell an Indian how an Indian should think.

Charlie Longsong concludes that if a man has a son, even one who's far away, even one who's lost in the snow of a foreign land, that man cannot pretend he has no son.

Jean-René Goupil is certain Charlie Longsong is pining to see the country where the woman he loved once lived, where she dreamed of him, where she loved him in dutiful silence.

Charlie Longsong regrets having stayed in his desert. Alone with the thousands and thousands of stars that dance in the sky, he understands now that instead of shutting himself away in his grief, his pain, instead of lulling his pain by drinking bourbon, he should have done like that Indian in the old legend who set out in search of the precious feathers of a very rare parrot. Like him, he should have crossed the desert, traversed forests, scaled mountains. He should have found in his heart even more courage than the feather-seeker, because he would have found not a bird but a woman who was longing for him.

What had to happen, happened. In Arizona, Charlie Longsong and his son, Jean-René Goupil, are sitting together in the same airplane, on its way to Canada. The travellers, a little stiff in their seats, have a preoccupied air, as if they're afraid the plane won't be able to take off, and now Charlie Longsong announces:

"I want out of here."

He no longer wants to climb into the air and float in the blue void of the sky. Jean-René Goupil tries to reassure him. He doesn't want his feet to be separated from the ground. He was curious to see a plane up close, now he's seen it, he has even gone inside its belly. And that's enough. Men weren't made to float through the clouds like the souls of the ancestors. The gods gave men feet, not wings. Why should he risk falling from the sky and crashing into the desert like a big hailstone? The hostess comes running. No one can persuade him to stay quietly in his seat. He doesn't want to sleep, he wants out. No smile, no promise will alleviate his terror.

And so they have to get out. And rent a car. And drive to Canada. For three days, Jean-René Goupil has to listen to his father's dogged silence. Charlie Longsong doesn't open his mouth. He's absorbed in a wordless dialogue with himself. He doesn't look at anything. His eyes are fixed on a very remote horizon. Is it the past? Is it the future? His soul is elsewhere. He resembles one of those wooden sculptures of a pensive old Indian that you still see at the doors of certain craft shops. Charlie Longsong has agreed to come and visit the land of Blanche Larivière. Has his soul refused to leave his shack in Arizona? Could it have set out on a nostalgic journey to the rue Gît-le-coeur in Paris?

Three days later, they arrive in Quebec City. They drive into town along the Grande Allée. Jean-René is going to show him the house where he was born, the house of Blanche Larivière. The month of October is offering them a mild day. Before the snow and the ice and the north wind take hold of the city, people are savouring the last rays of sun with nostalgia for an already distant summer that won't return for months. Strollers who've taken off sweaters, jackets, windbreakers linger on a restaurant terrace over a beer or a glass of wine, relishing this moment of eternity.

Reluctantly, the notary had to give over his beautiful and noble house to the businessmen who've transformed the Grande Allée into a cafeteria. Even in the days when, a rebel on a motorcycle, he charged into time with his eyes closed, he liked the bourgeois charm of the Grande Allée. Nothing is stable; everything changes, as the ancient philosophers he studied at the Petit Séminaire already knew. Today, the terraces are overflowing with customers. In front of his childhood house, Jean-René Goupil looks away, but he points to the Pizzeria where Blanche Larivière marked her days as an honest and devoted wife: "the rosary of her days," in the words of one of her poems. In this house the poetess composed her opus. It was here that she found the courage to write the troubling words of her confession. In this Pizzeria she dreamed about Little Tornado Man every day. The Indian had given his arm to the war; she had given him a few nights of love. No doubt the poetess was in love with her dream, thinks her son, but instead of a shack in Arizona she preferred the comfort of a notary's house. Charlie Longsong isn't looking.

Jean-René wants to get back to the tranquillity of the Île d'Orléans as quickly as possible.

Autumn is painting the trees again. Welcoming and glad to finally see the father with whom her husband has been reunited, Isabelle rushes up to embrace him. The Indian pushes her away as if she were attacking him. The Indian from the desert walks warily; he's afraid of falling on the polished floor.

"Your papa needs a shower."

His son lends him a bathrobe, she takes out some towels.

"How does it work?"

He is used to washing himself in the rain when it rains. Jean-René gives him a demonstration: the taps, the hot water, the cold water, the shower-head, the soap. Then, back downstairs, he pours himself a whiskey and fixes a campari and soda for Isabelle. This is a memorable moment. Nothing will be as it was before. They have no idea what the old man will bring them. They'll have to adjust, but it will all go well. Jean-René is entering this complex and fundamental relationship between a father and a son when he himself is already a grandfather. What an experience!

"Usually we force a son to have a father when he's much too young!" he jokes.

How happy his mother would be if she could share this moment! It's impossible that the Indian and the poetess have not communicated frequently through thought, Isabelle assures him. There's a reason why the poetess and the Indian met on rue Gît-le-coeur in Paris. Heaven bestows special gifts on Indians and on poets.

"I think you'll like this guy, if I can make him a little more sociable. You know, when we were driving up to Canada he went three days without saying a word."

"You're behaving like a real son ... you ask, you make demands ... Has it occurred to you that you're turning his old age upside down? You still have years and years ahead of you. For him, it's already too late.... It's too late in his life. He can never become a father.... You, though, you have time to get to know his Indian soul."

"Imagine the wisdom he must have accumulated while he was dreaming between sky and sand, talking with the Elders, listening to the ancestors ..."

"He's a man of another century who's waking up in our modern nightmare. That's why he says so little."

"Isabelle, I love you!"

"We're so lucky! Our love is opening, expanding. Most people's love just melts away."

"We owe our happiness to my brother, Robert Martin; I'm going to call him."

The historian answers as if he's been waiting for this call.

"I'm glad you and your father are finally reunited. All's well that ends well, as the poet said. Some amazing things happened on the rue Gît-le-coeur in Paris."

"That's my mother's street."

"It's my street, too. You remember, my brother, I told you: the beautiful girl from Brazil who drew fantastic flowers. . . . I took her to Provence, on a scooter, remember, I told you . . ."

"Rue Gît-le-coeur is the street of my mother and father . . ."

"I'd like to see Gabriella again. . . . I wonder where she is."

"Gabriella? . . . My brother, have you started working on the biography of Blanche Larivière?"

"I've started, but I had to go back to Farmer Dubois. A book club in France has ordered a first printing of seventy-five thousand copies. . . . I've got no choice. I have to finish the book. Miss Camion won't accept the idea of abandoning a project we've already started. . . . I've decided I'll never go back to my wife. I'll lose everything, but my mind's made up. Miss Camion tells me you should never say never. What a woman! I told her about Gabriella, my brother. She's prepared to look for her with me."

"Wait till you've found Dubois. And don't forget Blanche Larivière. . . . My father is with us at last. And I owe it all to you, my brother. I just wanted to say thank you!"

"History is like oil. Both are born in the sediments of the past and come up to the surface of time to operate the machinery of the present. . . . Are you impressed? . . . How is your father, after his long trip?"

Just then, the ceiling tears open as if the St. Lawrence River were crashing down on Isabelle and Jean-René.

"Shit! A flood!"

They rush upstairs. The floor is inundated. Books and socks are floating in the puddles. Charlie Longsong is standing under the shower, thin, bony, eyes closed. He hasn't pulled the curtain.

"Papa, you're supposed to close the shower curtain."

"In the war, there was no curtain in the showers."

"The war's over. Nowadays we pull the shower curtain."

Did his father just say that he hasn't taken a shower since the Second World War?

At breakfast the next morning, Jean-René announces the plans for the day.

"First we're going to the cemetery to visit the grave of Blanche Larivière."

Without a word, Charlie Longsong rises abruptly as if he were running away. He goes up to his room. The notary, stunned, gives his wife a questioning look. Her smile reproaches him for not grasping the obvious.

"He doesn't want to go to the graveyard."

"If he wants to see my mother, it's the only place he'll find her. It's not my fault if she's in the graveyard. Is he afraid the undertakers will keep him there?"

Jean-René is growing impatient. He's still irritated by the fact that his mother is dead. Whenever he thinks of her lying in the ground forever, he feels a twinge of sorrow in his heart. His mother ought to be alive . . .

"Do you know if visiting graveyards is an Indian custom?" he asks.

"You're the one who should know. Of the two of us, you're the Indian. . . . In your father's mind, Blanche Larivière must be still alive. That's why he hates the idea of visiting her in the graveyard. . . . I don't know. Like you, I'm trying to understand."

Later, he manages to convince his father to get in his jeep. He's going to buy him some clothes. When he emerges from the store, where Jean-René has energetically made the salesmen understand that his father is to be treated with respect, Charlie Longsong looks like a notary in his elegant dark suit with its distinguished pinstripes.

Jean-René has to spend a few minutes in his office. He can't take the man of the desert into his notary's hutch. He would suffocate. He'd think his son wanted to put him away. Instead, shouldn't he take him to the terrace of the Château Frontenac? There, he'll be in the open air, he can look out at the river, the boats; he'll be free to walk around. His new shoes shouldn't hurt too much.

"Wait here for me. Walk to the end and come back. I'll pick you up in half an hour. Enjoy the fine weather. Here's my card. If you have any problems, call me at the office. The number's here. Can you see it? I'll give you some money."

Slowly getting out of the car, the old Indian makes his way to the terrace of the Château Frontenac. His gait is hesitant, as if he doesn't trust the sidewalk.

The notary, who has been in his office for a few minutes, is painstakingly examining a codicil to the will of poor old Madame Tremblay, who is leaving all her worldly goods to some lunatic church whose members are waiting for extraterrestrials the way others await the Messiah. The work of revising it is turning out to take longer than expected. He has to finish it. He'd rather be strolling through the city with his father, or doing target practice, or riding around on his motorcycle. Would his father agree to ride with him? The telephone interrupts him. He is really very annoyed. Didn't he tell his secretary categorically to hold his calls?

"Natasha wants to talk to you; she assures me it's personal."

"I don't know any Natasha. Tell her to go to hell."

"That's difficult, Mr. Goupil. She's with your father . . ."

"Give me Natasha.... I hope the poor Tremblay woman can stay alive till I've finished revising her donation to the Martians. . . . Hello!"

"Hello. My name is Natasha. . . . Sorry to bother you, Mr. Goupil. I know notaries are very busy people. As clients, they're always in a hurry."

"What kind of business are you in?"

"That's what I'm calling you about. I'm with your father. I've taken my clothes off like an honest girl, but all of a sudden I realize your father has nothing but the change in his pockets."

"That's what I forgot: to give him money . . ."

"I'm a professional, just like you. You know what the cost of business is nowadays. I have substantial expenses. The Château Frontenac isn't a low-rent place. Your father seems to think I give my services away for nothing. So I started to yell at him. Your father gave me your card. He told me to call his son. I'm surprised your father doesn't have any money; his clothes are so stylish . . ."

"Listen to me, Natasha. I'm a very busy notary. I'm asking you to spend an hour with my father. Natasha, can you make him happy? He's a man who's experienced some terrible setbacks. In an hour from now I'll be at the Château bar. I'll pay you well. And if my father looks really happy I'll add something extra."

"Your father looks like a kind gentleman. You sound like an honest person. . . . You're a notary. . . . I'm not wealthy, but I own two apartments and a little chalet in the country. Since nobody knows the future, it's occurred to me that I should make a will. Nothing too serious. . . . I'm not going to die tomorrow, but you have to think ahead. . . . Better I should have a little will. . . . You understand me. . . . Could you help me out?"

"Take care of Papa first. . . . We'll talk about your will at the Château bar."

"You could deduct my services to your father from your bill.

That way, you and I, we'd outsmart the tax department. I think that we taxpayers pay far too much taxes."

"As fellow professionals we should help each other, is that it?"

"Does your father have a good solid heart?"

"His heart's as solid as a rock, Natasha, and his soul's as sensitive as the petal of a rose . . ."

"Thanks, and don't forget my will. Goodbye."

"Goodbye, Natasha."

"Should I put a meeting with Ms. Natasha in your diary, Mr. Goupil?" asks his secretary.

That afternoon, Jean-René and his father drive back to the Île d'Orléans. The son shows the father his collection of firearms. Charlie Longsong isn't interested. He doesn't even brush with his fingertips the beautiful rifles that are asking to be stroked. He looks at them abstractedly. Jean-René invites him to fire a few bullets. It's as if he hasn't said a word. Jean-René takes him to see his motorcycles. Charlie Longsong demonstrates no more interest. His son thinks: "Either my father can't tear himself away from his memory of Natasha or else we don't share the same tastes."

"Let's go and visit an Indian village. It's not far. They're Hurons. The Grand Chief is one of my clients. He's a real Indian. . . . Like you and me. . . . He wears a braid . . . Like the old Chinese . . ."

"I want to watch television."

He settles Charlie Longsong in an armchair. He explains how to operate the remote. During the rest of the afternoon he stares at the screen without interruption. He doesn't move. He doesn't get up even once. He doesn't touch one button on the channel-changer. He doesn't yawn. His attention is so profound, it's upsetting. He resembles a man who could watch himself fall into a bottomless hole.

"I wish I could see what he sees," says Jean-René.

"The poor man must be watching the movie of his time on Earth."

"What can you and I know?"

"He lost his own father so young. How could he have understood at his age? He was wounded in the war and he survived without ever understanding why he'd fought. He had a son but he didn't know it. He was loved by a woman who preferred writing poems to seeing him again."

"Maybe he's seeing everything that could have happened to him . . ."

"They say the desert has astonishing knowledge to teach. Besides, Indians know secrets that are forbidden to Whites. Maybe he can foresee the future. . . . He's looking at what's going to happen to us."

The old man's eyes don't leave the screen, but he's looking at something besides the image. Each of his limbs is totally motionless. Not one muscle in his face is strained or relaxed. Once again, his son thinks he resembles one of those wooden sculptures of a pensive old Indian outside certain tourist establishments in the United States.

"Is he still breathing?" he worries.

"Don't bother him. Let him do what he wants. Learn something from him. Instead of always moving, it would be good if you could learn to meditate like your father. . . . Or maybe he's conversing with his ancestors, your ancestors. He's parked his body here while his soul is travelling. . . . You have a lot to learn from your father. . . . I want to learn from him too."

"Wait. I want to see if he'll react when I zap."

"Why? Leave him alone. You've imposed a whole revolution on him."

Jean-René approaches his father and surreptitiously, playfully, relieves him of the remote. He zaps. Another image, a different set, different people fill the screen. The old man doesn't notice the change. Jean-René presses the button again. The old man doesn't react. Imperturbable, as if nothing has been altered, he continues gazing at the screen with the same attention. Jean-René makes several stations file past: news, cooking, weather, interview, rock 'n' roll, televangelist, boxing. Charlie Longsong doesn't see these images. Yet his eyes are open. He's not asleep. To get a reaction, a crease of his eyelids, a blink, Jean-René turns off the TV. Charlie Longsong goes on looking at the dark screen. His attention is so intense. He sees beyond what the antennae can pick up.

"That man's not here with us," says the notary impatiently.

"Stop bothering him. Leave him his freedom."

"He comes to visit his son for the first time and he's farther away than if he'd stayed in Arizona."

Later on, early in the evening, Charlie Longsong comes back from his absence. He jumps up as if he'd bounced. Astonished to notice his hosts, he hesitates briefly and seems to be asking himself who these strangers are. Then he understands the situation, calms down, smiles, reassured.

"Son, I've followed the road of my days. Now I've come to the end. I've got seven days left to travel. I want to travel those seven days in my desert. I want to go back there. Blanche Larivière is dead. I am going to die. Rue Gît-le-coeur is too far away."

"There's no question of letting you go. If you have seven days left, you're going to spend them with us. Do you want to die without our having really got to know each other? I want to know who you are. If you insist on dying in seven days, you might as well do it here, in a comfortable bed. . . . Why go and pass away in your miserable shack?"

"In our tribe, it's the fathers who tell the sons what to do."

"Isn't it normal to want to know my father?"

"You know you have a father. I know I have a son . . ."

"Isn't it normal for a son to want to take care of his father?"

"I'm at the end of my time; I want to go back to my desert."

"You're right," Isabelle interjects. "Jean-René will drive you back to Arizona."

"Let's go then!"

"Be patient."

"Can I take my new suit?"

"Take whatever you want, just be a little patient."

"We've invited Jean-René's children and grandchildren. They'll be here in a few minutes. They all want to meet you. Do you know you're a great-grandfather? You've got seven great-grandchildren."

"Great-grandchildren?" Charlie Longsong repeats, not under-standing.

"Jean-René's grandchildren are your great-grandchildren."

He is dazed.

The door opens and the doorway is filled with men, children, women who push and shove and bustle about. One boy brandishes a bow and arrow.

"Can we play cops and Indians?"

"Grandpa, show me how you shoot an arrow."

Nearly all Jean-René's family is there: his daughters, his sons, their husbands, their wives, some ex-wives and a few ex-husbands. They're all talking to him at once. Charlie Longsong is submerged by these people who speak the language of Blanche Larivière. They shake his hand, they touch him, they take his photo. They hurry to recount to him, as if he were someone else, his own love story with Blanche Larivière; they ask him questions about the desert;

they explain the twists and turns in the family genealogy. He takes refuge in silence, like a lizard in the crack of a rock. There he is, once again, elsewhere. He has left the guests. Is he in his desert? Has he joined Blanche Larivière? Is he with her on the rue Gît-le-coeur? Is he taking part with his ancestors in a powwow of his tribe? As he is no longer with them, little by little the children and adults feel as if they're together here as a family. Charlie Longsong stays by himself while, in the other room, they're celebrating the arrival of Jean-René Goupil's father. They drink champagne, they drink fruit juice. They're as happy as if the late notary René Goupil had come back from the dead...

"We're all Indians!"

"And nobody can say we aren't proud of it!"

Then, when everyone has taken a place around the long table, Jean-René goes to extract his father from his solitary dreaming. He brings him in to join his descendants, all these strangers who are watching him with their big *bohana* grins. The lined-up glasses and utensils sparkle. He wants to go back to his dream, to his vision. He wants to go back to Arizona. His son holds on to him.

"Papa, tell us a story."

The old Indian, strapped into his new suit, calms down and gets back in his chair. As he often did on the mesa, he starts to unwind his story:

"In the Arizona desert, there was once a boy called Little Tornado Man..."